A WHISPER
ON THE WIND

Book 3 of the
AMBER LEAF TRILOGY

a novel by

SANDRA H. ESCH

A LAMP POST BOOK

A WHISPER ON THE WIND
BY SANDRA H. ESCH

ISBN 10: 1-60039-213-X
ISBN 13: 978-1-60039-213-9
ebook ISBN: 978-1-60039-727-1

www.lamppostpubs.com

A WHISPER ON THE WIND

BY

SANDRA H. ESCH

ACKNOWLEDGEMENTS

A Whisper on the Wind is the final book of the *Amber Leaf Trilogy*. Writing these stories has greatly expanded my understanding of the histories of World War II, my hometown, and even my own family. It has been a fascinating journey.

My heartfelt thanks to Brett Burner, Publisher at Lamp Post, for seeing potential in this work and guiding me through the publishing process.

Thanks to my writers critique group (Martha Gorris, Ann Larson, Jean Mader, Mary Kay Moody, Diana Wallis Taylor, and others) for their selfless editorial help and ideas. Thanks also to Sue Duffy and Beverly Nault for their excellent input.

And then to Bonnie Aase-Roach, Cindy Belshan, Roselyn Collver, Marilyn Damien, Anne Fletcher, Del Glanz, Erika and Pablao Hartman, Lorraine Hooks, Fran Jenkins, Lois Kuehnast, Lori Lobnitz, Ellen Sheldon, Lynette Torrey, Patti Tzannos, and Nadine Washburn, among others, thank you for your inspiration, input, and encouragement.

Last but definitely not least, my profound thanks to my husband Fred; my sisters, Ardena Okland and Lois Williams; my nieces, Jaime Garvick and Sheila Okland; and my father-in-law Bernie Esch for their amazing input and support. I could not be more blessed.

You'll never get the Purple Heart hiding in a foxhole!
Follow me!

— Captain Henry P. Crowe

CHAPTER ONE

J o Bremley panicked. In a vain attempt to outrun the storm, her '31 Chevy fishtailed around the corner on two bald tires.

Steer into the skid! Steer into the skid!

A truck flashed past, horn blaring. She missed it by inches, her car spinning out of control. Trees and bushes jumped out all over the place, threatening. She fought for breath, her frantic heart pounding.

Pump the brakes, don't ride 'em!

She eased out of the skid, pulled to the side of the road, and stared at her trembling hands.

Thumping wipers half-cleared the windshield before rain filled it again. Then through the blur a fuzzy figure emerged—a black umbrella canopied over a wide-girthed elderly man shuffling along the sidewalk with a cane. Jo edged her car up the shoulder and rolled down the window, but a brew of violent wind and pounding rain muffled her shout. "Mr. Harrington—"

Big Ole Harrington tipped his umbrella. Not only did he arch a bushy brow, he bore the distinct demeanor of someone who wanted to be left alone.

Jo pointed to her door and cried, "You're gonna get pneumonia. Get in."

"How's a geezer supposed to get any exercise when you dote over him like a milquetoast?" Big Ole grumbled as he maneuvered into the front seat. "Honestly, you young women are all alike. You're far too protective. And speaking of being protective, I hadn't realized that was you skidding around the corner a minute ago. I thought that truck was going to have you for supper."

"I know," Jo said. "I can't stop shaking."

"It all happens so fast—doesn't it?"

She cringed at his penetrating gaze. "If you're referring to Tryg Howland, you're right. This is what it must have felt like for him. But for Tryg, it was a snowstorm. A deer he missed by inches. A ditch he didn't miss.

"And my husband was killed."

Jo blinked away threatening tears. She downshifted and the car once again puttered up the hill, a row of two-story clapboard houses ticking past one by one.

A brilliant lightning bolt sawed open the black Minnesota sky followed by deafening thunder that rocked the car. "That's quite some ruckus." Big Ole gaped through the windshield. "Can you imagine what the South Pacific must be like about now? Bombs falling like hailstones. Only there, people don't run for their basements—they run for their lives. The concussions? They don't teeter your car. They bust your eardrums and blow buildings to smithereens. Why, this little storm's just child's play."

"Speaking of this not-so-little storm, what on earth were you doing out there?" Jo said. "Clouds like these drop tornados."

"Which begs the question, my dear Mrs. Bremley, what are you doing out in this storm?"

"I'm on my way home from the office."

Ole broke a grin. "And I'm on my way home from town. Anyway, it's the weatherman's fault. He told me this storm wasn't coming until later tonight."

"Told you?"

"Yes, ma'am. On the radio this morning." Ole leaned to the side, pulled a monogrammed handkerchief from a pocket, and wiped it across his dripping brow. "So how are things at the office these days?"

Not too good. Jo's mind spun faster than the wheels on the car. The office. Tryg. The unexpected emotional trap she found herself embroiled in. Forbidden feelings. What were they all about? She couldn't decide whether she was indulging in unwanted infatuation or loneliness. *Honestly! Agreeing to work for that man was the sorriest decision I ever made.* "Not too bad. I'm meeting some interesting people, learning a lot about the legal profession."

When Ole indulged a moment's silence, she gave him a sidelong glance. "You look as if you don't believe me."

"Can't say as I do."

Jo's eyebrows drew together.

"You're troubled about something," Ole said. "I pick up on that sort of thing all the time." He winked. "It's part of my amazing charm."

Jo chuckled.

Meanwhile, the winsome father figure rested his hands on his generous middle and stared straight ahead. He smelled of fresh rain with a hint of aftershave. Massive frame, ruddy complexion, haphazard spidery veins sprouted on his ample cheeks like hairline fractures on a clay pot. The dear old man filled her car the way he filled her world—with warmth, purpose, and unparalleled respect.

"That's a pretty snappy tie you're wearing," Jo said.

"Thank you. But I'm a little color blind. What shade of green would you say this is?"

"Olive."

"And what about my cardigan?"

"Forest green."

"You don't say. They don't clash, do they? The missus used to lay my clothes out for me. Now I take a guess."

Ole's clothing complemented his sharp mind. His tie cascaded down a snowy white shirt. He wore rich brown trousers and shoes the color of walnuts. Even his black cane was polished to a high sheen. "They look perfect together."

Ole appeared pleased and then said in his matter-of-fact way, "I've noticed that your Tryg is spending a fair amount of time with my grand-daughter these days."

So Tryg is seeing Sarah. Although Jo's heart thump-thumped, she steadied her breath. "*My* Tryg?"

"I see the truth has distressed you."

"I'm fine."

Big Ole smacked the crook of the cane with his palm. "If you're so fine, why did you miss the turn onto River Lane? Isn't this your home we're pulling up to?"

A sudden warmth crawled up Jo's cheeks. She hit the clutch and brake, shifted the car into reverse, and backed up the wet gravel road.

"You know," Ole said, "we're a lot alike, you and me. You want to protect an old man from a nasty storm, and I want to protect a lovely young woman from herself."

Holding back a choke, Jo asked, "Why's that?"

"You're standing in your own way. Tryg is an exemplary young man. He's bright and knows the score."

"What does that have to do with me?"

"He's taken a fancy to you."

Quickly downshifting, Jo recoiled at the sound of grinding gears.

"And you to him," Ole continued. "Why, we'd all have to be blind not to see that. But—"

"But what?"

"But he also knows you're still married to your dead husband. The poor man doesn't stand a chance."

Jo drew in a decent-sized breath of the clammy Minnesota air and pulled up sharply to the curb in front of the stately O.M. Harrington

House. "I know you mean well, but nothing can ever happen between Tryg and me. In the first place, his ego is still smarting over Elizabeth. I mean, how does a guy ever get over being spurned by his fiancée? And even if he did have an interest, which he doesn't, you can bet it would be coming from a sense of obligation on his part. As for me, I've experienced the kind of love that comes once in a lifetime. That's not going to happen again. Besides, your Sarah is perfect for him."

"The way I have it figured, as long as you're around, he'll never be able to give his heart to her or anyone else."

Jo stared at the thick raindrops pelting her windshield. "Tryg's love life doesn't have anything to do with me. All I am to him is a reminder of his crushing guilt, and there's nothing I or anyone else can do to change that."

"I wouldn't be so sure. As for Sarah, you don't need to worry about her. My granddaughter is strong. She won't allow herself to get in too deep."

"Look, Mr. Harrington—"

"Big Ole," he corrected.

"If I ever got the feeling I was standing in the way of Tryg's love life, you can bet I'd catch the first train to New York."

"Still wanting to run away, are you?"

"Not running away. Pursuing a dream, Mr. Harrington."

"Big Ole," he repeated.

"I don't know," she said, staring off. "Maybe I was wrong all along not to have listened to myself. I should have gone when I had the chance. Besides, you're right. I can't give my heart to Tryg. I couldn't do that to Case."

"Aren't you forgetting something? What about your little girl? She needs a daddy and no one could fill that role better than Tryg."

"He couldn't do that to Case either. Subject closed."

Ole unlatched the door, popped open his umbrella, and turned to Jo with a playful grin. "No need to see me to my door."

CHAPTER TWO

Tryg monitored the summer storm from the office window. A torrent of rain was sweeping through southern Minnesota with the sound and fury of a freight train. Howling winds peeled shingles off rooftops and snapped tree branches, skittering them along streets like tumbleweed. Lightning bolts made fireworks of the sky. The thundershower was here one minute, gone the next, and laughing back at the town left trembling in its wake as it yanked the plug on Amber Leaf's power supply, then barreled on toward the east.

In the quiet that followed, Tryg returned to his desk and gazed at a teetering pile of paperwork. A ton to do, but little light left to get the job done. In an idyllic world, he would go home and enjoy a candlelight dinner with his beautiful bride. After eating their fill, they would retire to the front porch where he would enjoy a relaxing smoke. They would sit back, and watch the world go by. But he didn't smoke, his world was not idyllic, and he had no bride.

Alone with the sound of his footsteps, he went into the outer office and was surprised to see Ardena Okland still sitting at her desk. She was primping with a hand-held mirror, by far the smallest contraption he'd ever seen. He figured she'd have to powder her nose in quadrants to view it all. "How can you see anything with the power off?"

Ardena laughed good-naturedly. "I can't."

"I thought you'd left with Jo."

A warm smile lifted Ardena's forty-something-year-old cheeks. "I'm afraid not. Calvin should be stopping by any minute. Thought we'd go to The Copper Kettle for a quick bite. What about you? Are you heading home for the day?"

"Too much to do. Thought I'd close up shop for a while. Maybe grab a light supper somewhere and hope the power comes back on."

Ardena peered through the plate-glass window and her face lit up. "Here's Calvin now. Why not join us? You don't want to eat alone." She smiled. "Especially not on a dreary night like tonight when twilight can put a strain on a struggling soul."

Tryg laughed. "You think my soul is struggling, do you?"

Their footsteps clapped along the rain-washed sidewalk, the outside air heavy and moist. As they walked along, Tryg was struck by the affinity between Calvin and Ardena. Their presence seemed to add warmth to an otherwise cool evening. Yet he choked down an unwelcome pang of envy, but couldn't quite put a finger on why. Calvin had it all. Love. Passion. Purpose. Fulfillment. But, from all outward appearances, Tryg had it all, too. A budding relationship with an unusually lovely young lady. A successful law practice. Prestige. A bright future. Yet fulfillment was a gift he could not seem to unwrap.

When they arrived at the café, Tryg looked around. The place appeared more charming than ever with candles burning on its tables and counters. They ordered salads, cold cuts, and fountain drinks and shared highlights from their respective days. But then the conversation took a sharp turn toward Calvin's preaching, war, and the kamikazes.

Ardena placed a hand on Calvin's forearm. "Any idea where the name kamikaze came from?"

"If I have my history right, back in the fourteenth century, the Chinese launched an invasion on Japan, but a typhoon destroyed their fleet before they could get to shore. So the pilots are named after what they call a divine wind since it saved Japan centuries ago."

Tryg stabbed a fork into the last bite of salad. "That wind can't feel too divine if you're a sailor standing on deck, watching enemy planes take a nosedive, heading straight for you." Tryg looked up. "You know what I appreciate most about your preaching, Pastor Doherty?"

"No." Calvin released a warm smile. "But I am curious."

"Nothing is off limits with you. You cut to the heart. Make people think. Make us want to rise above the darker side of life."

"Be ye doers of the word and not hearers only, right?"

"Yes, sir. That's a tough one." Tryg found himself smiling unexpectedly. "You also have a gift for making your congregants squirm. Myself included."

"I can be every bit as challenged as my parishioners, Tryg. Do you know who gives me the hardest time?" Calvin wrapped a hand around a glass and lifted a soda, stopping shy of his lips. "Jo."

Tryg stopped chewing mid-bite and choked out the word, "Bremley?"

"Yes, sir. If it wasn't for her, I wouldn't be in the ministry now, and Ardena would not be sitting at my side."

"That's right," Ardena weighed in. "She introduced us right here in this very restaurant. A few emotional issues were holding Calvin back, weren't they, dear? He didn't get graying at the temples for no good reason. Our Jo conned him into facing what he didn't want to see. Helped him get past himself, you might say. We owe her a lot."

Our Jo? "I guess I'm not surprised," Tryg admitted. "She does have a knack for uncovering hidden truths."

"And pointing them out, plain and gentle," Calvin said, "all the while making her victims sweat. She's as sharp as she is beautiful. I understand she never was one to shrink from playing it straight. One of these days, I'm going to get her. What goes around ..." He grinned. "I do believe her number is nudging close to the top.

"Say, Tryg, how are you doing these days? I haven't seen you using your cane in quite some time."

"Not my cane, the cane. I never did want to take possession of a walking stick." Tryg slapped his thigh and gave his bum leg a slight shake. "I'm doing much better, thank you. Still have some nerve damage, but I've gotten a lot stronger.

"Every now and then I have a little setback, but with all of our boys overseas losing arms and legs and suffering shellshock, if not worse, you aren't going to hear me complain."

Ardena suddenly appeared distracted, oddly fearful, staring into a flame as if she and the candle were alone in the café.

"Ardena, if I didn't know any better," Tryg said, "I'd say something in that miniature inferno is distressing you."

She flinched, her eyes darting out and about the room. "I'm sorry. I don't mean to be rude. I don't know why, but all this talk about war reminded me of the robberies we've been having around town lately. Kind of gives me the heebie-jeebies. Amber Leaf is starting to feel like a war zone, too."

Tryg set his plate to the side. "I hadn't thought of them in that light before, but you're right." It had all started so innocently with a spattering of rumors about unimportant items mysteriously missing from a garage here and there. The robberies were sporadic. No apparent pattern. In no time at all, people were told to keep their doors padlocked and chained.

Calvin rested an arm on the table. "I didn't give it a thought either until news of actual break-ins hit the paper. I don't understand how anyone could even think to violate a bedroom community like ours."

Tryg considered Calvin's assessment. He was right. Serene lakes. Verdant wooded areas. Picturesque farms. Such a peaceful town.

Concern lines cut deep into Ardena's forehead. "There's something I haven't told you yet. Last night, around two in the morning, there was a loud racket outside. It was in the alley behind my house. Scared me half to death. Bet I jumped a good foot."

The fine hairs on Tryg's neck upended. "You must have been terrified."

"Why didn't you say anything before now?" Calvin reached for her hand. "We've got to be careful, Ardena. Those thieves are getting bolder. I hear they're breaking into houses during broad daylight now. Anyone catches them off guard, they could easily go on the attack. This is nothing to mess with."

"I know," she said. "I'm trying. One of my neighbors yelled out his window. Fortunately the commotion stopped, but I had an awful time getting back to sleep. I wish Chief Stout could catch those thieves. I feel on edge and can't seem to shake it. Now with the power being off —I mean, what if it doesn't come on again tonight?"

"Look," Tryg said, "if it doesn't, why don't you plan to spend the night at the O.M. Harrington? You know Big Ole. He'd be more than happy to put you up. If his place is full, you could probably double up with Sarah."

"That's right," Calvin said. "Come with me to the meeting. If the power isn't on by the time it's over, I'll drive you to the boarding house myself."

Seeing the raw caring in Calvin's eyes, Tryg found himself again feeling envious. With his present relationship with Sarah, that surprised him. He needed to get his expectations in line, he reasoned. After all, it takes time to develop that rich feeling of contentment.

"Speaking of Sarah," Calvin said, "words out you've been seeing her."

Tryg took his turn studying the candlelight dancing on the tabletop.

"Are you looking for your future in there?" Calvin said mischievously.

Tryg smiled. "I'm sorry. I didn't mean to be rude. You heard right."

"She's lovely, Tryg."

"She is beautiful, isn't she? We're seeing each other casually, but regularly—every Saturday night. Thought I'd see how it goes first and then take it from there."

Suddenly, without warning, Tryg's heart hurt. He sensed, even feared, it would never be possible to grow their friendship into the idyllic relationship Calvin shared with Ardena, or the idyllic relationship his best friend Case had once enjoyed with Jo.

Case.

Jo.

Tryg carefully positioned his fork at the side of his plate and nudged it, aligning it just so with his knife and spoon. "Does the guilt ever go away?"

"You have me at a disadvantage here," Calvin said. "What do you mean, guilt?"

"Case. His death."

Calvin's facial expression turned serious. "I wish I could say yes. Still having a tough time with it, are you?"

"Every waking minute of every single day."

A puzzling look washed over Calvin's face. "I don't mean to be inappropriate or to shock you," he said, "but frankly I'm surprised you haven't gotten together with Jo instead of Sarah."

"*Me* and Jo?"

"Why not? You certainly have enough in common."

Tryg let out a heavy sigh. "To be honest, there's nothing I'd like better. But you have to understand. Case was my best friend. I stole his life from him. I could never steal his wife from him, too. That would be unforgivable."

"But you didn't steal Case's life. That was an accident."

"I was the one behind the wheel, remember? I never should have been driving." Tryg wrung his napkin. "Case had burned the midnight oil one too many nights in a row. He was exhausted. He'd bought this beautifully wrapped gift for Jo before he picked me up. Between his being tired and wanting to show it to me in the worst way, I figured the least I could do was offer to drive. Besides, I was itching to get behind a wheel again. I was sure I could handle it. But when that deer shot out of the woods and I slammed my foot on the brake, the pain was excruciating."

"That's just it. You experienced the pain after you slammed on the brake, right? Like I said, it was an accident."

"Doesn't matter. I still couldn't do that to Case. Knowing Jo, she couldn't either."

Ardena reached for her jacket. "We'd better get going, Calvin, or we'll be late for your meeting."

With the power still off, Tryg relinquished any hope of getting more work done. Sauntering home in the diminishing light, he glimpsed up a darkened alley here and there and considered the plight of so many women alone these days with their husbands off to war. He then reflected on Sarah, pleased she lived at the O.M. Harrington where she was relatively safe, especially with Big Ole around.

But as quickly, Tryg thought about Jo and the guilt rushed back. Although the accident had been a cruel twist of fate, he couldn't shake feeling responsible for bringing an abrupt end to her life with Case.

He thought about Calvin and how passionate he was about forgiveness. The man preached about it all the time. Tryg never had much of a problem forgiving. Even during the heat of battle, he saw men's weaknesses for what they were and often looked the other way. When he returned state side, though, and drove Case's car into that ditch, Tryg learned forgiving others can be relatively easy. But forgiving himself?

His footsteps clapped against the sidewalk as he tortured himself with thoughts about Jo and Brue living alone. The vulnerability of their small asphalt-shingled home sitting on that dimly lit stretch of gravel road skirting the shores of Amber Leaf Lake. He looked up at the moonless sky, and he feared for them.

CHAPTER THREE

TWO NIGHTS LATER ....

J o stumbled to the telephone picking it up after the third double ring.

"Jo? It's me. Big Ole. You'll never guess who I got a call from."

She had no idea, but at this late hour, it must be good. "Who?"

"Charlie. Says he's at the train depot."

She extended the receiver an arm's length and gaped at it. "Not Doc's Charlie?"

"Yes, ma'am. Couldn't believe my ears when I heard the boy's voice on the other end of the line. Why, I assumed he was a goner."

Jo fidgeted with the telephone cord. "So did I."

"The young war hero said he wanted to surprise his dad."

"Does Doc even know he's still alive?"

"Not that I know of, at least not yet. I told Charlie someone would stop by for him right away. Seemed unconscionable for a brave young soldier to have to take a taxi. Couldn't reach our preacher, and Sarah's never met the lad before. Since I didn't know who else to call, I was wondering—"

"I'm on my way."

Jo nudged her seven-year-old daughter, Brue, out of bed and they hopped in her Chevy. A short while later Jo pulled into the parking lot. A handsome young soldier with a duffel bag plunked at his feet stood leaning against the red brick building. He was dragging on a cigarette and appeared lost in his own private world. She hesitated before gingerly stepping forward. "Charlie?"

The soldier jumped. He tossed a cigarette butt on the ground as if he'd unwittingly burned himself then mashed the smoldering butt beneath his well-shined shoe. "Jo! I didn't expect anyone to come so soon."

She wanted to reach out and hug him, but that felt awkward. Shaking his hand seemed too formal. So she stuffed her hands into the pockets of her cotton shift and stood rooted on the spot, taking in his once innocent-looking eyes that now emitted melancholy. What had the war done to this once vivacious young man?

Brue was seated in the back seat poking her wee nose out the open window when Jo and Charlie approached the car. He ruffled her flaxen hair, an act of pure affection, and then joined Jo up front. Appearing tense, he parked the duffel bag on his lap.

As the car pulled out of the parking lot and onto South Broadway, Charlie said in a strained voice, "How's dad?"

"Not too well, I'm sorry to say. He was doing fine until the day he got one of those vague telegrams."

Charlie cast his gaze toward the floorboard. "The kind you never want to get? The kind that tear up your insides?"

"That's right. It said your plane had gotten shot down, but that's all it said."

"Nothing about me being wounded?"

Jo shook her head. "No word about where or when or what happened to you, or if you were even alive. No indication he'd ever learn more. Your dad plunged into a deep depression."

"No wonder," Charlie said.

"From what I understand, he hasn't mentioned your name since."

Jo gave Charlie a furtive glance, hoping he would offer some sort of explanation, but he didn't. He appeared to be up to his shoulders in emotional quicksand. She could tell by his hollow stare. Straight ahead now. Thoughtful. Too quiet. Unfortunately, she didn't feel equipped to pull him out of it. "He seems better these past few months. I think trips to Jonathan's new place out in the country have helped some."

"Hey, Charlie," Brue called from the back seat, her voice bright and chipper.

"His name is Mister—"

"Charlie is fine, Jo," he said.

She nodded and then glanced back at Brue. "Go ahead, sweetie."

"Do you have any children?"

"No, I don't."

"Why not?"

Charlie chuckled. "Because I'm not married yet."

"Do you ever go fishing?"

"Yes, little lady. Why? Don't tell me you want to tag along."

"I fear you've opened Pandora's box," Jo said. "My little girl is fascinated with anything and everything."

A short minute later, Jo pulled to the curb in front of the O.M. Harrington and engaged the emergency brake.

"I'll get your door," Charlie said in a tone that warmed Jo's heart. What a breath of garden-fresh air to have Charlie, with the presence and confidence of a well-polished gentleman and the meekness of an average joe, make her feel like a lady again.

With duffel bag in hand, Charlie gazed up at the massive O.M. Harrington with its glowing French windows and wrap-around porch. He then took a step back and nodded for Jo and Brue to lead the way up the well-manicured pathway. "After you."

Jo felt jittery, as if she'd consumed one too many cups of coffee on an empty stomach. Thrilled to be included in the homecoming, she spilled over with anticipation.

They stepped up onto the porch. Charlie hesitated, inhaled a deep breath, smiled at Jo and Brue, and then pulled the door open expectantly and made his way into the great room. It was empty. No Doc. No guests. No Big Ole. Only Sarah leafing through a stack of papers at the registration desk.

Jo led the way across the quiet room, their footfalls thumping hollow against the hardwood. "Sarah, I'd like you to meet Doc's son, Charlie."

The instant Sarah stood and extended her hand, she appeared to melt at the very sight of him, her movements slow, her attention absorbed and distracted. Not only did it show in her blueberry eyes, the rapport between the two of them felt palpable. They went on to hold one another's hands, and one another's gazes, too many seconds too long.

Feeling uneasy, Jo was relieved to hear Big Ole surface at the far end of the hallway.

Good. The spell was broken.

"Charlie?"

Charlie lit up and hurried forward, meeting Ole at the great room's entry. "Mr. Harrington."

"What a sight for old and tired eyes." Big Ole clapped Charlie's shoulder. "Boy, you had us worried sick."

Still engaged in a firm handshake, Charlie scanned the room. "Where's Pop?"

"I'm afraid he isn't here. From the minute I got word from you, I've been busy making calls."

Charlie's eyes grew dark with disappointment. He looked like an abandoned little boy.

"We think he might be out at Jonathan's place," Ole added, the strength of his voice reassuring. "Jonathan's bought a nice little piece of land out in the country north of town here."

"Can we give them a call?" Charlie said eagerly.

"I'm sorry, son. Jonathan's taking his time getting a phone installed. Seems he's taken this peace and quiet thing a step too far."

Jo seized Brue by the shoulders and leaned in. "Say, Charlie. I think I know where Jonathan lives. We'd be happy to give you a ride out there if you'd like."

Charlie hesitated. He was looking at Sarah the way one craving sweets eyes a box of chocolates. Then Jo, Brue, and he dashed back to the car and headed north until the Chevy hit gravel at the edge of town. Bits of stone pelted the undercarriage, the heavy car rising, falling, and swaying over the deeply rutted roads. The corn was high enough to block the lights aglow at Jonathan's place until they rounded the bend. When they pulled into his pencil-thin driveway, Jonathan and Doc were sitting forward in their rocking chairs. From a distance, they appeared uncertain as to why anyone would enter their private rural world at this time of night.

Before the car pulled to a stop, Charlie unlatched the door, bounded out, and sprinted toward Jonathan's front porch.

And there, illuminated by the light of the car's headlamps, Jo watched shock register on Doc's gaunt face. He got up in slow motion and mouthed the word "son," trembling hands drawing Charlie into a tight embrace.

Jo swallowed hard against a painful knob inching up her throat, then drew Brue close and waited.

A long moment later, Charlie turned and waved Jo off with a grateful grin and a bob of his clean-cut head.

The car lights splashed over the rows of corn as Jo turned off the driveway and onto the gravel.

"Mom. Wait!" Brue shouted. "They're calling us back."

Jo eased to a stop by the ditch. Charlie was heading toward them at a full run. "Pop's car is in the garage having a little work done," he said. "Would you mind if we rode back with you? Seems silly for Jonathan to make a special trip to town."

As the car retraced the moon-bathed roads toward home, Jo

pondered the awkward quiet seeping from the backseat and shared a wondering look with Brue.

When the Chevy crossed onto asphalt, Doc broke the silence in a voice cracking with grief. "Charlie, why didn't you bother to let me know you were still alive? I thought I'd lost you."

Through the rearview mirror, Jo couldn't miss Charlie's grimace. He peered out the side window, away from his dad, as if shutting down. "I couldn't, Pop. I just couldn't."

"But, son," Doc said, his rough tone a plea, "I was worried sick."

Grieved by Doc's desperate need to know and Charlie's need not to tell, Jo interceded. "He didn't know you hadn't gotten the full story, Doc. And Charlie? We're all grateful to finally have you home."

She took note of the strained quiet from the back seat as the car lumbered down the darkened roads. She then glanced up at the moon hovering behind a layer of stratus clouds, too weak to cast a shadow on the wanting streets below.

Clearly, Charlie had serious issues that could easily require a lifetime to resolve.

At half past eleven, Jo pulled up to the curb in front of the O.M. Harrington where Sarah stood on the front porch leaning against a balustrade.

"What do you know about her, Dad?"

Engaging the emergency brake, Jo listened quietly.

"Nice girl," Doc said. "She's Big Ole's granddaughter."

"Married?"

"Not any more. I hear her husband got killed in the Netherlands. She's been seeing a successful young attorney uptown these days. Fellow by the name of Tryg Howland."

"I remember Tryg."

"Why are you asking about Sarah, son?"

"Cuz that's the girl I'm going to marry."

CHAPTER FOUR

Big Ole had been standing at the registration desk leafing through *The Amber Leaf Tribune* for the better part of an hour when Sarah tapped on his shoulder.

"Grandpa, you're gonna wear that newspaper out before Charlie comes down. For all you know, he could be a late sleeper."

Ole glanced at the open door to the coffee room. "Something isn't right with Doc. Did you see him when he walked by this morning? He didn't act like a man celebrating the return of his long-lost son. You'd think he'd be riding high. Didn't seem up to talking either. Kind of makes me wonder if something happened between the two of them last night."

"You can bet they're fine," Sarah said. "Now that Doc's had a chance to think about it, he's probably irritated with Charlie for not letting him know he was still alive."

Ole snuck another peek down the long hallway. "How I hate waiting. Dallying around makes me feel like an impatient adolescent."

"Why don't you go in and have a cup of coffee with Doc? I can attend the desk."

"No. I need to see if his boy's all right." He hesitated. "Perhaps I care more than I ought."

Just then a light swishing noise came from the far end of the hallway. "Here's our boy now. Mornin', Charlie." Ole's grin felt too wide even for his generous face. "I see you met up with your dad and made it home okay last night."

"Mornin'," Charlie repeated, but rather than meeting Ole's gaze, his eyes tethered onto a rosy cheeked Sarah who was standing at Ole's side.

"Mornin'," she replied demurely.

What is this anyway? Ole swore he could hear their hearts beating. Was he invisible or something? "If you're hunting down your dad, I believe you'll find him in the coffee room."

Charlie nodded his thanks, but continued standing in a daze, awkward, as if he didn't know what to do with himself.

Ole swept up the *Tribune* and found his way to a settee near the hearth, apparently the one place in the great room where this fine morning no fires burned. He peered over the top of the unfolded paper to see a confused-looking Sarah return to her post and Charlie disappear into the coffee room, looking as if he'd finally gotten his wits back.

Now what do you make of that?

Ole buried his nose in the paper. "Well, would you looky here."

"What, Grandpa?"

"Tryg's picture. It's in this morning's edition big as life. Come take a look. He's shaking hands with our mayor."

As Sarah hurried to peer over his shoulder, Ole considered how happy Tryg and Sarah appeared to be. Very well suited. Tryg was a far better catch than Charlie. With Tryg's war experiences a thing of the past, he was well established and knew where he was headed in life—professionally, that is.

But then there was Jo. He needed to wake up and make up his mind—either pursue Sarah with some sort of passion, or leave her alone and go after Jo, not that that ornery little heifer would give the man half a chance.

Ole reached for Sarah's forearm. "That Tryg is a good man."

"I know," she said with a far away look. "Sometimes I think he's almost too good."

CHAPTER FIVE

Immersed in her world of stenography, Ardena pounded away at her typewriter, stopping long enough to offer Jo a quick 'good morning.' She removed her seersucker jacket, which revealed an unusually thin, well-proportioned figure. Although Jo was several years shy of her thirtieth, an occasional client had asked if Ardena and she were mother and daughter. Same height, same delicate features, and straight white teeth, but the similarities stopped there. Ardena's hair was fine and reddish-brown, Jo's coarse and a dark shade of cocoa. Ardena's eyes were coffee-colored, Jo's midnight blue. And when Ardena got excited, she snickered with a snort.

Ten minutes past the hour, Tryg whistled all the way to the coatrack. Jo's heart did that crazy little fluttering thing again, but she ignored it. One of these days she would train that undisciplined contraption to settle down when in his presence. Six solid feet of tall, dark, and handsome—about to go to waste. Scrubbed look. Impeccable clothing. Wire-rimmed glasses. A hint of a limp from a war wound making him appear disarmingly vulnerable.

He strolled past her desk with a pleasant grin. "Word's out Charlie's back in town."

The keys on Ardena's Corona fell silent. "Charlie?" she said. "You mean fighter pilot Charlie? As in Doc's boy?"

"Yes, ma'am." Smile lines creased the corners of Tryg's liquid chestnut eyes. "I thought we'd lost him."

Jo swiveled her secretarial chair. "How did you hear about it so fast? Brue and I picked him up at the train depot late last night. No one knew he was coming."

"Jonathan. He told us all about it at our men's breakfast. That's why I'm late. So tell me, Jo, how did the guy look?"

Lovestruck—with your *girl.* Jo rolled a pencil between her fingers then inverted it and tapped the eraser on her desk. "He looks good, considering. Still the same Charlie. Quieter, maybe. No visible wounds that I could see."

"Where's he staying?" Ardena said.

"With his dad at the boarding house."

"You mean where Sarah lives?" Ardena grinned and turned to Tryg. "You'd better not get too comfortable in your relationship with Sarah then. You might have some stiff competition there."

Ardena's warning shot appeared to whiz past him. He didn't look threatened in the least.

"Is that a fact?" he said. "I'll have to stop by and say hello to the man. Better yet, maybe we should throw him a welcome home party."

"I don't think that's a good idea," Jo said. "Something's going on with him. I've got a feeling it's too soon for him to feel comfortable in the limelight."

Tryg turned thoughtful. "I guess I can understand that. It's not like I haven't walked in his boots. Maybe I can set up a small outing with the boys in the next month or so. Something sporty. Something to let him know we're here for him."

Ardena's eyes stayed fixed on Tryg as he disappeared into his office. The second the door closed behind him, she turned to Jo. "I can't believe I said that about Sarah."

"I'm glad you did. When I introduced Charlie to Sarah last night, they couldn't take their eyes off each other."

"How do you know you weren't misreading what you saw?"

"I overheard him tell his dad she's the girl he's going to marry."

"You've got to be kidding me."

"I wish I was. I wanted to warn Sarah, to tell her to guard her heart. Instead I felt like I'd hand-delivered Charlie to an unwitting yet apparent lady-in-waiting."

"She looked that eager?"

"You mean smitten. I couldn't shake the feeling of being complicit—of setting up the demise of Tryg's romantic future. What's worse, when you mentioned it to Tryg, I got the feeling he believes he's got little Miss Sarah Harrington comfortably tucked in his back pocket. He needed to be warned."

"Oh, dear," Ardena said.

"Oh, dear, is right. He's been cheated on before and doesn't need to go through that again."

"Tryg was cheated on? What woman in her right mind—"

"His fiancée joined the Red Cross. Went overseas. Ditched him for an Army doctor."

CHAPTER SIX

T he war had spread like a years-long tornado leaving the sun to shine on ruins strewn throughout the European Theatre. But still the black cloud crawled on its belly like a leopard sneaking up on its prey, growing increasingly ominous in the Pacific Theater. Rumors persisted about an atomic bomb, the man-made destruction the likes of which no one had ever before seen. Yet as the world grieved its destruction and feared its future, there were those giving and taking in marriage, one of which was Jo's next-door neighbor, Ned Wilder. Ned was home on a brief furlough to marry his childhood sweetheart.

Jo coveted a rest after an arduous week at the office, but refused to miss the shivaree out on the Walswick farm to the south and west of Glenville. When she and Brue arrived, the merriment was well under-way. An unusually happy character briskly pushing and pulling on the bellows of an accordion, a guitarist, and a fiddler stood atop a hay wagon, everyone stomping their feet rhythmically to the beat of peppy music.

Jo stood at the edge of the gathering content to watch dust trails swirl down the road and into the farmyard. Cars parked askew, half into ditches, half on the narrow road, many on the yard, while the crowd continued to grow.

When a familiar car angled in close, however, a filled up, nothing-is-missing-now feeling caught Jo by surprise. Tryg stepped around his car and got Sarah's door the way Charlie had gotten her door last Sunday evening. Tryg must have gotten past his fear of driving. Either that or he was putting on a very impressive show. To Jo's knowledge, he hadn't driven past the city limits since that dreadful accident.

Sarah clasped his hand. Her striking eyes glistened with a filled-up, nothing-is-missing-in-her-world look, too, the same look she had displayed when her gaze meshed with Charlie's. Maybe Jo misjudged Sarah after all, but she hadn't misjudged Charlie's intentions toward her.

Jo guided Brue on until they found a quiet spot at the far side of the yard. Suddenly Brue clasped Jo's arm with both hands and pushed onto her tiptoes craning to see past the crowd. "Hey, Mom. Look over there."

Jo followed Brue's gaze toward the charred remains of an outhouse.

"It's almost burned to the ground," Brue said. "Do you think it got hit by lightning or something?"

"No, not lightning," a masculine voice said from behind. "Looks more like an attempt at a controlled burning."

Pleasant and impressive-looking in his well-tailored uniform and wearing an arresting smile, Ned Wilder reached for Jo's hand. "Thank you so much for coming tonight."

"Ned. We wouldn't have missed it, not for the world. We're so happy for you. Look at you and how well you wear your uniform. You make your countrymen proud."

"Thanks, Jo, but you're going to make me blush." Ned turned to Brue. "About that outhouse. Methane gas forms in those structures, and every now and then a clever farmer has been known to drop in a match to burn off the waste."

"How come?" Brue said innocently.

"So he won't have to dig another hole and move it so often. He keeps a bucket of water handy in case the flames get out of control." Ned shook his head and with a glint in his eye, he said, "Poor Farmer Walswick. Looks like he didn't fetch enough water to get the job done."

Jo burst into laughter.

"Wait a second, Jo." Ned reached for the hand of someone in passing. She turned and gazed into the warm eyes of a well weathered, albeit shockingly good looking farmer.

"Have you met Frank Breck?" Ned asked. "He's one of the few eligible bachelors left in the county, if not the state."

Frank appeared taken aback, and gave Jo a brief nod.

"And this is Jo Bremley. By the way, Frank, thanks for helping my new father-in-law look after his farm while I'm gone. He says you've ...."

Understatedly excusing herself, Jo stepped away from their conversation. "Come, Brue. Let's give these men some privacy."

Just then the fiddler approached the microphone and asked everyone to find a partner. The square dance was about to begin.

Jo guided Brue toward the farmhouse. They were managing their way through the crowd when a young boy came running up from behind and grabbed Brue's hand. She giggled and marched out to the dance floor with him.

Jo smiled and walked on. Suddenly she felt a tap on her shoulder. "May I have the honor, ma'am?"

"Certainly," she said, but then she turned and choked down a gulp. The man, thirty years her senior if a day, was dressed in bib overalls, a checkered shirt, his face pocked with blackheads, several days' growth of whiskers, and his grin revealed a missing cuspid. The rest of his teeth appeared to not have experienced a brush bristle since birth.

Jo and her partner stepped into formation. A brief moment later, she found herself standing in a dance square opposite Tryg and Sarah. Tryg glanced at her partner then grinned at Jo and winked. She wanted to crawl into a gopher hole and hide.

Jo didn't mind bowing to her partner, bowing to her corner. She didn't mind allemande left. She didn't mind promenade. Nor did she mind do-si-do. She enjoyed them. It was the pull-by that gave her fits. Although she wouldn't allow her eyes to meet Tryg's, through her peripheral vision, she saw more than she wanted to see—the smoothness of his movements, that soft shock of brown hair bouncing gently against his forehead, and the warm and handsome grin that didn't appear to want to go away. She felt helpless to fight that unwanted magic, that tingling, those intoxicating sparks each time his fingers touched hers.

Casting her gaze toward the flattening grass, she willed it to stay there. What was the matter with her? Was it the contrast with her dance partner that spiked a sudden yearning for someone like Tryg? Whatever the reason, Jo needed to get past it.

Halfway through the dance, her ankle caught on a tuft of crabgrass and twisted. Sharp pain shot up her leg and she stumbled. Her alert and agile partner swept her up by the elbow and gently escorted her off the dance floor. "Are you going to be okay, young lady?"

"I'll be fine."

"Well, if it's okay with you then," he said with a grin, "there are so many lovely ladies, so little time, and my feet they can't a keep from dancin."

Jo found a folding chair and watched from the sidelines. Tryg and Sarah laughed merrily as they danced. Brue and her little friend happily dodged wild elbows and flying feet. The old man with the missing tooth appeared more agile and cheerful than anyone out on the floor. But Jo? She felt lonely, one step removed, and more determined than ever to get away. Make that move to New York. The sooner the better.

A too-long moment later, she felt another tap on her shoulder. "I'm sorry," she said, "but my feet—"

"Are hurting already? But the evening is so young."

Her breath caught. Tingles unexpectedly rippled from head to toe. "I'm sorry," she repeated. "I—"

"No need to apologize," Frank Breck said, his eyes glimmering. "Would a chat over a glass of punch suit you better?"

Her cheeks grew warm and her heart picked up its pace. "Yes. I'd like that very much."

"They're revving up their instruments," Tryg said, stepping up close from behind. "Why don't the two of you join us?"

Frank hesitated. "Are you—"

Jo stood, pressed weight on her ankle, and smiled. "I seem to be okay now."

Thanks to a dashing Farmer Frank and a quick recovery from her injury, she went on to dance until her feet hurt from dancing, her cheeks hurt from laughing, and she was very short of breath.

A few minutes past nine, dark descended, the stars growing even more numerous against the velvety sky. The music turned thoughtful. After yodeling *The Cattle Call*, the guitarist asked everyone to gather at the foot of the wagon. A silvery moon peeked over the barn and cast a soft glow, the barn and trees silhouetted against the darkening summer sky. During a brief moment's quiet, an owl hooted, a horse whinnied faintly out on the north forty, and then they sang *Home on the Range*, everyone swaying to the soothing rhythm of the music.

Looking around at the guests, everyone appeared so at home out here on the farm. How content and at home even Jo felt in this rural haven where worries of war were, at least temporarily, far from anyone's mind. Even Farmer Frank caught her eye and smiled bashfully. Jo stifled a grin when he looked away as if he'd done something wrong.

As evening drew to a close, the groom hopped onto the wagon and extolled the virtues of his beautiful young bride. He thanked his treasured family and friends for celebrating this joyous occasion with them, and thanked the musicians who then played an interesting rendition of *Anchors Away*. When their instruments quieted, Ned snapped to attention. His respectful salute to the soon-to-be-gone guests siphoned the air out of Jo's lungs. In the dead quiet, she swallowed against a painful lump rising in her throat that refused to go down. A tear splashed on a shoe here and there like fat raindrops on concrete, for in a few short days, Ned Wilder would once again head out into the Pacific where countless planes dropped out of the sky into shark-infested waters, and blazing ships sank into high rolling seas. Ned stood, the true sailor, ready and honored to do his part to protect his homeland.

Then the blushing bride and excited groom journeyed off in a well-polished Ford with *Just Married* scribbled all over its windows with homemade lye soap. Cans rattling on twine chased the car up the country road. The car, as it disappeared from sight, sounded more like a puttering tugboat than an old Model-T.

With the shivaree having come to a satisfying end, Jo quickly collected Brue, rolled down her window, and fired up the car. Before shifting into reverse, she jumped at the sound of a masculine voice. "Jo?"

CHAPTER SEVEN

Brue lay asleep in the front seat, fingers curled around gathers in her pink muslin dress, her head nestled gently against Jo's shoulder. The hustle and bustle of the shivaree had left her exhausted.

Not Jo. Driving through the country with the wind in her hair, she felt light and giddy. Arresting the attention of an extraordinarily handsome farmer certainly helped matters. Of all the unlikely places for dreams to unfold—a farm. The scent of hay and manure swirling about, an occasional cow mooing, horse snorting. Outhouses. Milk cans. She wanted to hold on to this evening's memories and never let go.

She smiled as she relived the square dancing. Her breathlessness. The banter, light and free. Good food. Too bad Tryg had to cut in before Jo and Frank got a good chance to talk, though. She recalled the last few minutes gazing through the open window of her car, and Frank's hopeful look when he asked if he could phone her. That look clicked in her mind like a picture she would not soon forget. The caring in his voice warmed her. As the car entered the southern end of town, she saw Amber Leaf through brighter eyes. In one brief evening her world had grown far more beautiful and promising.

But when her car eased over the hill on Charles Street, Jo gasped, her warm feelings suddenly waxing cold. Something suspicious lay at the side of the road ahead. It looked like a body. Lying face down, feet sticking out from under the bushes. She seized the steering wheel with a vice-like grip, her heart slamming wildly against her chest. "Brue! Get down on the floorboard ... fast!" she shouted.

Brue woke with a start. "Hunh?"

"Get down on the floorboard."

Jo's Chevy jerked to a stop, its headlights casting long shadows past the masculine figure sprawled half on gravel and half into the bushes like useless garbage. As she peered out her open window, a groan penetrated the darkness, prickling her flesh.

Brue pressed her nose against the windshield. "Who is it, Mom? Is he dying?"

Jo stared at the motionless figure, her voice quivering through shallow breath. "I don't know."

With trembling hands, she unlatched her car door then stopped and gazed at Brue. "If anything happens, sweetheart, I want you to run as fast as you can to Evelyn's. Got it?"

Brue nodded, wide-eyed.

Shoving open the heavy car door, Jo slipped out into the night. She hesitated, took a reluctant step, first back and then to the side. With slow, calculated movements, she ran her trembling fingers along the top of the door as if that could protect her. Rounding to the other side, she craned her neck and peered past the left front fender.

A single mother and daughter.

Alone.

And not another soul in sight.

Jo looked up into the inky sky. *God, I'm terrified. Help us. Please!*

The sound of the car door slamming rattled her. An instant later, she drew a quick breath as Brue clutched her arm.

"You need to get back in the car."

"I'm too scared, Mom."

Jo pulled her daughter close.

For a brief moment she might have seen a flicker of movement. Was this a setup? A drunk who'd passed out? A hobo who'd wandered too far from the railroad tracks? She glanced behind her, into the bushes, past nearby trees. Was anyone watching?

All the while looking, looking, looking around, she maneuvered Brue behind her and took a reluctant step forward. In the stillness, her penny loafers crunched loudly on gravel. What should she do?

Then through the dim wash of the street lamp, the man with ripped clothing, covered in dirt and blood, moaned and twisted toward her. He started to rise, then fell back down.

Stealing a closer look, she gasped. "Mr. Harrington! Big Ole!"

CHAPTER EIGHT

T he old man moaned.

Jo fell to his side. "What happened? Are you okay? Stay right here." Clearly Jo wasn't thinking straight. Stay right here? Where was the man going to go for heaven's sake? He was barely conscious. Couldn't even move. "We'll get help."

Jo steadied her rapid breathing. "Brue. Run. Fast. Over to Tomlinson's. Tell Evelyn to call an ambulance right away."

As Brue bounded out of sight, Jo bent over Big Ole's twisted, beaten-up body. "Who could have done such an awful thing to you?" she said more to herself than to him. "Mr. Harrington? Mr. Harrington? Is there anything I can do for you? Anything to make you more comfortable until an ambulance gets here?"

A sudden rustling sounded from somewhere nearby, possibly the lilac bushes. Jo tensed. Her breath caught. "Who's there?" she cried with feigned courage, praying she wouldn't get an answer. What if someone was there? What could she possibly do? Her only means of protection was her purse, and she doubted she could do much damage hurling it around like some crazy person trying to get in a crippling whack. Besides, her purse was in the car. She listened intently for a moment then backhanded her forehead and let out a breath of spent air. It was probably a rabbit or a squirrel, she told herself.

Jo felt for Ole's pulse. Weak, but definitely there. Or was it weak? How could she possibly know? She'd never had occasion to feel for a pulse before. She searched for signs of serious bleeding. Other than slight oozing here and there, she found nothing that needed a tourniquet.

Hurry, Brue. Hurry!

A forever moment later, Evelyn and Brue stood at Jo's side, hovering over her shoulder too dumbfounded to speak. "Brue, would you mind running over to the O.M. Harrington?" Jo said. "We need to get Sarah, sweetie."

"Evelyn, would you mind watching after her?"

Evelyn gave Jo a dazed nod.

"Thanks. And Brue? Tell Sarah to come quick."

"But they were still at the shivaree when we left, Mom. Don't you remember?"

"That's right, they were. Just leave word for her then, okay? Ask whoever you can find to tell her to get to the hospital the minute she comes home."

Brue's footsteps faded, and then a short while later her padding grew louder again when she rounded the corner on Charles Street.

In the distance, the scream of a siren also grew louder. When the ambulance screeched to a halt, neighbors poured out of their homes in bobby pins, robes, slippers, and bare feet. Gasps. Groans. Whispers. Necks stretching for a better look. Everyone aghast at the appalling sight before them.

Near the park's edge, something glinted in the rotating light. Evelyn gripped Jo's elbow. "Do you see what I see?"

Jo nodded. "I think we'd better take a look."

They meandered across the road with all the enthusiasm of one being forced at gunpoint to approach the jagged edge of a steep cliff. Jo crouched down and reluctantly seized Big Ole's cane. She then studied the road. Gyrating lights exposed the disturbed gravel like a lighthouse flashing an ominous warning. When she looked up, her gaze locked with Evelyn's horror-filled eyes. Big Ole had been dragged from the park, dropped, and left unconscious.

After a swift examination, the ambulance crew hoisted him onto a stretcher. A moment later Jo watched its closing doors. "I think I'd better follow them. Brue, you go home with Evelyn. Would you mind, Evelyn? I'll call as soon as I know anything."

Jo shadowed the emergency vehicle up the sleepy streets of Amber Leaf toward Naeve Hospital, wondering. How was it that no one had come to Big Ole's rescue? She didn't recall seeing lights on in any of the nearby houses until after the ambulance came. Maybe his groans had been muted by radios broadcasting war news, or the neighbors were in their back rooms preparing for bed and couldn't hear him.

The shock of finding him intensified with every passing streetlight, every passing car. She shuddered to think that had she not gone out for the evening, he might have lain on the gravel for the duration of the night, and worse could have happened. Or was the worst over yet? At his vulnerable age, Ole might not make it through this ordeal. How bad were his wounds? How could he not have internal bleeding? Broken bones? Punctured organs?

What kind of thugs had it in them to do such a despicable thing?

She shook her head. Man's blatant brutality to man.

An older couple stood at the street corner at East Main. Laughing lightheartedly about who knew what, they covered their ears as the ambulance wailed by. The contrast seemed stark, not right somehow—people carefree and laughing while others suffered and fought for their fragile lives.

The instant Ole disappeared through the doors of the Emergency Room, Jo called the chief of police. "I'll be right there," he announced. Not five minutes later his larger-than-life frame with jaws set like a bull-dog stormed into the hospital, the doors crashing against the aseptic walls behind him. He fired questions at Jo faster than she could answer them.

Several hours later, Jo and Chief Stout knocked on the doorjamb of Big Ole's room. He was already sitting on the side of the bed, glaring at his hospital slippers. Snowy gauze covered the better half of his swollen face. Scrapes and bruises colored his uncovered flesh like a bad tattoo. One arm was wrapped snug in a sling, and yet there he sat, alert and cross.

"Ole, what are you doing sitting up?" Chief Stout said, his tone mingled with unnerved compassion.

"I may be sitting, but my insides are standing taller than a redwood."

"I think you'd better lay back down."

"I think not."

Chief Stout cut a half grin. Jo felt certain that he admired Ole's spunk, too. The chief raised his double chin and stuffed a thumb in his belt. "Anything I can get for you?"

"You can get me out of here."

"I don't want to get in trouble with your doctor."

"You let me worry about him." Ole tried rearranging himself on the bed. Jo doubted it possible for him to find a comfortable position.

The chief appeared to take his time feeling out Ole then asked in a gentle voice, "What happened tonight, Ole? Who did this to you?"

"I know I'm an old man, far past my prime," he said matter-of-factly, "but I'm going to have to ask you to take a back seat for now. Something doesn't add up. I need to think things through. This may be one time when I need to handle things my way."

Jo's eyes froze into a stare. What was Ole thinking? He suffered a severe beating she doubted a lesser person could have endured.

"You're right," Chief Stout said taking on a more commanding tone. "You are an old man, and a lucky old man to boot. You could've easily been killed."

Ole's bushy brows snapped together. "It wasn't my time." He then reached out to Jo. "Now give me my walking stick. Where'd you find it?"

"Lying on the grass at the edge of the park."

Chief Stout rocked his ample weight on the heels of what appeared to be size thirteen shoes. "Whoever the ringleader is who did this," he said matter-of-factly, "and I do believe I know who that is, they have schools for that these days. That's where that boy's heading, along with that hoodlum friend of his. Straight to reform school. I'll give you a day or two to think things through. In the meantime, I'm going to chase those boys down."

Ole started to stand, but grimacing with pain, he flopped back on the side of the bed only to grimace again. "You leave him alone."

"Him?" The chief sounded taken aback. "Or did you mean to say them?" When the chief's request met with prolonged silence, he added, "I think you'd better get some rest."

Immediately outside Ole's room, Jo said to a fast-walking Chief Stout, "We can't reach Sarah. Brue and I just came from Ned Wilder's shivaree out at the Walswick farm. I think Sarah and Tryg were still there when we left. Brue left a message for Sarah at the boarding house."

The chief stopped and pulled out the keys to his squad car, fidgeting with them. "Did you see anything, Jo? Anything at all?"

She shook her head. "You might want to drive out and take a look at the road, though, before too many cars have a chance to drive on it. Evelyn and I could tell by the way the gravel was disrupted that Mr. Harrington was dragged all the way from the park. I may have seen tire tracks from a couple of bikes, too, but couldn't swear to it. It was awfully dark."

"I'll do that. Need a lift home?"

"No. I have my car. About Sarah, though—"

The chief hurried out, glancing back as though he hadn't heard her correctly.

"Thanks for trying to find her," Jo said to the slamming door.

CHAPTER NINE

With hands shoved deep into the pockets of her flared skirt, Jo trudged out into the night. Like a protective mama bear, she ached to get her paws on the devils who brought down Big Ole. She didn't care who they were—how big, tall, mean, or small. She had no idea what she would do if and when she found them. All she knew was that she wanted them, and she wanted them bad.

She drove slowly down Fountain Street—a young woman alone with no means of protection. Yet she scanned every alley, looked past every house, around every tree, looking for anything that moved as if she were some kind of Dick Tracy. A few blocks up the road, she turned onto the well-lit streets on Broadway. To her surprise, lights poured through the windows of Tryg's office.

Not only was Tryg in his office, the door was open. Once inside, she heard Sarah's feminine voice.

Jo knocked lightly, peered in, and met with two startled faces. "I didn't realize I'd find you here."

"What's going on?" Tryg said. "You look like you've seen a ghost."

"I think Chief Stout is out looking for you, Sarah."

Color drained from her rosy cheeks. "Chief Stout? Whatever for?"

"It's about your grandfather." Jo stepped farther into the room and folded her arms across her cotton blouse. "I'm sure he'll be okay, but he's been roughed up pretty badly."

Sarah's eyes swelled to twice their size, her chest visibly heaving. "He what?"

As Jo shared the details, Sarah groaned and leaned hard into Tryg. "Any idea who would do such a thing or why?"

"No, and for some reason your grandfather refuses to talk."

"He's at the hospital?" Tryg asked, through a severely clenched jaw. Jo nodded.

"We'd better get going, Sarah." He swiped his keys from the desktop and turned to Jo. "Want to come along?"

She shook her head. "I'll leave word at the boarding house about finding the two of you, and then I think I'll head home."

As she hopped into her Chevy, she watched Tryg drive away with Sarah. Giving him time to figure things out on his own was a lot harder than she could have imagined, but so be it. They had more important things to deal with now.

Returning her attention to Big Ole, she drove on, resuming her watch, searching diligently for misplaced shadows or movement, indignation overriding any fear.

A few minutes later she picked up Brue at Evelyn's and drove home, the utter darkness on her desolate road giving her an eerie chill.

CHAPTER TEN

S huddering at the sterile environment, Tryg sniffed the fresh hospital air. What was that pungent odor? Rubbing alcohol? Reminded him of one too many surgeries, being laid up for painful, boring, and lonely months—months listening to the groans of fellow soldiers and enduring the brave, silent tears shed by their loved ones. The memories strangled him. No one liked feeling broken or weak. As they walked along, he pulled back his shoulders. This visit was about Big Ole Harrington, not about him.

A wispy young woman wearing a white uniform and starched nurse's cap led them along a wide corridor. He listened to the swishing of her hose and choked down more painful memories, these memories of Elizabeth—the rejection and lost future still cut like a razor.

The nurse stopped shy of Ole's room. "You can go in now," she said sounding sympathetic.

He and Sarah hesitated long enough to collect themselves. Tryg tried not to react visibly to the appalling sight before him, Ole sitting up in bed covered head-to-toe in bandages.

"Bring me my clothes," he said gruffly without bothering to look at them.

Tryg forced back a pride-filled grin. With all that old man's swelling, scrapes, and bruises too numerous to count, while he looked fragile in the harsh light of the private room, the tenor of his voice was anything but. He remained unquestionably the invincible O.M. Harrington.

Sarah rushed to his side. "Well, hello to you, too, Grandpa. What on earth happened? You look a fright."

"I want to go home," he snapped.

"No, you can't. Look at you."

As Sarah reached for the sheet to cover him, Ole quickly tossed it aside with an abrupt flick of his wrist. "I'm fine," he insisted, but his controlled grimace as he reached for an arm snugly wrapped in a sling said otherwise.

Tryg sidled up to the bed. Resting a comforting hand on Sarah's shoulder, he caught a whiff of another familiar scent. Sarah's hair smelled like Elizabeth's had.

He took a step back, willing his past life to stay where it belonged—in the past. "Ole, you might want to listen to your granddaughter. You need rest. At least stay until morning. What if you get a blood clot, or have a fall?"

"Oh, for heaven's sakes," Ole hissed.

Sarah lowered onto the bed and scooched up close. "You grimaced again. I thought you said you were fine."

"I am."

"You haven't told us what happened yet. Who did this to you? And why? You've got to let us know."

"I don't have to let you know anything. Just take me home. I want to be left alone."

The sight of Ole in obvious pain after a brutal beating sparked questions too numerous for Tryg to count, and a building rage. "Do you think this relates to the string of robberies we've been having around town lately?" he asked.

Ole stared straight ahead.

Come on, man. Say something.

"Bring me my clothes."

"No," Sarah said. "You could hurt yourself."

"Don't go worrying about me. I have too much padding to break any bones."

Sarah scowled at his sling. "What's that?"

"It's a simple sprain for crying out loud! Now bring me my clothes," he said with an insistent point, but as he waved his huge hand, a groan slipped out.

"Grandpa, you're not getting your clothes until you get clearance from your doctor."

"Then get him in here."

Sarah looked to Tryg, her eyes summoning help.

Bruised, beaten, and emotionally battered, the old man didn't need any more stress, so Tryg gave Sarah a go-ahead nod and said to Ole, "Forgive us for trying so hard. When you're ready, you'll talk."

Since Ole appeared to settle down, Tryg headed for the door.

"Where are you going?" Sarah asked.

"I know it's last minute, but I want to see if it's possible to hire a nurse so he can go home."

Tryg left the room, his troubled thoughts knotted with fascination and horror. An hour later, he stood on the porch of the O.M. Harrington saying good night to Sarah. "I can't stop thinking about your grandpa, how bad he's hurting, and all that pent-up anger. Can you imagine how humiliated he must feel?"

"I know," she said. "I can't stop thinking about that either, and after such a long and vibrant life. I feel so sorry for him."

"Something's kind of hard to understand, though."

"What's that?"

"His actions. You know him. He couldn't have been in shock. He's too tough for that, and if anyone doesn't fear bullies, it's your grandfather. I've got a hunch there's more to his obstinacy than meets the eye. A lot more."

CHAPTER ELEVEN

T aking care not to awaken any bruises or abrasions, Ole shoved aside the breakfast tray and stared at the picture of his late wife sitting atop the dresser. "Good morning, mother," he said the way he greeted her morning and night, seven days a week, his tone always loving and sincere, but this time he added, "I need you. I've got a real battle on my hands here. Don't know which side is going to win, compassion or hate. You know me. Never did have much use for hate. Least not 'til I lost you. I really cut loose then, didn't I? Took it out on anyone who crossed my path. Hated getting up in the morning. Hated being bothered. Hated life. The only thing I looked forward to was going to bed so I could sleep it off. I finally regain my will to live and this happens. I'm ashamed to say it, but feeling violated, it's almost ..." He shook his head.

"That one boy, though, the one they call Wil. I don't know what to make of him. After he stood by and watched his friend beat me senseless, it wasn't so much his coming back that night that surprised me. It's how he came back. Now I don't know what to do."

Ole was smoothing a pucker out of his bed sheet when a light knock rattled the door.

Calvin Doherty peeked in. "Mind if I come in? I can only stay a minute. There's a sick man at the hospital who needs me, too."

"Too?" Ole said.

"That's right." Calvin grinned, pulled up a chair, then looked around. "Must be my imagination. I could swear I heard you talking to someone."

Ole glanced at the picture. "The wife. Imagining what she'd say if she were here."

Calvin nodded as if he understood. "How are you getting along? I stopped by yesterday. Didn't want to wake you. You were sound asleep."

"Been better, I guess. How about you? How are you doing?"

Calvin chuckled. "Always got to be in control, don't you? Even of the conversation."

"I've always felt at home taking the lead, yes. Isn't that what leaders do?"

"Looks like your wounds are mending well." Calvin hesitated then got up and strolled to the far side of the room, rested a shoulder against the window frame, and peered out as if looking for something. Time, maybe?

"What's on your mind?" Ole said. "Might as well spit it out."

"I'm trying to be considerate."

"Then let me say it for you. If you're wondering about the wounds you can't see, you don't want to hear what I have to say about them."

"That's why I'm here." When Ole did not respond, Calvin said, "I assume the scales have tipped hard toward bitter. I'd say that's understandable. Under the circumstances, who could blame you?"

"Humiliation's really something, isn't it?" Although Ole carefully shook his head, he still endured another stab of pain. "I don't like it, not one little bit. You should hear the whispering going on out there in the hallway. Makes me feel like I've got some kind of contagious disease. Somehow, some way, I've got to get my dignity back."

"You aren't hurting for dignity, Ole. Never have. Never will."

"Easily said for someone who wasn't left out on the dirt like roadkill. I want all of my dignity back."

Calvin returned to the chair, flipped it around, and straddled it, forearms resting on its back. "How are you planning to do that?"

"I don't know yet. You're the preacher. Got any good counsel?"

"As a matter of fact, maybe I do. But I doubt it's going to make much sense."

Ole smoothed yet another pucker out of the bed sheet. "Let's have it."

"Okay," Calvin said. "There's a scripture that comes to mind. You're undoubtedly familiar with it. *And we know that all things work together for good to them that love God, to them who are the called according to his purpose.*"

"Even in a situation like this?"

"That's right. Giving thanks and, believing that all things can work together for good changes our focus. Lifts our eyes toward a solution. Awakens our hope. But then you already knew that, didn't you?"

Ole nodded. "I've given it some thought over the years, I guess. But I want answers here. This is a problem that needs a good fix."

"Have you thought of looking for the answer in the problem?"

"*In* the problem?" Ole repeated. "You might have something there. I'll give that a try."

Calvin got up and stood quietly, as if finding it difficult to leave.

"Chief Stout is stopping by this morning," Ole said. "He's going to ask questions. I don't know what to say to the man, at least not yet. I can't let him take over my life."

"What do you mean?"

"The more information I give him, the less control I have. I need to handle this one myself."

"You've whetted my curiosity. I'd like to hear more, but, unfortunately, I've got to run. Try not to worry about it. When the chief comes, you'll know what to say."

Ole watched the door close and then looked around the room. Although a light breeze danced with the sheers and the sun filtered through the open windows brightening his surroundings, it was quiet, too quiet, and the walls were closing in on him. He eased out of bed and plodded toward the mirror with an uneven gait. When he caught sight of his gaping image, he grimaced. Small stabs of pain shot up in places he didn't know had nerve endings. He gripped the water basin until the throbbing subsided, then examined his face from top to bottom and side to side. Why did they have to make bandages so blindingly white? Why did bruises have to turn so revoltingly dark? At least the swelling was subsiding.

Unable to tolerate a shut-in's existence for another suffocating second, he gazed longingly at the bedroom door. If his image scared the living daylights out of him, what would it do to everyone else? He sighed. What was a caged-in old man to do?

Not only did Ole give himself an extra-close shave, he patted on a two-day supply of aftershave and redressed his wounds with smaller bandages, whiter than snow though they were. He slipped on a crisp dress shirt, his best-tailored trousers, and the snappiest suspenders he could find. He buffed his cane to a spit shine, then hobbled around his bedroom until his raw muscles limbered.

He took one last look at himself.

Not too bad.

At the top of the staircase, an attack of light-headedness hit him harder than a cinder block. Whirling around like a drunk on stilts, he reached for the wall and steadied himself. He then pulled out a handkerchief and wiped the perspiration leaking from his forehead and hands as if gushing from a broken pipe. Making it to the bottom of the stairs was going to be tough. Regaining his equilibrium, he seized the handrail and planted his cane on the top step for extra support. The first step riled him. His foot went out, but refused to go down. Wrong leg. He rested the bulk of his weight against the banister and tried again. To his relief, he managed to make it to the bottom of the stairs one clumsy step at a time. Chiding his legs to keep moving and his knees not to buckle, he eased down the long hallway with his head held high.

"Grandpa!" Sarah shrieked when he rounded the corner of the great room. "What on earth are you doing out of bed?"

A maid in the far corner let out a gasp then gaped at him. Was it really necessary for her to take a step back, too? Crazy woman.

"A better question would be what have I been doing loitering around in bed so long? Any coffee left?"

Suddenly the front door swung open and Chief Stout walked in at a brisk pace. "Ahh! Just the man I came to see," he said. "Ready to have that little chat now?"

"Not really, but if we must." Ole looked around then led them to the game table where Chief Stout pulled out a chair for him.

"How are you doing?" the chief asked.

How was Ole doing? When Calvin had asked, Ole didn't give his response much thought, but now that he was up and around, it niggled at him. Every time he saw his image reflecting from glass, he relived that runaway bike racing toward him, the burning slide across dusty gravel, and the incessant kicks slamming against his aging body. Every whisper reminded him he'd been violated. Every movement reminded him of the cruel, senseless blows to his face and body.

"I can handle the pain any day of the week, but it's the ..." Ole looked past Chief Stout, trying to distance himself. The pain those boys inflicted sliced deep, but those thoughts were private. "Let's say that I've learned more than I want to know about hate. It came marching in like a warrior. Don't worry. I'll deal with it. So tell me. How are you doing with your investigation?"

The chief chuckled. "I'm the one who's supposed to ask the questions here."

"How's it going?"

"I'm not getting far," the chief said, sober faced. "Those boys are smart."

"You're assuming it was boys?"

"That's right. There were bike tracks on the gravel. No one wants to talk. Seems the two in question are members of a bicycle club. I can't get any of the boys in that club to talk either. Now tell me what happened. Like I told you in the hospital, if Wil Thompson was one of the thugs who attacked you, he'll be the first one to make a one-way trip to Red Wing."

"Reform school?"

"That's right."

"Want a cup of coffee?"

"No. I'm fine."

"What's the story on that Wil boy anyway?" Ole asked.

"He's a renegade. Always getting into trouble. Truant from school. Bad mouth. Bad attitude. Comes from a rough home. His dad's the town drunk."

"That I did know. What makes you think Red Wing would be the best place for a boy like that?"

"What are you getting at?"

Ole folded his hands. "Sounds like the boy's troubled. Maybe he could use a helping hand."

"So it was him, wasn't it?"

"We've already had this conversation. You're on your own, Chief."

"Look, I don't care how troubled anyone is. There's no excuse for beating up people."

"If I did tell you all about what happened," Ole said, "whoever did it would get sent away. Is that right?"

"That's right. So what happened? Why don't you start at the beginning?"

Ole shook his head. "Sorry. Seems I don't remember a thing about that night."

The chief scowled. "Well, if you don't beat all!"

"Now if you'll excuse me, I'm behind on my chores here."

"Ole? What's going on with you? Did they knock you senseless? I need answers."

"Like I keep telling you, you're not getting them from me."

Chief Stout thrummed the table as if waiting Ole out. A few long moments later, he stood. "Okay, have it your way. I don't know what to make of you, but I am going to shake those boys down, and you will be getting a subpoena. I will get answers from you one way or another."

Ole poured a steaming cup of coffee, swiped up a copy of the early morning paper, and then occupied a rocking chair at the far end of the wrap-around porch. He sipped the warm liquid and fixed his gaze on Harrington Park. Things tended to look better in the daylight. Fresher. Brighter. But not today. At least, not yet. Today's brightness was tinged not only by his night of terror, but also by Chief Stout's rush to judgment, appropriate though it may be.

Yet, after his chat with Calvin, Ole sensed opportunity. A Harrington could not allow a single event to turn his world upside down. Calvin's words played again in his mind. 'Have you thought of looking for the answer in the problem?' If the answer was in the problem, was Ole's burgeoning thought to make good of the incident feasible?

"Well, hello, sir."

Ole peered over the railing. "Charlie!"

"Nice to see you're out of bed again," he said as he strutted up the sidewalk and onto the porch. "You're looking a lot better this morning."

"Tell that to the maid."

"Why's that?"

Ole shrugged.

Charlie pulled up a rocking chair next to Ole's and crossed an ankle over a knee. "I wouldn't worry about it. It'll take time, but people will get used to seeing you. All that's important is that you get better."

Time. That was a luxury Ole could ill afford. "You've been out and about before the crack of dawn, I see," he said.

"That's right. Had breakfast at Hotel Albert."

"No problem with our food here, I hope."

"Not at all. You can't beat Bernie's cooking. I needed to get out for a while. Little case of cabin fever, I guess."

Ole chuckled then lifted his cup, stopping shy of his lips. "You should try playing shut-in some time."

"No, thanks." Charlie looked out toward the park as if something or someone had arrested his attention.

"What am I missing?"

"That couple over there. They've been craning their necks. Looks like they're trying to get a gander at you."

"Maybe I should stand and take a bow," Ole said flatly. "That's the way it's been around here."

Charlie stared after the couple as they walked on. "They aren't the only ones nosing in, Ole. There's a lot more whispering going on. Everywhere I go seems strangers can't resist approaching me. Must know I live here. They're asking questions like it's their right to know all the gory details of your assault."

Ole set his rocker into motion. "I have broad shoulders and can handle a lot of things, but whispers behind my back get my dander up." He slowed his rocking. "After your stint in the Army, you understand what it's like to make a temporary stop on the losing side of life."

"Tell me about it. First, you endure the hit, and if that's not punishment enough, you get the privilege of enduring peoples' opinions about the hit. Don't let 'em get you down, sir."

Ole considered Charlie's words. Although broken, Ole was on the mend, and having been treated as if he were worthless did not diminish his value in the least. True, his body showed visible signs of some rather interesting wounds, but they were superficial, and his mind was razor sharp. "Problem is," Ole said, "in my search for answers, I'm flirting with taking on a considerable risk here, a risk I fear will further unnerve those revoltingly small minds. I need to make absolutely certain I'm doing the right thing."

Charlie plucked at the cuff of a pant leg. "You're never going to find out unless you try."

Ole mulled over the people who had believed in him before, but now chose not to. What was worse, his granddaughter and Chief Stout numbered among them. Few had the wherewithal to see a broader picture.

Well, that was about to change.

Ole got up and pushed through a few stiff, painful steps then strode down the porch stairs and onto the sidewalk.

"Hey, where're you going?" Charlie asked.

Ole turned and grinned. "I've got a job to do, a home to visit, and a score to settle."

As Ole walked away, he swore he'd heard Charlie mutter, "Go get 'em, Ole."

Jo sat outside the office in her Chevy, mapping out her route. Tryg needed a package for a hearing at the courthouse. It was her job to pick it up from a private residence on East Ninth Street, down near the south end of town.

The south end of town.

She smiled.

Farmer Frank. He lived closer to the south end of town and should be calling any night now.

Firing up her car, she headed down Newton, turned left on First, then right on Frank Avenue. While slowing to check the traffic at a quiet intersection, she did a double take when she saw a familiar-looking figure walking down a side street. Big Ole? Out and about mere days after the assault?

He was tottering along with a slower than usual gait as if nothing out of the ordinary had happened. She pulled her car to the side of the street and observed a redheaded girl with freckles, poking her petite nose over the railing on a front porch.

Jo quietly rolled down her window and leaned out, hoping to get an earful like a proficient snoop.

The little girl twisted a braid and pointed. "It's that house down there at the end of the road," she said, her voice loud enough for Jo to hear.

Oh, no! That was the house where that Thompson boy lived. The kid had the reputation of being a renegade. What was Big Ole thinking?

Jo frowned at her watch. Unfortunately, she had a package to pick up and no choice but to get there. She rolled up the window and drove on. The houses passed by in a blur as she deliberated on the one thought she couldn't get her worried mind to comprehend. A frightened old man doesn't approach an adversary by himself, not even in broad daylight. An assaulted old man doesn't protect the anonymity of his attacker at the expense of other would-be victims. Big Ole knew something, but what? Who was he protecting? What was he hiding? And for heaven's sakes why?

CHAPTER TWELVE

The shabby screen door sprung back at Ole's knock. He waited for a drawn-out moment, listening. After an extended silence and several more muted raps, the shout, "Go away. Nobody's home," bawled through the door.

As Ole inched closer, rotting boards creaked beneath his feet. "I need to have a word with you. It's important."

A few indistinguishable utterances and several rasping coughs later, the door grated open, and Ole stared into the bloodshot eyes of a hollowed-out-looking man. Lucky Strikes rolled up the sleeve of a grimy tee shirt, pudgy beer belly, three-day growth of whiskers, can of beer in one hand, a cigarette butt dangling from loose and generous lips with smoke curling up into his nostrils. Dull and greasy hair that cried for a good washing.

"Are you the man they call Harry Thompson?"

Harry let out a rude, disgusting belch. "Near as I can tell. What d'ya want?"

"Good morning. I'm O.M. Harrington."

Harry lifted a wary brow and pulled back, conspicuously rejecting Ole's outstretched hand. "Oh, yeah? I heard 'bout you. You're the old codger, the one that got roughed up the other night. Can't say as I'm surprised. That worthless, no-good-for-nothin' kid of mine didn't take a shine to you, either. Wanna beer?"

"No, thanks."

Harry pulled the inside door back and after kicking a beat-up work shoe against an even more beat-up threshold, he waved Ole into his dank house with his beer hand, pale liquid spilling over the can, foam splashing onto the grubby floor. "Well, what d'ya want?"

"I want to have a word with your boy."

Harry riveted plucky eyes on Ole. "He ain't here."

"Then I suggest you get him here."

"Anything you wanna say to my kid, you can say to his old man."

Not to be bested, Ole clenched his jaw. "Like I said, I want to have a word with your son. I'm trying my best to keep him out of reform school."

"He doesn't need your help."

Ole planted his walking stick on the filthy floor, and rested his weight on it with both hands. "You might want to rethink that."

"Say, you ain't implyin' my kid had anything to do with your clock cleanin', are you?"

Ole glared eyeball to eyeball while he waited the man out.

Harry took a step back as realization drained the red from his ruddy face. "You better not go blamin' me. The boy's the spittin' image of his ma. It ain't my fault he didn't get her warm ways. Always did have a mind of his own."

Ole looked around. "Where is your wife?"

"Ain't here. Lost her the day he was born. I warned him," Harry huffed. "Told him he was gonna get sent up some day, but would he listen to his old man? No."

Ole had known men like Harry in the past. All talk. They bully the weak and shrink from the strong at the drop of a scowl. "I think you'd better get him," Ole said, raising his voice several decibels.

Harry Thompson threw his hands up quicker than a blowhard

staring down the wrong end of a switchblade. "Okay, okay, don't get testy. He's out back in the tree house. You wait right here."

Ole stood in the archway between the kitchen and living room, repulsed by the dismal surroundings. He rubbed his aching neck and looked around. This was a place he couldn't get out of fast enough. Smelling of sweat, stale smoke, and beer, the small shack of a house lacked a feminine touch. Gloomy. Shades drawn. So filled with trash, it would take a detective to find the sofa.

Seeking only to get answers about why a wayward teen would want to harm an old man, Ole got far more than he bargained for when a too-long moment later, Thompson returned shoving his kid through the door before him. The boy bristled at the sight of Ole and cringed at the tenor of his dad's condemning voice. "Your ma would roll over in her grave if she got wind of what you did," Harry derided, swinging a fist in anger. Wil cowered, instantly shielding himself with a forearm, and pulled away as if trying to make a run for it. Harry caught a hard grip and was about to strike again when Ole pressed the tip of his walking stick hard against Harry's chest.

"You touch that boy again, and you'll live to regret it. Do I make myself clear?"

"You want 'im?" Harry scoffed as he backed down, "well, here he is."

Ole ran his fingertips lightly across a still-too-generous bandage covering his thinning hair and lightly rubbed the nape of his neck again, buying time to think. He wasn't ready to take on this project. But if he didn't, how would the boy stand a chance in life? "Son, if you want to stay out of reform school, stop by the O.M. Harrington." Ole pulled out his pocket watch and glanced at it, thinking. He may need a few days to plan. "How about Thursday morning? You know where my place is?"

Wil nodded reluctantly.

"Be there at ten o'clock sharp."

"What for?" Wil said, looking far tougher than he sounded.

"We'll discuss that then. And don't even think about being late."

With Tryg's signed documents in hand, Jo drove back down the narrow avenues of town. Anxiety gripped her as she passed the street where she'd last seen Ole. She still hadn't sorted her thoughts about watching him amble up the sidewalk let alone hearing where he was headed. What happened when he entered that rundown house? Was he safe? Should she have sought help, or was she right to have left well enough alone?

When she reached the O.M. Harrington, she pulled up to the curb and had only taken a few steps when a masculine voice cried out from behind.

"Well, hello there."

Taking a look back toward the park, Jo's shoulders relaxed.

Ole was sitting on a shaded bench. "What brings you out this way?" he said. "Shouldn't you be at the office? I thought you were one of those nine-to-fivers."

She strolled through the freshly mown grass to greet him. "I needed to know you were okay."

"Is that a fact?" He straightened. "Why wouldn't I be?"

"I saw where you went."

"No, you didn't see where I went," he said forcefully. "Are we clear on that?"

Caring too deeply for the old man, and respecting him too much to take offense at his sharp retort, Jo released a smile and folded onto the bench beside him. "Yes, sir. We're very clear. So how did what I didn't see go, if you don't mind my asking, that is?"

"Oh, but I do mind."

She chuckled. "I understand. But after what you've gone through, I didn't know how you'd be received at that place or ..." Jo stopped herself.

"Or what?"

"Or if you'd take another beating."

Ole picked up his cane and held it out, staring down the shaft as if checking to see if it was in precise alignment. "I can count on you to respect my privacy?"

"Without a doubt. You won my respect some time ago, you know that, and that does include my respect for your privacy. Sir."

He hesitated. "On second thought, I'd say that's all either of us need to know, wouldn't you?"

CHAPTER THIRTEEN

J o?"

Jo focused on Ole's bruises that had turned a deeper shade of black. "Hmm?"

"That is all either of us need to know, right?"

She shrugged then stared out across the tranquil waters of Amber Leaf Lake, thinking. "Playing your not talking game feels right, and I do want to please you."

"But?"

"You've certainly earned that," she said.

"But?"

"But knowing now who one of your attackers is, I need to consider the cost—trusting you, covering for you, keeping quiet about something that has a huge impact on others. I don't know how I could live with myself if someone else got hurt and I could have helped prevent it."

"I know," he said. "But this is me. Remember? Big Ole Harrington."

Jo could not in good conscience say yes, neither could she in good conscience say no, so she nodded. "You're right. If anyone has earned my trust, it's you—and that is all either of us need to know."

"We both have unfinished business, don't we, Jo?" Ole said.

"I'm not sure what you mean."

"I have unfinished business with that Thompson boy the way you have unfinished business with Tryg. The only difference between us is that I recognize it, but you? You refuse to come to terms with it."

Jo shook her head.

"About the Thompson kid, though. I know I'm putting you in a tough spot." Ole lightly massaged what appeared to be a smarting knee. "How about if I tell you only what you need to know? Would that be helpful?"

"It really isn't necessary."

Ole looked up into the powder blue sky. "I went to his house to feel the boy out, to confirm my suspicions. Now I know my instincts were right. There were two of them, Jo."

She cringed at the thought.

"Wil Thompson and his friend Teddy Anders." Ole looked away. "That Anders kid is a mean one. He's hiding behind Wil's reputation to save his own hide."

"How do you know that?"

Ole gave Jo a furtive glance. "Because Wil didn't have it in him to beat the tar out of me, that's how. I heard it in his voice and in his sobs when that Anders kid wasn't around. Wil needs help. You should have seen him this morning. When his dad hunted him down and shoved him into the kitchen where I stood waiting ..." Ole looked away. His voice trailed off.

"I'm feeling my way through this whole thing," he continued. "If I do blow the whistle, Chief Stout let me know in no uncertain terms where Wil is going to end up. A kid like that won't make it in reform school. He'll either get hardened or destroyed. If I turn Teddy Anders in, Wil is going to get hauled in, too, and that will be the end of it. I can't allow that to happen."

"How are you planning to control Teddy? What if he hurts someone else?"

"I've given that some serious thought. Taking it one step at a time. My gut tells me Teddy and Wil overplayed their hand, that they'll both back off for a while. Meanwhile, the senior Anders needs to have some skin in the game. I figure a little nudge might encourage him to control his son's actions."

"What kind of nudge?"

"Money. It needs to cost him something. Thought I'd start by seeing how he responds to paying my hospital bills. I figure a man with his ego will want to pay up, if for no other reason than to keep his son's name from being plastered all over the front page of *The Amber Leaf Tribune*. I'm counting on that to also put a damper on any more costly mischief."

"What if the boys don't back off?" Jo asked.

"I've thought about that, too. Don't worry. I intend to keep a close eye on them. I won't allow either one to get out of hand. I know I'm taking a risk here, a big risk, but I believe it's well worth taking or I'd never do it. Wil and Teddy also need to pay back their debt to the town. Thought I'd begin with Wil."

Jo clutched her handbag to her waist. "How do you plan to do that?"

"Keep an ear to the ground. You'll hear soon enough if and when it happens. If I don't see immediate improvement in the boy, then I'll turn both of them in. That's a promise. By the way," he said, "thanks for choosing to believe in me."

Ole stopped short immediately inside the great room where Sarah stood surrounded by workers and guests. Assuming they hadn't heard him enter, he cleared his throat. When they turned, he looked into a sea of guilt-ridden eyes, and that violated feeling welled up within him once again. People feeling entitled to their opinions, whether or not they were right—and at his expense. He needed time, but they were unwittingly pilfering it from him and turning up the heat on his already pressure filled world.

"Grandpa, where have you been?" Sarah asked.

"I was out. Now I'm back."

"But where'd you go?"

"I already told you," he said with a scowl. "Out."

"I've been worried sick about you. Come. Let's go to your office where we can have a private chat."

Big Ole stood his ground. "I know you're only being protective, but at the moment I don't particularly appreciate it." He looked directly into the accusing eyes around him and the guarded glances and ears tuned in to their not-so-private conversation. "What's more, I don't want to go to my office. You've already opened Pandora's box in this public forum. Anything you have to say, you can say right here."

Sarah looked taken aback. "Alright, if that's what you want. People are talking, Grandpa. They're asking questions, reasonable questions."

Ole grimaced, his bruised and swollen cheeks smarting. The word reasonable coupled with the plurality of the word questions stuck in his craw, further violating his right to personal privacy. He looked at the gossips about the room spreading rumors over steamy cups of coffee, and considered those across town whispering half-truths over baby carriages and passing judgment on rocking chairs in sun-streaked porches, all in the name of reason. Half-truths they knew nothing about. Teddy and Wil wouldn't boast about what they'd done. That would implicate them. And no one else had a clue about what happened, no one, that is, except Ole.

"Questions, you say? No. Not reasonable questions, Sarah. Unreasonable judgments. I was the one violated, not any of you," Ole said as he looked into the retreating eyes surrounding him.

Although hurt appeared to ripple through Sarah's eyes, he went on just the same. "You are all treating me as if I were weak and helpless, which I definitely am not."

"Who are you protecting, Grandfather?" Sarah said. "And why? Does someone have something on you?"

"My business is my business," Ole said, suppressing a glare. "Are we clear on that?"

Looking unmistakably corrected in front of a roomful of spectators, Sarah muttered a deferential, "yes, sir."

Turning his back on the retreating slumped shoulders and guarded gazes, Ole returned to his office, hoping the meddlers would have the decency to show more respect to a beleaguered old man.

CHAPTER FOURTEEN

There wasn't a place Tryg would rather be tonight than visiting with Big Ole. Were his wounds healing? Was the swelling subsiding? Was he still sore? Had he come to terms with the beating? Tryg fingered the box on the scarred wooden table. Cuban cigars. *Big Ole is going to love these.* But as he picked them up and headed to the door, he got a call from a friend asking if he'd planned to attend tonight's town council meeting, which he hadn't. His curiosity was aroused, though, when he learned the Big Ole Harrington mess had made it on the agenda. "Isn't that a bit premature?" he asked.

"That's what I thought," Jim said.

The cigar box hit the table with a thump. "I'm on my way."

Jim met Tryg at the door. They found chairs at the back of the smoke-filled room. Light coughing and idle chatter had a hollow ring throughout until the mayor dropped the gavel, called the meeting to order, and looked around. "Chief Stout isn't here?"

Henrietta Braddingly, by far the most outspoken member of the town council, took a nose-dipping gaze over her bifocals. "We didn't think to invite him," she said. "Besides, I don't believe his presence is necessary."

Tryg's brows shot up involuntarily.

Just then the chief hustled in, his voice strong. "Sorry I'm late."

Jim grinned and said in a low voice that only Tryg could hear, "Thought the guy deserved a heads up."

The mayor rearranged the agenda to accommodate Chief Stout's schedule and asked him to begin by sharing the latest developments. "I'm talking hard evidence here," the mayor said." Last I heard, you were on the trail of a couple of wayward teens."

"One wayward teen," Mrs. Braddingly corrected, still peering over her bifocals. "That Thompson boy."

The chief hesitated, then said, "In all due respect, there are two boys we're looking at. If Thompson is guilty, you can bet Teddy Anders is complicit."

"Surely you can't believe that," Henrietta said. "The Anders boy comes from such a good home."

"I'm afraid we can't rule him out, neither can we make an arrest on circumstantial evidence alone. I've had stakeouts, been to the boys' homes, questioned victims til I'm blue in the face, but try as I may, I haven't been able to secure a thread of hard evidence yet."

"With all due respect, it's wartime," Henrietta said. "There must be something you can do to put that boy behind bars."

"I assure you, Mrs. Braddingly, those boys are my top priority."

Since the chief had no further information, the mayor asked him to keep the council updated on developments as they happened and thanked him for his input. The moment he left, however, things heated up when Henrietta turned to the mayor. "Someone needs to light a fire under the chief, and it's the council's job to do it. If Big Ole Harrington could be attacked, we're all vulnerable."

"But it's only been," the mayor looked at the ceiling confoundedly and scratched his chin, "how many days now?"

After a back and forth about Big Ole's refusal to cooperate, no substantive proof of who the attackers actually were, things not having turned violent until Big Ole got attacked, and no further incidents since, Henrietta stepped up her charge. "That's my point," she said. "Mr.

Harrington *was* attacked, and it appears the trauma has had a nasty effect on the poor man's thinking. He used to be a man of such good sense. Now he's acting like a feeble old man who's lost his marbles."

Henrietta stopped long enough to scowl at a room full of gasps then continued. "Mark my words, these things escalate. There will be more incidents if we don't find a better man to handle the job."

"You aren't suggesting—"

Henrietta's condescending look did not sit well with Tryg. Not only had she become rude, she was rushing things, especially with the chief. Why? What was her hurry? This was not a court of law and no one was on trial, especially Chief Stout. She needed to cool down the rhetoric.

"Mrs. Braddingly," the mayor said, "aren't you being a bit premature?"

"I fully understand why you might feel that way, but this is broader than the Big Ole Harrington assault. What about the robberies? By the chief's own admission, there hasn't been a resolution to those either. If he doesn't solve these cases soon, it's our responsibility to begin looking for a new chief of police."

Tryg's jaw dropped. *She has an angle.*

Henrietta held the floor. "Let me be clear about this. Our chief of police is not acting fast enough." She slammed a flat hand on the table. "We must act, and we must act now."

Her flare-up met with uncomfortable quiet.

After the meeting, Jim plucked a Lucky Strike from his cigarette pack and lit up. "Tryg? Where did that dame get the brass to talk about Big Ole and Chief Stout like that?"

"I don't know. My gut tells me she's up to no good. It doesn't make sense that she would be calling for a new chief of police. It takes time to gather evidence to solve crimes. What's gotten into her that she would do such a thing?"

Making their way up Broadway, Jim exhaled a lungful of smoke. "I have no idea. One thing I can tell you, though. That dame could not care less about the people she's hurting."

Tryg nodded as he switched his briefcase from one hand to the other. The damage one woman could inflict by saying and doing whatever she wanted and not questioning herself unnerved him. He stopped abruptly in the middle of the sidewalk. "There's got to be a way to ease her off her throne."

CHAPTER FIFTEEN

Ole pulled a gold watch and chain from his inside vest pocket. He shook out a handkerchief from a pants pocket and mechanically polished the crystal. Five past ten. No Wil. Ole could have sized the boy up incorrectly, he supposed, but he didn't think so. Where could that young lad be?

At fifteen past the hour, still no Wil.

Ole poked through the morning's mail, but found reading futile, the words registering no deeper than black ink on white paper. He thoroughly cleaned his pipe and stuffed in a generous amount of fresh tobacco. After lifting it to his lips, he set it down and frowned. The mere thought of a good smoke held no interest. Maybe feeding the squirrels would help. Besides, he needed thinking time and seemed to think better out in the park. With the unobstructed view of nature, he felt closer to his Maker's divine wisdom there. So, he went to the kitchen to gather a bag of peanuts.

"Grandfather!"

Something about the way Sarah said grandfather gave Ole the feeling he wouldn't appreciate hearing the words that followed.

"I'm awfully sorry. I was sure you'd gone up town."

"I was in my office."

"I know that now. A boy stopped by to see you a little while ago."

Ole caught his escaping breath. *I knew it. I just knew it. I should have said something, but how could I? That would have invited questions.*

"I think he said his name was Wil."

"Why didn't you send him to my office?"

"I told you," Sarah said. "I was sure you'd gone to town."

"What did you tell him?"

"I told him you weren't here."

Ole looked around the great room and started toward the coffee room, as if the boy would materialize there. "Where'd he go? Did he say? Will he be coming back?"

"He didn't say, but he did look irritated. Who was he anyway? What did he want with you?"

Big Ole sat on a bench and eyed the span of the park, tossing an occasional peanut to a hungry squirrel.

His opinion of that boy had to be right. He obeyed. He stopped by the boarding house as requested. Although that was a positive sign, Ole had let Wil down, bungled an opportunity. Five minutes with the boy was all it would take. If he couldn't command respect in that critical window of time, it would all be over with. Seeing him in his dingy home during the raw light of day, and seeing the devastated look on his face when he accidentally wet his trousers sealed the boy's fate. He wasn't a hardened miscreant destined for a wasted life. He had a moldable heart if Ole had ever seen one, but could Ole ever gain Wil's trust now?

He shook a few more nuts on the grass. Recognizing the loud scrape of a bicycle fender a half block away, he smiled to himself. The bike rolled into the park and pulled up alongside him. Ole didn't look up. He didn't need to. "Lean your bike against that tree over there, boy—"

"I'm not a boy. My name's Wil."

"And have a seat."

Wil took an inordinate amount of time propping his bike against the towering tree.

"We have some tools over at the boarding house," Ole said. "Be happy to help fix that kickstand if you'd like. Maybe we can do something about that loose fender at the same time."

Wil appeared to ignore Ole's offer. He jammed his hands into his trouser pockets and studied his dirty sneakers. Lanky. Medium height for a kid in his mid teens. A clump of mousy brown hair accented his street-hard eyes, which were a shocking peacock blue. Skinny arms protruded from a threadbare long-sleeved shirt with only one sleeve rolled up to an elbow. He acted like a frightened two-year-old who didn't quite know what to do with himself. "I did what you told me to," he said, "but you wasn't there."

Ole shook his head slowly, deliberately. "Oh, but I was there, son."

"I'm not your son."

"My granddaughter thought I'd gone to town. I apologize. I should have told her I was expecting you, but I thought it would be best to downplay our meeting." By the stunned expression on Wil's face, Ole wondered if anyone had ever had the decency to apologize to the boy for any mishaps before.

"Why?" Wil asked, his tone leery.

"I have my reasons."

Wil kicked at the grass a few times the way his dad had kicked at the worn threshold, and then meandered to Ole's bench. He plopped down at the far end, keeping a healthy distance. "I 'spose you squealed to Chief Stout."

"No. Can't say that I did."

"How come?"

"You sound skeptical."

Wil shrugged.

"It's none of his business. This is between you and me."

Ole reached for the cane and mindlessly rolled it between his large palms. "So tell me, were you disgusted with me when I didn't fight you and that ... friend of yours the other night? Did you find me disgustingly weak?"

Wil shrugged again.

"Somehow I get the feeling you did." Ole waited the boy out, giving him ample time to relive the incident in his mind. "How'd you feel about yourself when you got home that night? I'll bet you hated me even more when you found you couldn't get a lick of satisfaction over what you'd done. You only felt worse about yourself, didn't you?" Ole flexed his hands. Reliving the incident, he felt the need to put a stranglehold on his rising anger. "While we're at it, tell me how you felt about yourself the next morning after you had time to think."

Wil squirmed as if wriggling could quiet a tormented conscience. At least he appeared to have a conscience, and a fired-up one at that. He looked like a cornered animal ready to bolt.

Although the squirrel had scattered when Wil rode up and Ole could hear it flitting about high above in the tree, Ole leisurely tossed several more peanuts on the grass and said in a soft, thoughtful tone, "That wasn't me you were taking your hate out on, you know."

"What're you talkin' about? You don't make no sense."

"You probably see me as a weak old man who smells like pipe tobacco and wiles away the hours out in the park feeding wild critters." Ole deliberately tapped the sidewalk with the tip of his cane. "I'm not. I may not be as strong as I used to be, I'll give you that, but I definitely wouldn't consider myself weak either. You haven't answered my question. How did you feel about yourself after taking me down?"

"If you ain't weak, how come you didn't fight back?"

Ole angled his head. "So that's it. Well, if you will recall, it was dark out, and I wasn't expecting your friend to kick my cane from under me or knock me down when he came charging at me full speed with his bike. Can you tell me it wouldn't be difficult for a pipsqueak like you to fight off two attackers when you're the one on the ground and they're on their feet?"

Looking as if he didn't know how to respond, Wil mopped the lock of mousy hair away from his forehead.

"Words escape you, boy?"

Wil hopped up. "You don't know what you're talkin' about. You're crazy." He jumped on his bike, the fender again scraping loudly as he tore off.

CHAPTER SIXTEEN

Ole didn't know how long the wait would be, but one thing he did know—he had to wait Wil out. Whether it took an hour, a day, or a week, the boy would be back. Ole felt it in his gut.

For the better part of an hour, he'd been sitting again on the park bench beneath the shade of the old elm, its leafy branches hovering above like an oversized umbrella. He wondered more about himself than Wil, wondered what made him think he could make a difference in a lost boy's life. How could he go about teaching the boy to value others, let alone value himself? Wil needed to set high standards if he wanted a decent future and a fulfilling life, but it would take time to teach him those things—time, which, Ole knew, was quickly slipping away.

Twenty peanuts and fifteen minutes later, Ole packed up his bag of nuts and returned to the boarding house. After lunch, he foraged for sandpaper, a brush, and a quart of white paint then busied himself touching up spots of chipped paint along the outer porch railing. He was picking up the paint can when the distant sound of a bicycle fender scraping loudly against its wheel again caught his attention. Ole set down the paint so fast, it sloshed over the side of the can and onto the porch floor, but he didn't care. He picked up the bag of peanuts, swiped the cane from the railing, and made a tottering beeline for the park. Wil rode past, doubled back, and rode past again, looking straight ahead as if Ole wasn't there.

Ole eased onto a bench and cracked open a peanut shell while keeping a close eye on the sidewalk. Several passes later Wil steered his bike into the park. He didn't say anything, merely rode circles around and around Ole's bench. Tiring circles. With each lap, the fender of the bike scraped, making an increasingly louder ruckus. Ole tolerated about ten full orbits then said, "You win, boy—"

"Name's Wil."

"I'm getting dizzy looking at you. Come. Sit down."

Moving slower than a three-legged turtle, Wil wedged the bike against the tree. He stood with his hands shoved deep in his trouser pockets, one dirty shirtsleeve still rolled up to a bony elbow, the other buttoned at a wrist. He must be minus a button, Ole decided, with no caring mother to sew it back on. He studied Wil, contemplating his silence for a generous minute, then passed the half-empty bag of peanuts to the boy.

Wil looked at the sack indifferently then reached for it and plopped down at the far end of the bench again. His sullen look told Ole the boy was there in body only, but for now that was enough.

"Toss one out. He'll come."

Wil tossed a peanut onto the shaded grass, then another. He looked up. With an expression of wonder, he watched a squirrel nervously skitter around high on the sturdy trunk.

"Have you fed any squirrels before?"

Wil shook his head.

"Stay quiet. Keep tossing them out. Don't move too fast. You don't want to scare him. When he's ready, he'll come down."

Seven or eight peanuts later, a faint smile broke when the fluffy-tailed creature scampered down the tree trunk and onto the grass. The squirrel appeared cautious, peering at Wil then peering at the peanuts scattered a comfortable distance from his scuffed up shoes. It struck Ole that Wil, so busy fending for himself, had been robbed of the childhood joy of appreciating nature and its beauty. When the squirrel gazed up at him a second time, Wil slowly tossed another peanut on the ground. The squirrel snatched the nut then skittered across the grass and back up into the safety of the tree, Wil watching in awe.

"If we're going to work well together," Ole said, "I have two demands you're going to have to meet."

Wil's head jerked toward Ole, exposing a confused you-don't-mean-to-tell-me-you-honestly-care-about-me look. "You ain't told me why you're doin' this," he said.

"I have my reasons." How could he not understand? Ole then considered Wil's world. His mother had died bringing him into the world. His father abused him. Rarely, if ever, a caring word. Wil's hometown spoke ill of him, but then, given the boy's actions, what were the townspeople supposed to think?

Hearing the sound of a car passing by, Ole waved at the driver.

"Who's that?" Wil said indifferently.

"You don't know him? Why, that's Reverend Calvin Doherty. I thought everyone in Amber Leaf knew him." Ole glanced over his shoulder. "He pastors Village Church up the hill there," he said, indicating the direction with a nod.

Wil's countenance soured. He jumped up and stomped on a peanut shell. "I ain't gonna go to no church."

Pardon me? "Where's that coming from?"

"Aww, church is for softies."

"I don't know about that. I don't think I'd call Calvin Doherty a softy. No, sir. Not in a million years. I don't think you would either if you knew the man."

Wil's eyebrows raised half the height of his forehead. "What's to know?"

"You're a little on the snoopy side, aren't you, boy?" Ole teased.

"So're you. So tell me how come you wouldn't call the preacher man a softy."

Ole sobered and easing his back heavily against the park bench, he said, "Because he's one of the bravest men I've ever known. He was a chaplain during the two worst wars in our world's history. First World War I, and then this war. He volunteered to go down into the trenches with our fighting men and crawled through ditches and open fields to rescue the wounded while bullets were whizzing past him. Think about it. Grenades blowing bodies apart. The constant shelling of machine guns. The screams. Young men crying out for their mamas. The ugly stink of death. Then one day he took a hit and got sent home."

Wil lifted his chin, his forehead creased with hard lines. "Why would a preacher volunteer to go off to war anyway? That's kinda stupid, ain't it?"

"Somebody has to do it."

"Yeah, but a preacher? I thought they ain't supposed to believe in war. I thought they were 'sposed to help save people an' stuff like that, not kill 'em."

"I doubt he believes in war, Wil. But he does believe in ending war. He was on the helping side. If he wasn't absolutely certain it was God's calling in his life, he would never have done it."

"Oh, yeah? That preacher may got guts, but he ain't too bright."

"Now why would you say a thing like that?"

"Why'd anyone want to help out a god who lets war happen in the first place? I don't believe in no God," Wil announced, sounding prideful.

Ole slowly shook his head and cut loose a warm yet bewildered grin.

"What're you grinning at?" Wil asked. "Don't you hear what I said?"

"Oh, I heard you alright. So what you're telling me is that I should be more impressed with your opinions about our Maker than with our Maker himself. I don't know what to make of that."

Surprised they were even engaged in his conversation, Ole continued, "Imagine living in a house with a radio, a telephone, and lights in every room," he said, taking ample time to think his words through. "Now imagine deciding they don't work because you can't see the invisible energy flowing through them. Then take it a step further. You're so proud of your stance, you choose to live in the dark with no news or entertainment or connection to the outside world. That wouldn't be what I would call wise living, would you?"

Wil shook his head, appearing bewildered.

"So how is your choosing not to believe in God any smarter?"

Ole studied Wil, but couldn't read him. The boy merely stared at the road abutting the park, the same road where Ole had been dragged, dumped, kicked, and left writhing in pain.

"There's something inside you, boy. Something awfully good."

Wil looked at Ole, puzzled. "Hunh?"

"That's why I didn't snitch to Chief Stout. Lying out there the other night," he cast his gaze toward the road with a bob of his bruised and scraped head, "I wasn't quite as far gone as you might have thought. I heard you come back." Ole wanted to say more, to tell Wil he'd heard his sniffling, too, but that might be too much. He refused to chisel off any more of the boy's dignity. Ole feared the poor kid was barely holding onto what little he had left by a thin and rotting string. "I heard every word you said. It was that friend of yours who was heartless, not you. You were worried about me, scared I might have been badly hurt, right?"

Wil shrugged.

"You stopped him when he started kicking me in the head. For a little while there, it was like the Anders boy had the devil in him. But not you. You had the guts to stand up to him, and you didn't back down."

Although Wil looked away, Ole didn't stop. "You were going to go and get my cane, too. But then we heard the rumble of Mrs. Bremley's car and saw her headlights shining over the top of the hill. I also heard the lilac bushes rustling on the side of the road. You were there, weren't you, son, lying low in those bushes the entire time until the ambulance finally hauled me away?"

"How many times do I gotta' tell ya? I ain't your boy, and I ain't your son."

Ole listened to the quiet before continuing. Working with Wil was like working with that untamed squirrel. Skittish. Unstable. Ready to run off any second and disappear.

"What do you want to be when you grow up?"

Wil didn't hesitate. "I wanna be a soldier."

"I thought you didn't believe in war."

"You didn't hear right. I meant I don't believe in preachers goin' to war." Wil sounded contrite, his voice softening. "I was wrong 'bout that one, I guess."

"I see. So tell me. Why do you want to be a soldier?"

"Cuz soldiers get to carry rifles an' travel all 'round the world." Wil looked up, his eyes and voice suddenly filled with longing. "They get respect."

"You're never going to make it into the military if you have any kind of record." Ole inhaled a deep breath of warm summer air. "They won't take you. But, then, you probably already knew that, didn't you?"

"They won't?"

"Why would they? They've got their hands full enough teaching good men how to fight, and you of all people need to be especially careful. You're already walking a tight rope with Chief Stout."

As Wil searched Ole's eyes as if taking his words to heart, Ole drew a handkerchief from a trouser pocket and buffed smudges from his walking stick. "These past few days I've spent a considerable amount of time trying to sort things out in my mind."

"What's to sort out?"

"Well, near as I can figure, you had it tough early in life. Didn't you?"

Wil flinched, his eyes darting toward the ground as if he'd been stripped of his emotional clothing.

"Judging by the stiff way you're teetering at the edge of the bench there, I'd say I nailed a nerve." Ole lifted his chin. "That's really not the problem you might think it is."

Wil hesitated. "It ain't?"

"No, it isn't. Boys like you may have to try harder, but boys like you also have an advantage."

"Advantage? Aww. What you talkin' 'bout? That's the stupidest thing I ever heard. My dad's the town drunk."

"I knew that. I'd say that gives you a solid edge." Ole carefully folded his handkerchief and slipped it back in his pocket. "There's something else you need to know." Taking intense care not to show any signs of vulnerability or pain, Ole got up and stepped in front of the boy. "There's no question that what you did was wrong, horribly wrong, but what you did wasn't entirely your fault either."

Wil looked up at Ole as if he had three heads.

"I see the way your father treated you. You can bet he was treated the same way."

"That don't make it right," Wil hissed.

"No, it doesn't. On either count. But, then, what's a boy supposed to do with the rage he feels when he's been told and shown repeatedly that he isn't worth a hoot?"

Wil bristled at Ole's words. If he was trying to hide the pain in his eyes, it wasn't working. Ole felt as if he could see the boy's heart weeping. Still he continued. "You've never had someone care for you, and I mean really care. You know, son, in that church up on the hill there, the one that I go to, the one you refuse to enter? That God you don't believe in said that one day the last shall be first. You need to carry that in your heart, and believe it. Because one day you will come up from behind, and the kids who have everything now will be looking up to you. Not because you're any better than they are. You aren't. Not because God loves you more. He doesn't. He loves all of us. You will come up from behind simply because God promised it. We're not responsible for what happens to us in life. It's how we respond to what happens that counts. Sometimes it takes a mighty long while to learn how to do that effectively."

Ole pulled his gold watch from his vest pocket and glanced at the time. "It's getting late."

"What do you want from me?" Wil asked, his words, almost plaintive, slipped out softly. "Those two things?"

Surprised by the hint of hunger in the young boy's voice, Ole repeated, "Not two things. Two demands." He pulled an envelope from an inside vest pocket. "First, I want you to deliver this to Mr. Anders at his office uptown."

Wil reached for the envelope, his eyes growing larger than oversized grapes.

That was good.

"You need to know that I'm taking control of your fate as well as that of that renegade friend of yours, and I have no intentions of making this easy. Are we clear on this?"

Wil nodded.

"Good. Now about Anders," Ole said. "We both know who he is. I checked a short while ago. He'll be in all day, and he's expecting you."

"How'll you know if I deliver the letter or not?"

"Oh, I'll know alright."

Wil plucked the envelope from Ole's large hand. "What else?"

"I think we might be able to use a little help in the kitchen across the road there at the O.M. Harrington. I'll pay you a generous wage. The minimum these days is forty cents an hour. How about if we start you off at, say, fifty-five cents? Will that be okay with you?"

Wil looked at Ole dumbstruck.

"Of course, initially you're going to have to share some of that wealth to pay back the people you stole from. After you've paid them in full, the rest of the money will be yours to keep and spend however you want."

Wil appeared shot down. "But then they'll know I was in on attackin' you, and I'll get sent up."

"Don't worry. We'll make certain your contributions are anonymous." Ole grinned. "That might even make it more fun. How about putting in four hours a day to begin with? Say four o'clock until eight, Monday through Friday. You be there, son."

Big Ole walked on, certain he'd left the young boy in a daze on a bench in the middle of Harrington Park.

A few minutes before closing time, Tryg asked Jo to come into his office. "I went to the town council meeting last night," he said.

Folding arms over her champagne blouse, she took a slight step back. "And?"

"I get the feeling Henrietta Braddingly is trying to get the entire town in an uproar about Big Ole. Seems word about his reluctance to talk has been ripping across the cornfields of southern Minnesota faster than a hailstorm," Tryg said matter-of-factly. "Unfortunately, Henrietta is using that against him."

Jo's breath caught as Tryg casually loosened his tie. He unbuttoned and rolled his sleeves. Smoothly. First one and then the other, up his forearms. "People are upset enough about it without her fueling the flames," he continued.

Jo watched his lips move, but realized she hadn't heard his words. "What?"

"I said people are upset about it," he repeated.

"Oh."

"To put it impolitely, Henrietta thinks Big Ole's lost his marbles."

"She actually said that?"

Tryg nodded. "In a way, you can't blame her or anyone else for thinking that. People are afraid. A boy's name keeps popping up. She repeated it again last night. Wil Thompson, I think it is. You wouldn't happen to know anything about him, would you?"

"No more than you or anyone else."

"Do you think he might have been in on Ole's assault?"

Without a doubt. "I'm not sure."

Jo's conscience yelped. She couldn't hold out on Tryg. Clearly this wasn't the same Trygve Howland who had come home from the war a broken hero. He appeared increasingly comfortable in his own skin, almost boy-like, these days. But how could she draw him in? Help him figure it out himself? Could he help Ole buy time? Ole needed all the help he could get and time had swiftly turned into an enemy. "Tryg?"

"Hmm?"

"I don't mean to tread on sacred ground, so let me know if I'm out of line, okay?"

He nodded hesitantly.

"Remember when you were dating Lauren, and she was manipulating us behind our backs?"

"How could I ever forget? What about it?"

"Did I do right by not telling you what I knew?"

"Aren't you getting a little off subject?"

"Did I do right?" Jo said, pressing the point.

Tryg intertwined his fingers. "I think you did fine."

Fine. What a nondescript word. It was right up there with all the other tactful words people use, words that say nothing, words like all right, okay, and okey-dokey. "But what if you would have married her, not knowing who she really was, and I could have helped stop it?"

He chuckled. "That didn't happen, but I guess I would have paid a hefty price for not paying closer attention, wouldn't I?"

Tryg wasn't taking the bait.

"Maybe it would be a good idea if you had a chat with Big Ole yourself," she said. "He likes you."

"Not all that long ago, I wouldn't have hesitated. But now I'm not convinced." Tryg shook his head, his eyes downcast and his tone pensive. "Why would he be so tight lipped, Jo? Doesn't make any sense. Why would he protect the thugs who could have ended his life?"

Sharing only what she had witnessed personally, information that wouldn't violate Ole or show her hand, she said matter-of-factly, "Two kids did it."

"That's what they were saying at the meeting last night. How do you know that?"

"Tire tracks. Bike tires. I saw a couple of patches where the gravel was shaved clean. Only bike tires could have done that."

"I guess I'm not surprised," Tryg said. "Ole's too big for one kid to take on alone. Knowing what they did to him, though, you'd think he'd want to turn them in, if not to avenge himself, at least to protect everyone else. What's that old man thinking?"

Later that evening, a hint of relief washed over Ole. His plan might well be working. He received a call at a quarter to eight, as requested, from a shaken Mr. and Mrs. Anders. They didn't hesitate to agree to the terms of Ole's note. They would reimburse him for his hospital expenses the moment they received an itemized billing, and they would immediately assume full responsibility for keeping a keen eye on their wayward son's future actions in exchange for Ole's continued silence. Fortunately for Big Ole and the people of Amber Leaf, protecting the Anders family's name appeared to carry weight, and for now, at least, Ole felt confident he had stopped the hemorrhaging.

In the middle of the night, however, he awakened with a start when an animal yelped and a distant siren screamed. What if those boys were up to no good again?

CHAPTER SEVENTEEN

lthough the morning sun shone bright, the assault on Big Ole had cast a shadowy mist on Amber Leaf that even the sun's heat could not burn away. Everywhere Jo went, she heard talk about Big Ole Harrington. Even vendors who stopped by the office were talking, their stories twisting and turning and taking on lives of their own. The conclusion was always the same. If a street-smart man of Ole's stature could be victimized, everyone was fair game.

Tryg stepped into the outer office, lines of apprehension scoring his otherwise young-looking face. "Jo? Chief Stout wants to meet you, me, and Sarah at The Copper Kettle at noon today."

"What about?"

"Big Ole."

Jo balked. "I already told him everything I knew the night it happened." *Why did I have to see Big Ole tottering along to Wil's house? How am I going to keep that quiet?*

"The chief needs all the help he can get, Jo. The town council meeting has him on edge. Henrietta is working overtime to get him replaced."

A few strokes before twelve, a distressed-looking Sarah rushed in and the three of them plodded next door to the café.

That man can definitely fill a booth, Jo mused when the chief eased in beside her. After a polite sentence or two about nothing important, he wrapped a large hand around a coffee mug. "Day before yesterday I stopped by to have a chat with Wil Thompson. Talked to the boy's dad." Chief Stout set the cup down hard and shook his head. "That Harry is one rough character. You should have heard him when I asked about his son's whereabouts the night of the attack. He was more interested in himself. Said he'd been out on a good drunk. Bragged about it. Then he turned around and insisted his boy had spent the night at home in bed. I guess it's possible the man could have been more disagreeable, but I don't how."

"What did you do?" Tryg asked.

"Told him I was there to talk to his boy. Asked to see the kid. He insisted Wil wasn't home, so I set up a time to come back. When I did, Harry insisted he hadn't seen hide nor hair of the boy to even get a message to him. I've stopped by several times since. Got the same hare-brained story. I swear tracking that kid down is like trying to find a speck of pepper on a dirt floor."

"What about the other kid?"

"Stopped by his place, too. I understand Anders and Thompson are inseparable. Anders' dad also swears his boy was home that night. I did question young Teddy. He's got a cold and mean streak that's kind of hard to figure. I couldn't get him to crack. Seems I can't get cooperation from anybody these days. When I do get my hands on that Thompson kid, though, he will talk."

"Why was Big Ole roaming around after dark in the first place?" Tryg said.

Jo's defenses reared. "Why would that be a problem? Why would Ole or anyone else have been afraid to go outside after dark? We've definitely had enough thefts recently, but this was the first time anyone's been attacked."

Sarah placed a thin hand on Tryg's forearm. "Jo's right, Tryg. When the weather's nice, Grandpa always takes a walk out to the park for some fresh air and a cigar to relax before he turns in for the night."

When Chief Stout turned toward her, Jo bristled.

"I know we've covered this before," he said, "but I want you to think hard. When you found Big Ole lying on the road, did you see anything? Hear anything? Did he give you any indication at all about who might have done this to him? Or why? Did he mention any names? Say how many there were? Anything that could possibly give me a clue?"

Looking into the questioning eyes of Tryg and Sarah, Jo reached for her napkin and played with its edges strikingly similar to the way she was about to play with their minds. "Other than what I told you before about the tracks on the gravel, all he did was groan."

"Has he said anything to you since?"

Yes. "Did you ever get a chance to talk to any of our neighbors?"

Tryg's eyes lit up. "That's right. Somebody had to have heard something."

Thank you, Tryg. "I know the Wilders were down in Iowa spending a few days with their daughter, so they weren't home."

"No one else heard anything either." Chief Stout raised a brow. "Seems everyone was sitting in front of their radios about the time it happened."

"But there had to have been a loud racket," Tryg said.

Chief Stout choked down a swig of water. "Big Ole make a racket? He'd be about as likely to cry for help as General Patton. That ain't gonna happen."

The chief zeroed in on Jo. "I noticed you didn't answer my question. Has Big Ole said anything to you since?"

Jo picked up her napkin again and refolded it. Ignoring the tightening in her stomach, she refused to talk.

Chief Stout's gaze was penetrating, his voice strong yet controlled. "That's what I thought. Your silence is screaming. I'm the authority around town here, Mrs. Bremley. Not Big Ole Harrington. Now let me cut to the chase. You were right about the bike tracks we both saw out on the road. There had to have been at least two attackers. There were several solid sites where the gravel was scraped clean. The way I see it, those boys must have torn out of there like bats out of Hades, their bike tires spitting up stones. One of his attackers was Wil Thompson, wasn't it? And the other one was that Anders kid."

Feeling Tryg and Sarah's hopeful stares, Jo hesitated. "I was so terrified when I found him," she said finally, "I didn't know what to do. I do remember looking all around, though. I didn't hear or see a thing. No. Wait a second. I did hear something. A rustling sound. It was coming from Evelyn Tomlinson's lilac bushes. I remember feeling scared. I forced myself to look, but didn't see anything. I blew it off as probably being a rabbit or a squirrel. I was too afraid to think anything else. Other than that, I get the distinct impression Big Ole wants to handle this himself, and if that's the case, he has a good reason."

"Let me remind you again that as chief of police, I'm the authority in town."

"He's right, Jo," Tryg said. "If you know anything else, it's your duty to come clean."

Jo stared at her sandwich and the slices of bread that were growing dry. She felt as if she were back in grade school, listening to the public chiding of unrelenting schoolmarms, but silently held her ground.

"All right," the chief said finally, "have it your way. But I aim to find out who did this if it's the last thing I do and, mark my word, if I can prove that Thompson boy was the ring leader, he'll be learning far more about reform school than he ever wanted to know."

CHAPTER EIGHTEEN

J o stepped out into the early morning and smiled at a robin singing in the apple tree. The tree's branches sagged from the weight of sprouting green fruit the way her spirits sagged. Concern for Big Ole. Not hearing from Frank. She gazed at the glistening lake, the cattails poking up haphazardly in the marsh, and a lone rabbit hopping along the thin three-wire fence lining the perimeter of the backyard. Peaceful. Beautiful. The kind of morning she needed to lift her spirits. How she would love to preserve this day in a Mason jar, only to open it for another pick-me-up when the weather became dull and dreary again.

She was the first to arrive at the office for what she thought would be another run-of-the-mill day. Ardena strolled in as the coffee finished perking, and Tryg breezed through the door a few minutes later, looking as if he'd been up half the night.

At twenty to ten, however, Jo noticed a florist pulling up in front of the office window. A deliveryman rounded the side of the truck carrying a colorful summer bouquet. She glanced at Ardena and smiled. "Looks like someone's about to get a very pleasant surprise," she said. The door swung open and a middle-aged man with larger teeth than mouth strutted in with shoulders back, chest puffed out, and his manner radiating purpose. He appeared unusually happy for someone who undoubtedly needed directions.

"I'm looking for a Mrs. Jo Bremley," he said brightly.

Jo's breath lodged deep in her lungs and stayed there. "I'm Jo Bremley."

He greeted her with a tip of his cap, then caringly placed the arrangement on the middle of her desktop. He took a step back, his gentle eyes glistening. "These are for you, ma'am. Good day to you."

Jo sat speechless then reached for the card wedged deep inside the blossoms. Ardena, meanwhile, appeared front and center as excited as a kid on Christmas Eve. "Who are they from? Who are they from?" she repeated.

"You've got me." Jo plucked a card from its dainty envelope and gazed up at Ardena, amazed. "It says, *Thank you for the dance. Frank.*"

"That guy you were telling me about? The one from the shivaree?"

Jo nodded.

"Boy. He sure is something," Ardena said, gushing. "I wish he'd give Calvin a lesson or two."

Frown lines tightened Jo's forehead. "I was beginning to think I wasn't going to hear from him. I know it hasn't been that long, but I was expecting a phone call, not flowers."

"Maybe he felt bad about not calling yet."

"But we barely had a chance to talk. Besides, it was only a group dance."

"No," Ardena said. "Not to him, it wasn't."

Jo suddenly felt joyfully frightened, not certain what to think or how to feel. Frank knew nothing of her beyond a pleasant evening on a crowd-filled lawn. He knew nothing at all about her heart. At this point, it appeared he was declaring his intentions. She needed to exercise caution. How far should she walk into a relationship she wasn't ready for?

Just then Tryg breezed past. "I'm on my way to the courthouse. Be back in a few hours."

"But you didn't see Jo's flowers," Ardena said.

Tryg turned back, giving Jo a quick glance. "Yes, I did. Not too bad."

Jo stared through the window as he disappeared from view. His tepid response felt like a practiced thief snatching her baffled pleasure. How was it she could allow herself to feel even the slightest bit diminished? Shaking it off, she returned her attention to the beautiful bouquet and sniffed its fragrant perfume. At least someone out there valued her for who she was, not who her husband had been.

Tryg couldn't get off his own back. *Yes, I did. Not too bad?* What a cad he'd been. He sauntered down the sidewalks of Broadway unthinkingly stepping on cracks the way he'd done when he was a kid, the balls of his feet enjoying a lickety-split massage with every footfall. Catching himself, he looked up, hoping no one had noticed his childish whim.

Who gave Jo the flowers? Was it her birthday? Or was someone staking out his claim? Whoever it was, he'd better be good to her. Frank Breck, the farmer? Tryg jingled his change. It had to be him. He certainly looked as if he was in hog heaven when he danced with Jo at the shivaree. Tryg mindlessly flexed the other hand that had tightened into a fist as he walked along. What was the matter with him? Why did he feel as if he needed to hold back a wagonload of resentment? The farmer hadn't even taken Jo out yet. Or had he? If he was planning on seeing her, he'd better have honorable intentions—or else. Tryg stifled an uneasy chuckle. Or else what?

No. That wasn't what was gnawing at him. Even if Jo was seeing Frank, the dashing farmer had a roving eye. He wasn't the kind of guy who knew what he wanted, and he certainly didn't appear ready to settle down. With so many men overseas, Frank's sense of selection was undoubtedly muddied by too many choices. Jo deserved better. Tryg didn't need to worry about her, though. Not Jo. She was too smart to get hoodwinked.

It was Sarah. That's what gnawed at him. He fell short by not sending her flowers before getting shown up by a near stranger. Tryg could still send them any time, he reasoned, but not until he was certain he'd won her heart and she'd won his. Then, as afternoon follows morning, he would make that special trip to the best florist in town, find the largest, freshest bouquet in the shop, and have it delivered along with a generous box of chocolates to seal his intentions.

But for now he was content to spend time with her every Saturday night—wasn't he?

CHAPTER NINETEEN

Later that evening Tryg sat near the window of The Copper Kettle staring at the empty chair across from him. It reminded him of Big Ole's famed 'table for two, party of one' tables. Only this time Tryg was the one who was dining alone.

Sipping his cooling coffee, he thought again about Jo and the sparkle in her eye when she had gone home for the day. When Case was killed, Tryg had learned about the fragility of life, how nothing stays the same. Why hadn't it dawned on him that one day Jo might get involved in a relationship, and why did that day have to come so soon? The possibility of being wrong about Frank Breck, their relationship advancing toward marriage, and Jo leaving the office for a new life out on a farm left him feeling colder than the dish of ice cream he'd finished.

This was about more than Jo's running off, though. It was also about Sarah. Ardena had fired a warning shot about Charlie, about the competition. Tryg knew she was teasing, but Sarah had appeared somewhat distant the night of the shivaree, not warming up until they got to the farm. Or was that his imagination?

Tryg pulled out a few bills, tossed them on the table, and headed back to the office. He needed to take action, set his foolish thinking aside. Picking up the receiver, he called Sarah and invited her to the Canton Café for a quick fountain drink.

At seven o'clock he headed for the O.M. Harrington. As he reached for the handle, the door popped open and out stepped Charlie. They shook hands and exchanged an awkward hello. Jo had been right about him. He wasn't the same guy who'd gone off to war. He appeared troubled, withdrawn, and his eyes hadn't met Tryg's. "It's good to see you home again, Charlie. How about coffee one of these first days?"

"We'll do that," Charlie said distractedly, then scurried down the steps.

A moment later, Sarah hurried toward Tryg, her shiny auburn hair flowing softly about her narrow shoulders. His heart warmed as she seized his hands. "Before we go," she said, "you might want to say hello to Grandfather. You'll find him in his office."

Tryg winked at Sarah who blushed.

After a few pleasantries, Tryg said, "On the way in I finally got a chance to say hello to Charlie. Seemed a bit preoccupied."

"That Charlie's a good man." Ole smiled. "And Doc? At first something didn't seem right with him, but now he can't stop grinning. It's nice to see again."

"Has Charlie said anything yet about where he was all those months?"

"No, and no one feels right asking."

"Not even you?"

"If he's not about to tell his dad what happened, even I know enough to leave the lad alone." Ole emptied an overfilled ashtray into a wastebasket next to his desk, keeping his gaze fastened on it. "I've been thinking, maybe it wouldn't be such a bad idea if you had a word with him. He puts up a good front, but there's no question he's troubled. If he doesn't let go of the poison pumping through his veins, it's going to destroy him."

"I doubt I'd be the best one to take him on. In the first place, I'm not a professional—"

"A guy like Charlie has too much pride to see a professional. That would be admitting he had a problem."

"I don't know him all that well either. Besides, my situation was far different from his. I'm one of the lucky ones. I didn't get captured, and my wounds are the kind that heal."

"Yes," Ole said forthrightly, "but you still have that limp. Think about it, okay?"

Tryg did think for a moment. Charlie couldn't be a threat, not if Ole wanted to Tryg to befriend him. "You know, maybe we could take Charlie out by the dam on the north side of Fountain Lake for a little fishing. Just us boys. Then when the war is over and we don't have to bother with gas rationing, we could always make a follow-up trip to the north woods. Maybe Cass Lake. Catch ourselves some walleye and northern pike. You game?"

"Let's plan on it."

Suddenly feeling restless, Tryg said, "Say, Ole."

"What is it? You look like you got a sour stomach."

"Are you familiar with the name Henrietta Braddingly?"

"The she-devil Braddingly? I believe that name is overly familiar to a lot of folks and, unfortunately, I fear very little of that familiarity is good. So what's that old ... what's she up to now, or dare I ask?"

"She has it in for Chief Stout," Tryg said.

"And your point would be?"

"My point is ... you can't hold out on the town much longer. I thought you might want to know you were on the agenda at last week's town council meeting."

"That was a bit premature, wasn't it?"

"That's what I thought, too, but people are nervous. Rumors are flying." Tryg inhaled a breath. "And Henrietta isn't helping it any. She's spreading word that the chief's inept because he can't make you talk, and he still hasn't made an arrest. I doubt she has a leg to stand on until enough time passes, but people are also upset with you for refusing to come forward. In a way, you can't blame them. They're afraid they could be next. To be direct, people are not taking kindly to your silence."

"But about Chief Stout," Ole said, "why implicate him? He's doing the best he can."

"You tell me. She mentioned something about the robberies in the same breath that she mentioned your situation. For some reason, I get the impression she's either using him to get at you or she's using you to get at him."

"Why do you say that?"

"She's the one taking the lead in this whole thing. She also said some rather unflattering words about you in the context of your unwillingness to help the chief."

"Word gets around, doesn't it? I'm running as fast as I can, Tryg," he said, the ache in his voice unmistakable.

"I believe you, but people are cranked up."

Ole shook his head. "That Henrietta. She always did consider herself the town matriarch. Well, you tell those busybodies, Henrietta included, they don't have a thing to worry about. I know what I'm doing."

The misery in Ole's look wrenched Tryg's heart.

Ole paused then said, "When our Maker divvies out problems, He doesn't hesitate to make them tough, does He?"

"He knows the tough can handle them," Trug said confidently, then added, "But what if something happens to someone else because you refuse to talk?"

Ole plucked up a small piece of notepaper and smoothed its edges. By the way he monotonously tapped it against the cherrywood, Tryg could see this conversation distressed him. He then gave Tryg a penetrating look that appeared misplaced and said, "Is that your only concern?"

At that moment Sarah strolled past the door, and Ole raised a brow as if Tryg should be able to read his thoughts. To Tryg's misfortune, this was one time he knew he could.

"Look, I don't know how to say this other than straight out." Tryg lowered his voice. "But your competency is being brought into question, too."

"Do you question my competency, Mr. Howland?"

Mr. Howland? "Absolutely not."

"Then what's the problem?"

Minutes later, Tryg and Sarah headed up the road for close of day.

"You're awfully quiet," she said.

With a tight grip on the steering wheel, Tryg nodded. "Sorry. I'm rehashing my conversation with your grandfather."

"What did he want?"

"Nothing much. Asked if I'd talk to Charlie."

"What about?"

Noticing her tone had taken on a defensive edge, Tryg glanced at Sarah. "Getting wounded. I don't know what I could say that would make a difference."

Neither am I sure about you—and your friendship with Charlie.

The knock at the door was light. Jo kissed Brue softly on her forehead. "Get some sleep now, you hear?" then cried out, "Coming!"

Big Ole stood on her back stoop with an embarrassed yet confident grin and hat in hand.

"Mr. Harrington."

"Why must you insist on calling me that? It's Big Ole, remember?"

Jo chuckled. "Why the back door?"

"We have some private business to attend to. Mind if I come in?"

Jo led the way into the kitchen. "Can I get anything for you? Iced tea maybe?"

"No, I'm fine, thank you. Let me be direct." He reached into a pocket and pulled out a fistful of bills. Twenties, tens, and fives, and a note with sizes scribbled all over it. Boy's sizes. "I need your help. The boy could use some new clothes."

Jo eyed the money. She was getting into the Big Ole mess much deeper now, but there was no pulling back. Not only was she withholding vital information from the chief of police, she was also aiding and abetting, and in a flagrant way. She felt compromised, but she couldn't turn him down. Not Big Ole.

"You look reluctant," he said, "almost resentful."

"I'm fine. Really. But in helping you, I'm also helping Wil. He is one of the boys who attacked you, remember? Don't worry. I'll get past it."

"You're a good woman, Jo Bremley." Ole began pacing, but then stopped and frowned.

"What's the matter?" Jo said.

"Charlie. Sarah. Things are heating up at the boarding house, and it looks like there's no stopping it."

Jo shook her head. "I was afraid of that."

"Tryg stopped by a little while ago to pick up Sarah. I tried to get his attention."

"You want to protect him from hurt the way you want to protect Wil from reform school, is that right?"

"I guess you might say that. Why won't you and Tryg give each other a chance, Jo? He's an awfully good man. I don't mean to be crude here, but your dead husband can't keep you warm at night."

Feeling a chastened grin escape, she said, "But it's summertime, and we're in the middle of a heat wave."

"You know what I mean."

Jo turned serious. She considered Frank Breck and those beautiful flowers. At the moment, what an unwitting life preserver. "I know. But my dead husband aside, I need someone who will love me and want me for me, not for some displaced sense of duty."

CHAPTER TWENTY

J o stopped at the O.M. Harrington with an oversized bundle in hand.

"Let's see," she said as she ripped open the tightly-strung package, pulled out clothing one item at a time, and made a neat stack on the chair next to Ole's desk. "Three pairs of trousers, one pair of oxfords, five long-sleeved white button-down shirts, five pairs of socks, and three neckties. These are awfully nice for work clothes."

Ole grinned like a mischievous schoolboy, his proud eyes glistening. "Nice clothes for a nice place. I hope my plan works."

Jo eyed Ole.

"They say clothes make the man," he said reassuringly, as if he could read her unsettled thoughts.

Ole painstakingly looked over the goods, his heart in his eyes. He was so alone in his stance that it grieved Jo. Now that she'd had time to think about it, she didn't care if Wil had gone back to the crime scene crying over what he'd done. What were those tears really about? Were they for himself? For fear of getting caught? What was it that Ole saw in the boy that no one else could see? Painting the stripe on a skunk would not change its character, but it could certainly make for one unhappy skunk. Was it possible to find in the end that Ole was right and the whole town was wrong?

Ole turned toward Jo and smiled guilelessly.

Knowing him as well as she did, she would not be surprised. She held out her hand. "Here's your change."

"Keep it, my dear."

"But—"

"I may need to call on you again." He looked at her with the innocence of a child. "I'd feel far more comfortable if you knew you'd be paid well for your efforts."

It was great knowing he felt comfortable, but Jo certainly didn't. "It was no bother at all. I ran over to Skinner Chamberlain's ..." Ole's gaze was so fastened on the clothing, Jo doubted he was listening.

"Go on," he said.

She continued with a smirk, "... during my lunch hour. It's only a few doors down on Broadway."

"Just the same—"

"Sorry to bother you, Mr. H—"

Ole looked up. "What is it, Wil?"

A mousy-haired, ill-dressed young man was stepping into the office. When Jo's eyes met with his, a jab pierced her heart, for in those eyes she gained unexpected understanding. She now saw what Big Ole had seen—years of loneliness, pain, and grief exuding from the eyes of a lost young man who desperately needed and deeply appreciated someone who cared.

Before the boy could answer, Ole said, "Wil, this is Mrs. Jo Bremley. She used to do our laundry here at the boarding house." Ole looked as if he wanted to say more, but appeared to stop himself. Of course, Jo thought. He wanted to protect Wil from knowing she was the one who had found him on the road.

"Nice to meet you," Jo said.

Wil looked at her extended hand reluctantly before seizing it, as if he'd never shaken a young woman's hand before. "Nice to meet you, too."

"What seems to be the problem?" Ole asked.

"Bernie told me to tell ya that the refrigerator konked out. He's worried some a' the food is gonna spoil before a repairman gets here."

"Tell him not to worry about it. We'll make sure the food finds a good home before we even think of throwing anything out."

"Thank you, sir."

After Wil disappeared into the hallway, Jo said, "I never saw him up close before. He was so respectful. I didn't expect that."

"Neither did I. The boy seemed to change over night." Ole gazed at Jo, his eyes compassion-filled. "And now you understand."

Ole peered into the spacious kitchen. Curious. Surprised to find Wil alone. The chef nowhere in sight, Wil hurled warm dinner rolls into a woven basket at the far side of the brightly-lit room. His speed and aim were phenomenal, every roll finding a precise place to rest. After watching Wil toss a half dozen or so rolls, Ole stepped into the room. "That's quite some aim you've got there, son."

Wil jumped and spun around. His cheeks and ears sprouted a brilliant shade of crimson, reminding Ole of the scene at Wil's home when Wil had cowered at his dad's touch.

"I'm serious." Ole moved in closer. "Let me have one of those things, will you? How'd you learn to do that?"

"Aww, it's nothin'."

"I wonder about that." Ole plucked a warm biscuit from the counter, slowly wound his arm, then lobbed it the way Wil had only to have it bounce off the far wall and find its final resting place dead center in the garbage can.

Ole glanced back at a voice sounding from behind. The chef strutted in carrying a large cardboard box, which appeared leaden, and lugged it to the counter.

"You checking up on us, are you, boss?"

"I wanted to have a word with Wil here."

"Looks like Wil's the one having a word with you." The chef chuckled. "He's teaching you his craft, is he?"

"I guess you might say that. Say, what do you have there, Bernie?"

"Oranges."

"I thought those things came in crates."

"They do. I know how much you love your fresh-squeezed juice first thing in the mornings, so I ordered these special."

Ole glanced at the oven. "What's for supper?"

"Prime rib."

"Is that a fact?" Ole pulled open the door and took a peek. "What are you serving with it?"

"Baked potatoes, coleslaw, green beans, biscuits, and warm cherry cobbler à la mode for dessert."

Noticing a bewildered look on Wil's face, Ole gave his shoulder a light pat. "After you finish for the day, why don't you plan on stopping by my office? I have a few things you might be able to use."

"What kind a' things?"

"You'll see. Stop by at eight."

Ole turned to the chef and motioned for him to come along into the great room. "Is it my imagination or does that boy have good aim?"

"It's not your imagination." Bernie's eyes twitched the way they did whenever he got excited. "His hand-eye coordination is amazing, like what you would expect to find in a professional athlete."

Ole smiled. "Keep an eye on him for me, will you?"

CHAPTER TWENTY-ONE

Y ou'd better be careful with that watering can or you're going to end up watering my books."

Sarah pulled back with a start. "Sorry, Grandpa."

"You know how I hate reading soggy books." Ole scoured his pipe with a cleaner and tapped residue into an ashtray. "That plant looks piti-ful, by the way. What do you think about replacing it one of these first days?"

"I'd be happy to."

When she headed for the door, Ole said, "Sarah?"

"Yes, sir?"

"Is there anything you'd care to talk about?"

Her cheeks took on a light shade of pink as she set down the water-ing can, her steps appearing awkward as she slowly made her way toward him. "Am I that transparent?"

Ole grinned coyly. "No. I'm just that perceptive."

"What am I going to do, Grandpa?" Sarah's eyebrows knitted together. "I feel so stuck. Stuck and guilty."

"About?"

"Tryg."

Ole rocked back in his chair and thoughtfully folded his hands.

"I adore him," she said, "and he's so good to me."

"But?"

"I sense I'll never be able to have him."

"How so?"

"That accident. His best friend dying. Jo. They're bonded, but I don't think they even know it. I always get the feeling I'm on the outside looking in. What's worse is I don't think he'll ever get over it. If things did get serious between us, I doubt I'd ever have more than a part of his heart. Case and Jo would always come between us."

"Don't you think you're jumping the gun a bit?" Ole pressed fresh tobacco in his pipe then gave her a sympathetic look. "You sound defeated. It can't be all that bad. Give him time. But the guilt, what's that all about?"

"Charlie," Sarah said without hesitation.

"Charlie, huh? That's what I thought."

"I don't know that he would ever pursue me, but if he did?"

"You'd feel tempted, is that it?"

Sarah nodded.

"Charlie has wounds, too, my dear."

"I know, but there's something about him. We seem to connect at a deep level. I don't know that I could ever feel that connected with Tryg."

Ole looked up. At eight o'clock sharp, Wil grinned like a baby who'd taken his first step. He glimmered with perspiration and appeared utterly exhausted. After a few short hours of tedious work, the joy in his big blue eyes filled Ole with guilty pleasure. Wil emanated fulfillment, his transformation amazing. But it was all so new. How long would it last?

"Finished with the dishes, son?"

"Yes, sir."

"How was the prime rib?"

Wil's smooth forehead wrinkled. "Sir?"

"The prime rib. You enjoyed it, I'm sure."

"No, sir. I didn't have any."

"Why not?"

Wil shrugged. "Didn't know I was 'sposed to."

"Is that a fact? I guess that would be my fault then, wouldn't it? I neglected to tell you and Bernie that supper is a mandatory part of our deal here." Seizing the top of his desk, Ole pushed himself up. "I'll be right back. While I'm away, why don't you take these things into the laundry room where you'll have some privacy? Try them on for size then meet me back here in, say, five minutes."

Wil gaped at the pile on the chair looking as if he'd never seen new clothes before.

"Go ahead, boy."

Five minutes later, Wil strutted through Ole's door like a pompous rooster past a henhouse crammed with admiring chickens. The clothes were a perfect fit. However, one shirtsleeve was again buttoned at the wrist, the other folded neatly up to an elbow.

Ole reached for Wil's arm, but he snapped it back lightning fast.

"What's going on here?" Ole asked, taking care not to sound too demanding. "Why roll up only one sleeve?"

Wil tugged at the buttoned sleeve, hiding more of his already covered wrist. The poor kid looked as if he couldn't hide his inner shame any more than an adolescent could hide an outbreak of acne. How could Ole help him? If only Wil could see himself through Ole's eyes. Value himself the way Ole did. He was unspoiled and had no idea how rich that made him. Even with his fighting spirit, he epitomized innocence.

Ole pivoted around, rested his backside against the desk, and crossed his arms over his generous middle. "You know, when I was growing up," he said, "must have been about seven or eight years old at the time, we had these old wooden school desks. Back in those days, they all came with inkwells. One day, a schoolmate of mine spilled his ink. Completely by accident, of course. Black liquid splattering all over the place. And I'll never forget that calloused teacher. Doubt I will for as long as I live." Ole shook his head. "She made a mountain out of a foothill, scolding that poor kid the whole time she helped clean up. Teachers can be cruel at times, can't they? You should've seen the boy. He dropped his head like a whipped puppy, not looking anyone in the eye. That got my attention, let me tell you. After that episode, do you know what happened to me?"

Wil shook his head, his eyes widening.

"I learned to fear that teacher. The other kids have to have feared her, too. How could you not? No one said boo about it, though. I figured if I kept my desk shipshape from that moment on, that would never happen to me." Ole lifted one foot over the other and crossed them at the ankle. "And then do you know what happened?"

Wil shook his head again.

"After a while things got away from me. I couldn't keep up. My desk got messier and messier all the time. It got to the point where I could barely find a hole to stuff a flimsy piece of paper. I wasn't one to spill things, but I never did open my desk when the teacher walked by.

"Then one day the unthinkable happened. The girl sitting in front of me, her name was Martha as I recall, she dropped her pencil, and it went rolling. When she bent down to pick it up, I got distracted by her silky long hair and missed the inkwell with an open bottle. It was full. I was mortified. Black ink dripping all over the place. My teacher flew into a rage. Stumbled over her own feet trying to get to me. She helped me clean it up all right, scolding me the entire time, like that other poor sucker. Made me stay after school, too. I felt lower than a viper's belly."

"What did ya do?" Wil asked. "Did ya tell your ma an' pa?"

"No. I was too embarrassed. But then, one day many years later I ran into an old fraternity buddy of mine. Guy by the name of Hap. Hap had gone on to become a schoolteacher. One night over a hamburger, we were rehashing old memories and one thing led to another. With him being a schoolteacher, I decided to suck it up, find out how inept

I'd been back then. Asked him if he ever had any students with messy desks." Ole grinned at Wil. "And do you know what he said?"

"No. What'd he say?"

"He said, 'yes, and they're always my best students.' Now, son, I say that to say this. Whatever's under that sleeve of yours, when you're ready, I'd be happy to take a look. Maybe we can talk it through."

Wil changed the subject faster than Ole could blink. He stuffed his hands in his pockets, greatly expanding the width of his new pants, and did a three-sixty. "How do I look?"

Ole shook his head. The kid hadn't heard a word he'd said. "The fit looks good on you, but how do the clothes feel?"

Wil's eyes were shining. "They feel good, sir."

The clatter of a serving cart wheeling into Ole's office broke into their conversation. Wil looked at the chef who grinned and bowed to him, his hand sweeping, palm up. "For you, my lord!"

Ole let out a gleeful chuckle. "Thank you, Bernie. That will be all."

The chef backed out of the room with a grin so wide it must have hurt.

"What's that?" Wil sounded astonished.

"My workers eat supper. Always. Now grab a chair and dig in."

Wil looked unsure of himself.

"You've had prime rib before, haven't you?"

"No, sir. I ain't."

Wil pulled the tray close, his gaze latched to the steamy food. One bite of the prime rib, and he slowly closed his eyes, inhaled a slow whiff, and visually savored every chew.

"Not too bad, is it?" Ole said.

Wil simply shook his head and kept chomping.

"Since you probably would prefer eating in peace, let me have a word with our fine chef. I'll ask him to pack a plate for you to take home. Stop by the kitchen on your way out."

Ole stepped into the hallway, stopping long enough for a quick look back. When he entered the kitchen, the chef asked, "How'd the boy like the meat?"

"I've got to tell you, Bernie, I've never seen anyone take to food the way that boy took to your prime rib. He can't have eaten anything more exotic than a hotdog or a hamburger. And it shows."

CHAPTER TWENTY-TWO

O le tapped a smattering of ashes into the ashtray for the umpteenth time. He straightened it, perfectly aligning its square sides parallel to the sides of the desk, moving it a few inches, and realigning it just so, before giving it another nudge as if realigning the cold hunk of glass could realign peoples' opinions—Henrietta's opinion, the chief's, and everybody else's around this scaredy-cat town.

He mulled over the whispers he'd quieted at the O.M. Harrington. Problem was, he hadn't counted on his efforts being so effective. Not only had the whispering stopped, the talking stopped, too. The place was quieter than a potter's field in the still of night. He thought about the townspeople, Henrietta Braddingly, Chief Stout, and their displeasure with his lack of cooperation. Those he could handle. But unleashing his anger at Sarah while simultaneously browbeating the onlookers niggled at him. Respect isn't something that can be taken. It has to be earned. How could he undo the damage he'd done during a deliciously careless moment of self-expression? He mashed the cigar in the ashtray as if that could help blot out his blunder. Why beat himself up? Everyone was entitled to a mistake now and then.

He ambled to the bookcase, dusted off a dog-eared copy of *For Whom the Bell Tolls*, then plopped back on his chair, and began reading when light knocking captured his attention. Ole looked up to see the chef with a grin as wide as the doorframe.

"I think you'd better come with me, sir. It's about our boy and his natural gift for pitching. Can't seem to stop himself. Come," Bernie said, excitedly leading the way.

When they drew near the kitchen, the chef twisted around, and pulling a finger to his pursed lips, he tiptoed forward. "Shhh!"

Wil was lobbing sticky globs of biscuit dough at the far wall. Biscuit upon biscuit hitting the wall with a dull splat and forming a perfect horizontal line above the counter, until one by one they sagged by their own weight.

After several fascinating minutes of unimpeded observation, Ole said in his deep baritone voice, "Son?"

Wil jumped and twirled around looking like a caged cat itching to flee. "I'm sorry. I'm sorry," he repeated, the words flying off his fear-drenched lips. "I won't do it again."

Ole erupted with mirth. He stepped to Wil's side and reached out. "No need to apologize. We were admiring your artwork."

Wil appeared to relax beneath Ole's caring touch, his eyes widening.

"You have an amazing arm there," Ole said.

"You mean, you ain't mad at me?"

"Not a chance." Ole thought about his old friend, Hank. At least there was one person he was still in good standing with. 'I've been feeling company-starved these days,' Hank had said a few days ago.'

Ole studied Wil for a moment. Now here was a boy who could use some broadening, and Hank enjoyed more connections in the sports world than the bank held dollar bills.

"Say, Wil, have you ever thrown horseshoes?"

He looked taken aback. "Course. Who ain't?"

"I'll bet you're pretty good at it, too, aren't you?"

"Ain't too bad, I guess."

Wondering if Hank had delighted in a formidable opponent in

years, Ole grinned. "There's someone I'd like you to meet. A gentleman by the name of Hank. Stop by Monday morning. Say ten o'clock straight up. We'll take a ride over to his place. There's no question he'd like to meet you."

"Who's Hank?"

"Meet me here at ten."

Pulling at his earlobe as he walked away, Ole couldn't help but wonder. Even after his talk with Wil, the boy still had one shirtsleeve rolled up to an elbow. Now why would he roll up only one sleeve on a brand new long-sleeved shirt? Didn't make a smidgen of sense.

CHAPTER TWENTY-THREE

Tryg emptied the wine goblet with one last swig. After wiping a dribble of golden liquid from the side of the crystal, he placed it gently on the table. "How was your chicken?"

"Excellent." Sarah leaned to the side clearing the way for a server to pick up the near-empty plate. "You can't beat Stables Supper Club when it comes to great food."

"Main course, yes. Dessert no."

"Ahem." Sarah exposed a flirtatious grin. "You can't be serious. Where can you possibly find a better dessert?"

"Oh, I dunno. I've heard there's a little hole-in-the-wall a few blocks from the heart of town called Tryg's Kitchen. Been meaning to try out the place."

"I see. This Tryg guy, he bakes incredible desserts, does he?"

"Can't bake a thing you'd want to eat, but he can pour chocolate syrup on vanilla ice cream like nobody's business."

Sarah chuckled.

"And then," Tryg said, reaching for her hand, "I thought we might enjoy a cup of coffee over a game of chess. If you'll remember, you whooped me the last time we played. I'd like to gain my honor back, that is, if you wouldn't mind. You up for it?"

"What if I win again?"

"We'll have to schedule another match. What do you say? You can't win 'em all."

Ten minutes later, the car cruised south on Broadway and made a turn on Main.

"Say," Sarah said. "That boy over there—"

Tryg followed Sarah's gaze. "What about him?"

"He works at the boarding house now."

"Wil Thompson? You can't be serious."

"Of course, I am. You sound as if you don't believe me."

"But that's not possible. Chief Stout's positive he's the ring leader that roughed up your grandpa."

"Chief Stout is wrong," Sarah said emphatically. "I'm telling you that's Wil Thompson. Look at his shirt. Every time I've seen him, he's worn only one sleeve rolled up to his elbow like that kid there. Has the same color hair, same gait, same everything. Grandpa would never hire him if he was in on it."

"You're right," Tryg said. "He wouldn't, would he? But if that's the case, Chief Stout needs to know he's yelping up the wrong tree. Mind if I pull over for a minute? I'd like to see where Willie boy is going."

Tryg pulled to the curb and waited until Wil was out of sight then followed along, careful to stay several full blocks behind. When they reached the ballpark, Tryg parked a comfortable distance away. Meanwhile, Wil sauntered across the field and pulled a bat and half a dozen or so balls from underneath the bleachers then headed toward home plate.

With his gaze cemented on Wil, Tryg rubbed his chin. "I wonder if he's waiting for Teddy Anders."

"The other kid Chief Stout thinks was in on the whipping?"

"That's right. I understand the boys are inseparable."

"Speaking of the boys being inseparable, did you know Grandpa's out roaming the streets again?"

"You aren't serious."

"Oh, but I am."

Tryg leaned closer to the windshield.

"What are you doing?"

"Nothing much. I'd like to watch Wil place the balls for a second here."

"What's that supposed to mean?"

"It means he decides before he takes a hit where the ball is going to land. The harder he hits the ball, the farther it flies. If he hits it early, you know, before it reaches home plate, the ball veers to the left. He hits it dead center, the ball goes straight."

"And if he's slow to hit it, it goes to the right, right?"

Tryg chuckled. "That's precisely correct. See how he's hitting them in a near perfect line straight up the center past the pitcher's mound? He's doing a good job of spacing them, too."

Sarah swatted at a mosquito. "Pesky thing." She quickly rolled up her window. "Wil does the same thing at the boarding house, only with biscuits."

"Your grandpa allows that?"

Sarah nodded. "He sees something in Wil. You should have seen that kid the other day. Even I was impressed. Grandpa was in the great room showing Wil fencing moves. He had his sword outstretched, nearly lost his balance for a split second, and knocked a vase off the mantle. Wil caught it in one hand just before it hit the floor."

"That is good. So your grandpa is aware of his skill then. I'm surprised he doesn't have the kid playing with the Packers."

"You know Grandpa. I think he's angling for it. He's introducing him to an old friend of his on Monday morning. He mentioned something about the guy having outstanding connections."

"Not Hank?"

"You know Hank?" Sarah said, sounding surprised.

"Who doesn't? He was quite a ball player during his day."

Sarah grinned. "Any bets on how long it'll take to see Wil on the team?"

"That one's too easy. Any bets on how much you're going to enjoy eating ice cream at Tryg's Kitchen?"

CHAPTER TWENTY-FOUR

While Ole stood on the corner waiting for a taxi, he prepared himself for disappointment—just in case. "Have you seen anything of that Anders boy lately?" he asked.

Wil cast his gaze downward. Kicking aimlessly at the sidewalk, he appeared too ashamed to look up. "No, sir."

"Would that have been your decision or Teddy's?"

"Mine."

Ole gazed up into the crystalline Minnesota sky, his gratified mind lingering on matters below. "I guess I probably don't need to ask why then, do I?"

Wil shook his head remorsefully.

"I was right about you, Wil."

"What d'ya mean by that?"

"There's a diamond inside of you. A big fat shiny diamond."

The taxi arrived at the corner of Charles Street and River Lane a few minutes past ten. Not long after, the driver pulled up to a curb on Fountain Street.

Wil balked at the residence. "What're we doin' here?"

"Like I said last week, there's someone I'd like you to meet."

Ole paid the fare, leaving a generous tip. "Stop back in an hour or so," he said to the driver and then led Wil down a path of flat stepping stones at the side of the large clapboard house. Without bothering to knock, he entered through a side door, headed down a long hallway, and stopped at the threshold of a pleasant-looking room with rich furnishings. A mahogany mantle lined with well-polished trophies canopied a large fireplace, and a small lamp burned in a far corner. A decrepit old man sat in a wheelchair staring out a window lined with a planter box bursting with red zinnias. "Finding anything of interest out there?" Ole asked.

The man wheeled around and his face lit up. "Big Ole Harrington. Why, aren't you a sight for ancient eyes? What brings you to my castle again in such a short window of time? I could get used to this."

"Got someone I'd like you to meet."

"So you brought the boy, huh?" Hank said. "Good. I've been looking forward to meeting him. Didn't expect him to come hand delivered though." Hank craned his neck and looked toward the empty doorway. "Is it my imagination or hasn't that young whippersnapper learned to respect his elders yet?"

"You catch on fast for an old coot, but he is making progress." Ole stepped out into the hallway, surprised to find Wil hugging the floral-papered wall, looking as if he wanted to slither into it. "What are you doing out here?"

"I ain't meetin' no shut-in," Wil said, his eyes run amok with fear. "You ain't gonna make me."

"What are you all worked up about, son?"

Wil stared down the far side of the hallway, his words appearing caught in his throat. "I know I messed up in the kitchen at your place, but you ain't gonna get me to bathe an' feed no cripple who lazes around all day smellin' like a old folks' home."

Wil's response stung. This was Ole's fault. He was moving too fast, way too fast, and had scared the boy off. It was clear Wil feared grownups. Now Ole had added another adult into the mix and, to exacerbate matters, in an unfamiliar setting. "Is that what you think? No, I'm not relieving you of your duties in my kitchen, and I certainly don't expect you to change anyone's bedpans. But I do need you to trust me."

Ole looked around and sniffed the sweet air. "As for this place smelling like an old folks' home, I think you'd better sniff again. Smells wonderful. Smells like home. Smells like someone's baking an apple pie in the kitchen down at the far end of the hallway, too. Don't be afraid to open your eyes, really open them and take a good look around. This place is cheerful. It's immaculate, and highly upscale. There's a lot of brainpower inside these walls. You'd do well to pay attention. You might learn a thing or two. Now come on. Step inside with me."

Wil shuffled into the room looking more like a terrified kid getting his first inoculation than a boy about to meet an accomplished old man.

"Wil, I'd like you to meet my good friend Hank."

Only after Ole nudged Wil forward did Wil reach for the man's hand.

Hank looked up at him and then at Ole and offered a warm smile.

"Hank knows how to throw a mean horseshoe," Ole said. "I thought maybe you could get to know one another, play a game every now and then. We can set it up out back. Can't we, Hank?"

Wil looked at Ole skeptically, then eyed the wrinkled and weathered man who had kind and alert eyes, but was sitting between two steel-spoked wheels. "He's in a wheelchair."

"Can you toss a biscuit sitting down, son?"

"How many times do I have to tell you I'm not your son, Big Ole?" Wil said with an edge.

"I want you to take a good look at me," Ole said, his tone impatient. "At the moment you may not like me, but you will learn to respect me. And by the way, to you it will continue to be Mr. Harrington, son. Now about my question, can you toss a biscuit sitting down?"

Hank reached for Ole's arm, his eyes filled with spunk. "Say, Ole. I know you mean well and I appreciate it, really I do. But I think I'd prefer playing with a man instead of a boy—if you know what I mean."

Wil dropped his shoulders and sighed. "Okay, I'll do it."

After an ill-at-ease good-bye, Ole and Wil awaited the taxi. Ole wasn't particularly happy with Wil or with the way the meeting had unfolded. "Not only will you learn to respect me, you will also learn to respect Hank," he said. "He deserves as much. Furthermore, after infecting everyone with your miserable attitude, I've changed my mind. I don't want you stopping by every now and then. I want you to report here every day from ten until eleven until I say differently. With the exception of some hefty storm clouds, if you miss even one day, I will blow the whistle. Loud!"

CHAPTER TWENTY-FIVE

Ole gaped at the poor kid standing before him spilling over with need. After giving it some thought, Wil had apologized for his childish behavior at Hank's place and spent the bulk of Monday trying to make up for it.

"I feel like an ogre deciding for you what you should spend your hard-earned money on," Ole said, "but if you ever plan to have any quality of life at all, it has to be done. Friday will be your first payday. I'll pay you in cash, but half of each week's salary is going to have to go for paying off your debt to everyone you stole from. Will you be okay with that?"

"Yes, sir."

"Good. Now here's what I want you to do. Tomorrow, bring in a list of all the items you took and what houses you took them from. Do you think you'll be able to do that?"

"Uh-huh," Wil said confidently.

Ole plucked a cigar from his desk drawer and snipped off an end. He struck a match against his thumbnail and, securing the cigar between his lips, he inhaled flame. He tossed the spent match in an ashtray and after a few quick puffs and an exaggerated blow, he said, "But how will you know the addresses and the precise things you walked off with from each house?"

"Aw, that's easy." Wil slid onto a chair as if taking ownership. "All the stuff was known."

"What do you mean by known?"

"Well," Wil said with a lift of his shoulders, "if someone left a garage door open during the daytime and we saw somethin' we wanted, we remembered where it was an' snuck back after dark an' picked it up. We snuck a few things from the hardware store, too. And the lumberyard. But only when there wasn't no one around."

"Do you remember what those items were?"

"Uh-huh," Wil said, sounding eager to come clean. "We still got the stuff."

Ole scoured his right ear with a forefinger as if it needed a cleaning. "You do?"

"Yup. We only took stuff we needed like sports an' fishin' gear an' stuff to build me a tree house. Oh, yeah, an' a raft, too."

Ole took a deep drag on his cigar, held it in for a while, then raised his chin and slowly exhaled the smoke, watching it swirl like steam from a cold muffler. "That's going to make this far easier than I thought. But what about the burglaries?"

Wil looked innocently surprised by the question. "You mean the ones inside peoples' houses?"

"That's precisely what I mean."

"I wasn't in on any a' that stuff," Wil said with an adamant shake of his head.

"You weren't? Do you have any idea who was?"

Wil looked away too quickly.

"Wil, do you mean to tell me the Anders kid did that all by himself?"

Wil nodded dejectedly.

"What's the long face all about?" Ole asked.

"You called me Wil."

"That's your name, isn't it?"

"You mostly call me son."

Ole smiled. "You've corrected me so many times, I didn't think you liked me calling you son."

"I changed my mind," Wil said, but not without a distinct frown.

Ole fidgeted with the ashtray. "Getting back to Teddy. Why don't you stand up for yourself? Why don't you tell Chief Stout what really happened?"

"Cuz I ain't no snitch," Wil snapped.

"But don't you understand? You could go to reform school for what you've done. That's what Chief Stout's angling for."

Wil looked at Ole, confused. "But I thought you said we gotta pay back our debts to society."

Ole's heart melted. The boy was soft, moldable clay in his trusted hands. "That's true. I did. But you're paying the debt all by yourself. What about that renegade friend of yours? Why are you bearing the brunt for him?"

"Aww, Chief Stout ain't gonna believe me noways," Wil said. "Besides, I'm guilty. I done way too much bad stuff on my own."

"But why? Why did you do so many bad things?"

Wil shrugged.

Ole got up and eased onto the chair next to Wil. "Was it attention you wanted or did you feel other peoples' things belonged to you?"

Wil stared at the floor for a long moment and shrugged again.

"Well, whatever the reason, I couldn't be more proud of you for owning what you've done," Ole said. "But I'm still concerned about that Anders boy. He's dangerous, Wil. He needs to get off the streets."

"Na'ah. When he's alone, he's a big, fat chicken."

"He can't be too much of a big fat chicken if he burglarizes houses by himself."

Wil looked disgusted. "He only burglarizes houses when he knows nobody ain't around."

"You don't say. Well, what about what he did to me? He was the leader, not you."

"The only reason he took the lead was 'cuz he knew I'd take the rap. Besides, he acts a lot worse than he is. You didn't get no broken bones, did ya?"

"No."

"You know why?"

Ole shook his head.

"Cuz Teddy wanted to hurt you and scare you, but not enough to break any bones. If he wanted to do that, believe me, he woulda. You don't gotta worry about him. The only reason he did it was cuz he—"

"Because he what, Wil?"

"I better not say."

"Why not?"

Wil displayed all the signs of having said too much—fidgeting, sweat glistening on his forehead, eyes riveted on the floor. "I better not is all."

"Are there more kids involved other than you and Teddy?"

Wil shrugged.

"So that's it. I'll bet you took an oath, didn't you?" Ole said then waited him out. "I heard you were in a bicycle club. My harassment wouldn't have been part of an initiation stunt, would it?"

Wil nodded. "Teddy was 'sposed to do somethin' that took guts, and he wasn't 'sposed to show no fear when he did it. I was 'sposed to be the one to watch him to make sure he done it right."

"So you chose to inflict bodily harm?"

"Not me. Teddy did. An' since you stood up to him in the park that day when he rode by too close, he decided you'd be a tougher target than most, cuz he thought you were mean. He figured he'd get more points for that. No one ever hurt nobody before. It never dawned on any of us Teddy would show off an' play rough. All the guys are pretty sore about it. You won't tell on us, will ya?"

"Did you hear what you asked me?"

Wil nodded sheepishly.

"All the boys in your club know what he did? And no one will come forward?"

"Can't. If one of us gets in trouble, we all get in trouble, and no one wants to be a snitch."

"Do they know you work here now?"

Wil shrugged. "I dunno. Maybe."

"Maybe that's a good thing."

"Why?" Wil sounded surprised.

Ole couldn't hold back a satisfied grin. "Because, I'll bet the little cowards are all trembling in their sneakers. Serves 'em right."

"About Teddy, Mr. H. You really don't need to worry about him. Honest."

"Why's that?"

"Cuz he ain't gonna be around much longer anyways. He's eligible for the Army next month. Says he's gonna join up."

"Is that a fact? Well, I'd still be happy to talk to the chief on your behalf. You think about it, okay?"

Wil made his way toward the door. "There ain't nothin to think about. I ain't gonna snitch. If I go to reform school alone, then that's what I gotta do."

CHAPTER TWENTY-SIX

Monday passed with little to no noteworthy events. But then came Tuesday. Shortly after Jo arrived at the office, Ardena stopped typing. "Are you holding out on me?"

"About?" Jo said.

"Farmer Breck. When I was brushing my teeth this morning, I remembered you telling me he had the whitest teeth you'd ever seen, and then I realized you've been awfully quiet about him."

The lead on Jo's pencil snapped. She pulled open her desk drawer and plucked out another one only to find the lead on it also as broken as her thoughts.

"He sent you that beautiful bouquet. So what gives?"

Jo's cheeks grew warm.

"You are seeing him, aren't you?"

Jo mindlessly twirled her leadless pencil and slowly shook her head. "Other than the flowers, I haven't heard boo from him since the shivaree. Makes me feel as if he's lost interest. If he hadn't, you'd think he would have called by now."

Ardena frowned. "That is unusual, isn't it? I mean, he did send flowers."

"Maybe he's too shy to come around."

"Did he say anything when you—"

"When I what? Thanked him for them? I could have given him a jingle, I guess, but somehow that didn't feel right. I was sure he'd follow up with a call. I thought I'd thank him then, but too much time has slipped by. Can you imagine how embarrassing it would be to do that now?"

"Don't worry about it. He'll still call. I know he will." Ardena resumed typing then stopped again. "I wonder what could be taking him so long."

Whatever his situation was, Jo was pleased to have gotten his attention for a little while anyway and thrilled to get his flowers, but there was a part of her that didn't want to hear from him. If he didn't call, she wouldn't have to worry about a budding romance she wasn't was ready for in the first place. She smiled weakly. "I don't know. I'm learning more about new love than I ever wanted to know."

Ardena smiled as she erased a typo, blew off the residue, and realigned the paper on her platen. "It's a beautiful and exciting time, Jo. Look at Calvin and me."

"But it's a scary time, too. When you don't have anyone, you don't fear the unknowns—the competition, the uncertainty, or even the rejection. Now I've got an awakened longing, and I can't help worrying about an endless possibility of hurt."

Jo returned to her work, purposely replacing the hope in her heart with feigned indifference.

Brue stared at her food as if it was spoiled, poking at it, swirling it, and taking a partial taste every now and then.

"Want more peas?" Jo asked.

"No thanks."

"Potatoes and gravy?"

"No thanks."

"Sauerkraut and fudge?"

Brue lifted her chin off a palm and broke a grin. "Aww, Mom!"

"Your supper's getting cold. Doesn't look like you have much of an appetite tonight. Why not?"

Brue shrugged.

"It isn't my cooking, is it? And here I thought I was getting so much better at it." Jo set down her fork. "Did something happen at school today, something that's bothering you? Everything okay with you and all your friends?

Jo considered Brue's silence. "Sweetie? Home needs to be a safe place where you always feel you can talk openly about anything that's bothering you. Am I doing anything to make you feel uncomfortable in any way?"

Looking at her plate, Brue shook her head.

"Do you mind my asking what's up then?"

Brue lightly tapped the tip of the fork against the wooden table and dropped a cheek on a fisted hand. "It's Annie," she said softly.

"What about Annie? I thought the two of you got along well."

"Her dad came home yesterday."

So that was it. Why hadn't Jo thought of that before?

"Come here," she said, patting her lap. When Brue nestled in, Jo smoothed her hair. "Your friends' fathers are coming home from the war, but your dad will never come home. That's what's bothering you, isn't it?"

Brue hesitated then nodded.

"It's true, Annie's going to see her dad again," Jo said, "but we have no idea what kind of condition he's going to come home in, do we? He might have scars we can see like a missing limb, maybe, or worse. Or he could have the kind of scars that can't be seen, but are definitely felt. Scars like Char—"

Charlie. No wonder Brue lit up around that man. Why hadn't Jo thought to link those lines together before? "Charlie reminds you of your dad, doesn't he? He isn't as tall or slim, but he certainly has the same sandy-colored hair and the same warmth and appeal. Brue?"

She looked up, her midnight blue eyes seeping with sorrow. "Hmm?"

"I know you're missing your dad something awful." Jo blanketed her hand on Brue's. "I miss him, too. That's natural, for both of us. Don't worry. I understand it gets easier with time. About Annie's father, though—it's wonderful that he's coming home, and we need to be happy for her, but she might have a hard time of it. Take a look at Charlie. He's a good, good man, but he seems sad inside from whatever happened to him in the war, doesn't he? And remember when Tryg came home? He looked empty and dazed, too, and he still has that limp."

"Why doesn't Mr. Howland ever come to see us, Mom? When Dad was here, he used to come over all the time. He used to play with me and bring candy and stuff. Doesn't he like me any more?"

"His not coming around has nothing to do with you, sweetie. He's still hurting over your dad. Don't worry. He still likes you very, very much."

Just then the phone rang. Brue ran and picked up the receiver after the second double ring. "Mom, it's for you." She mouthed, "I think it's Mr. Breck."

CHAPTER TWENTY-SEVEN

J o glanced at the receiver dangling from Brue's small hand. Suddenly the supper in her stomach turned sour. *Just when I thought I no longer had to worry about a budding romance, the man had to call. Honestly!*

"This is Jo." She didn't particularly care for how she felt—inexplicably ungrateful, resentful, and borderline rude. She absently threaded the telephone cord through willowy fingers. "Yes. I don't know how to thank you. The flowers were beautiful, but you really shouldn't have. Thank you so much. You've been out of town a lot? I understand. Saturday evening? Yes. I guess I could go. Okay. I'll see you then. What? Oh, yes, what was I thinking? Our address is 537 Charles Street. Right. I'll see you then. Yes. I'll be looking forward to it, too," she said, willing those feelings into existence, but they stubbornly turned to dread.

Several hours later, Jo blew Brue a goodnight kiss and quietly pulled the bedroom door closed, leaving her to sleep once again in Jo's bed. The last window tightly secured, she plucked a light shawl from the sofa and stepped onto the front porch to relax a while before calling it a night.

She dragged the rocking chair toward the wall-to-wall windows, its runners complaining indifferently against the wooden floor. After settling in, she looked out toward Amber Leaf Lake where the moon shimmered across still waters. Countless stars speckled against a pitch-black sky, a sky without cloud, a sky pure and innocent, a sky depicting beauty the way her life once had.

She smiled at a squirrel flitting along the gravel road. It stopped, looked around, and then scampered into the park. A brief moment later, her rocking chair slowed as she happened upon the silhouette of a young couple sitting on Big Ole's favorite bench. They were deeply engaged in conversation. Overshadowed by the huge branches of a tree, Jo wasn't able to see their faces, only their profiles.

But there was something about them.

They didn't bear the swift movements of youth, nor did they exhibit the stooped over and trembling movements of the elderly. Rather they seemed serene, their motions relaxed and unhurried. The gentleman appeared to have a whiffle cut. He must be home on furlough, Jo decided. What an ideal night and place to enjoy one another's company, searching the heavens for constellations, and basking in the bliss of deep and true love.

Watching them from afar, Jo reflected on the floral arrangement she'd gotten, and Frank's call. Seeing the couple in the park so beautifully in love, she wondered what Saturday night might bring, how their date would go, and what she would learn about Frank. Was he the kind of man who didn't know what he wanted in life and leafed through women as if they were nothing more than pages in a telephone directory? Would he pick her up, set her back down, and walk off? At the mere thought, her heart constricted.

She thought about how fortunate she had been to marry the love of her youth, but what a tragedy it had to end so quickly. She'd lost her one true love. Jo pulled the shawl tightly around her shoulders. Did she have the courage to give love another chance? She had Brue to think about, too. Would it be right to subject her to the sort of distress a relationship might bring? Did Jo care enough to take a risk? And yet after so many months of being alone, she remembered how pleasant it felt being in

Frank's presence when they were at the shivaree. She remembered how flawless his smile, how raw and glorious his appeal.

But for now, with the exception of Sarah and Tryg, she felt content sitting back and observing the Ardena's and Calvin's of this world and, yes, even the couple in the middle of Harrington Park. Dating was work. Relationships required effort, responsibility, and sacrifice. She was torn—a part of her excited, wanting to take on a new adventure and another part wanting to turn and run away as fast as her size seven shoes could carry her.

Jo gazed out across the park one more time before calling it a night. Her heart warmed as the young couple stood and lingered for a moment, undoubtedly sharing a few more tender words. They then strolled in the direction of the O.M. Harrington, he with his hands clasped behind him, and she with her arms folded over her shawl.

But as they stepped beneath the glow of a coach lamp illuminating the pathway, Jo's hands flew to her lips. "Oh, no!"

Charlie.

And Sarah.

CHAPTER TWENTY-EIGHT

Wil handed the sheet of paper to Big Ole. On it was written, in unusually neat penmanship, an itemized list including the brand, how new or used, and the approximate value of each item Wil and Teddy had stolen. Ole had expected a much longer list. "Well done," he said. "But what are the check marks all about?"

"Oh, that's the stuff I still got. I wanna give 'em back. If it's okay with you."

"That's fine. Looks like you kept about everything you stole. This shouldn't be as hard as I thought."

"Borrowed," Wil said, his tone adamant.

"Hmm?"

"Borrowed. I'd like it better if you used the word borrowed."

"Which Olson is this? Would that be the Richard Olson place?"

"Yes, sir."

"Says here, two fishing rods and a tackle box." Ole tapped the paper with his pointing finger and looked up at Wil. "How are we going to return two fishing rods? I dug through our spare boxes this morning to see what we had around. The fishing rods might be too long to package."

"I got an idea," Wil said excitedly. "I could slip 'em under the merry-go-round up at Academy Park. Then I could send Mrs. Olson a note an' tell her where they are."

Ole plucked a blank sheet of paper from the desk drawer. "Good thinking. Now how about if we have you pen a nice little note, and we'll slip that and a couple of your hard-earned dollars in an envelope to pay Mrs. Olson for her trouble. I understand her husband is overseas, so she's all by herself. She must have been distressed."

"What do I gotta say?"

Ole picked up a fountain pen and handed it to Wil. "Start with Dear Mrs. Olson."

Wil nodded and taking the writing instrument, he nudged a chair up close to the desk, carefully penned her name, then looked up at Ole expectantly. "Now what?"

Ole got up and, clasping his hands behind his back, he paced in front of the windows while dictating. "Please—"

"Please," Wil repeated as he wrote.

"Forgive—"

Wil's head snapped up. "Hunh?"

"Forgive. Please forgive—"

"Oh, no." Wil shook his head vehemently. "I ain't gonna say nothin' stupid like that. That's somethin' some dopey sissy would say."

"Who's the sissy, Wil? The person who has the courage to ask for forgiveness or the person who doesn't have the courage to?"

A mortified look crawled over Wil's frowning features. "Okay. If I gotta, but I ain't gonna be happy about it."

"I'm not going to be happy about it, not I ain't gonna be."

Wil scowled, then returned to the paper and began writing again. "Please ... forgive—"

"Please forgive me for taking your fishing rods and tackle box," Ole continued slowly, keeping time as Wil painstakingly jotted down the words. "You will find them underneath the merry-go-round in Academy Park. Enclosed please find two dollars to help pay for your trouble. I'm sorry, but I can't tell you who I am, because I could get sent away, and then they won't take me in the Army. I want to serve our country soon. Yours sincerely, A reforming thief."

Wil's head snapped up again. "Thief? Hey, look. I don't care if we say the reforming part, but thief? That's a ugly word."

"That was an ugly thing you did, Wil. You need to have the courage to own it. That's the fastest way to get to the other side of this."

Wil nodded unenthusiastically and let out a loud sigh. "I guess."

"Now let's pen a couple of letters to pay off your debts to the lumberyard and the hardware store. Before we send them, you'd better double-check the prices of the materials you took. Then we'll itemize them and slip in an extra dollar to both places. The way I have it figured, they won't be expecting payment, let alone an overpayment. With a little bit of luck, that might help get them off your back. What's that look for, Wil?"

Wil pulled a carefully folded sheet of paper from his back pocket and smoothed it open. "There's more. Here's some a' the stuff Teddy took."

"Some of the stuff?"

"Yup! He bragged about it all the time. This is the stuff I remembered. He don't know I'm—"

"That's okay, son. Don't worry about it. I'll be more than happy to cover this with Teddy boy later. First we need to get you all squared away."

CHAPTER TWENTY-NINE

On Friday afternoon Wil entered Ole's office at such a fast clip he tripped, coming to within an inch of the floor before catching himself. His eyes were clear and his grin cut from ear to happy ear.

"We did it, Mr. H! We did it. I shoved the fishin' rods an' tackle box under the merry-go-round like we talked about. And the last two mornings I saw the mailman make his rounds. When he delivered the mail at Mrs. Olson's place today, I hung around for a while just in case. And d'ya know what?"

Ole shook his head. "I'm waiting."

"She came rushin' out of the house lickety-split. Looked like she was on her way to a wildfire or something I followed her all the way to Academy Park."

"She didn't see you, did she?" Ole asked, concerned.

"Na'ah. I was real careful to stay way behind. I hid behind a bunch of trees all along the way t' make sure she wouldn't see me. She got that rod and reel okay. And the tackle box, too. And d'ya know what else?"

"No. What, son?"

"She was smiling wider than I ever saw anybody smile before in my whole entire life."

Holding back a grin, Ole slipped a light hand on Wil's bony shoulder. "That's good to hear. Now, who do we have next on our list?"

"I dunno. I took a flashlight back to a garage over on St. Joseph and a hockey stick to a garage up on Third. I don't know the peoples' names, so I don't know how to send 'em a note. Do I need to give 'em money if they din't even know the stuff was missin'?"

"This exercise isn't just for them, Wil. It's for you, too. The money pales in comparison to the way you feel about yourself or your relationships with other people. You can't put a price tag on self-respect."

"But who should I send the letters to? And how much should I send 'em?"

"Can you get the exact addresses?"

Wil nodded. "Course, I can."

"Okay, let's start with that. You can always address the envelope to 'the family of.'"

"How much should I send 'em?"

"I think about a dollar to each place should do it."

Wil balked. "But ain't that a lot of money? I mean, the flashlight din't even work and the hockey stick was awful old, and they got 'em all back."

"I understand, but like I said, this isn't about money. This is about you learning to value people, their property, but most important of all, yourself."

"Okay," Wil said dutifully. "What about the stuff Teddy took? He did most of that on his own."

"Don't worry about Teddy. Like I said, I'll handle that with him later. So tell me, do you have anything else in your possession?"

Wil flicked a lock of hair from his brow. "Not a whole lot else 'cept for that stuff from the lumberyard and hardware store I was tellin' you about."

"Have you had a chance to check the cost of those items yet?"

Wil slumped against Ole's desk. "Yup, but I still got stuff from the hardware store in a box up in my tree house. I thought I could send a letter after I find a place to return it to. I gotta' find a spot out in their alley so no one can see me. I dunno what to do about the lumberyard, though. Teddy and me, we hauled the boards home on a wagon, and we already sawed 'em apart and made a raft with 'em."

"Do you know how long the boards were? What kind of wood?"

"Course, I do."

"Okay. Give me the details. I'll have Bernie take a drive over there and buy more of the boards you stole. Then in a day or two you can find a place to stash them so the lumberyard will find them. When you've done that, let me know, and we'll send another letter with a buck or two for their trouble. Sound okay to you?"

"Yes, sir. But there's one more thing," Wil said.

"What's that?"

"This is just 'tween me and you, okay? Teddy stole a bike from a house up on the north side of town."

"Can you get it back?"

Wil shook his head.

"Why not?"

"Cuz he was showin' off one night and shoved it off a dock, right smack dab into the lake."

"Which lake?"

"Fountain."

"I see. That is a problem, isn't it?" Ole pulled at his suspenders and rocked on his heels. "The Anders boy is going to have to cough up the money on that one."

"But if you say anything, he'll know I snitched."

"Don't worry about it. When the time is right, he'll take care of his business, all of it, one way or another."

CHAPTER THIRTY

G randpa, I've been hearing stories. Unbelievable stories."

Ole looked up. Sarah's gait was purposeful, her expression cloaked with apprehension.

"Seems stolen property is mysteriously being returned all across town these days. Everyone's thrilled about it. Some of the stuff the people didn't even know had been taken. Crazy concept, isn't it? Thieves paying back their debts?" She steadied her gaze on him. "Or should I say thief?"

Ole looked at her blankly.

"The whole town's abuzz, you know," she went on. "What a baffling bandit. Only one making restitution. Whoever he is, along with the pithy notes he's been writing, he's included a dollar or two for his victim's trouble. You wouldn't happen to know anything about that, would you?"

Although Ole sat quietly and watched her lips move, she touched a nerve.

"Grandpa? Why aren't you saying anything? People think the thief might be Wil and some boy named Teddy Anders. I've been standing up for Wil, telling them they're wrong—including Tryg. I knew you wouldn't bring a thief into your boarding house. You wouldn't put your guests at risk. You wouldn't put you or me at risk. Can you tell me the rumors aren't true? Can you tell me you wouldn't consider bringing Wil under our roof if that was the case? Can you tell me he isn't one of the thieves who's been terrorizing our town? Terrorizing you? He isn't, is he? Not our Wil."

Not our Wil! Ole swiveled his chair, giving Sarah his back, but she stepped around the side of the desk, arms still crossed. "Okay," she said. "Let me tell you what I think is happening. Correct me if I'm wrong.

"Knowing you, if Wil was one of the attackers, you would have good reason for protecting him, or you'd never do it. You probably figured hiding him in plain sight was a clever strategy, a strategy you knew would be short lived, but a risk you were willing to take to buy time—time to counsel Wil, help turn his life around, and have him make amends. How could anyone begrudge a repentant thief, right? You knew you and Wil wouldn't get by with what you're doing, at least not for long. People would catch on. Chief Stout would catch on. And the floodlights would shine bright on the O.M. Harrington House—on Wil and on you."

You would have made a great attorney, Sarah. Finding himself stuck between a huge rock and a bigger boulder, Ole further disengaged. What could he say to help her understand?

"Grandfather? It's one thing to tell us about the thefts, but if you confirm that Wil is one of the thieves, are you afraid people might push about the incident that landed you in the hospital? Are you afraid that if you came clean even a little bit, you'd have to come clean all the way? That problem hasn't gone away, and it's not going to without stirring up controversy. Are you worried about me? Afraid I might feel betrayed by a grandfather who opened doors that made us all easy prey?"

Ole was in a pressure cooker now, the flames growing hotter. He fidgeted with the edges of a sheet of paper as he fidgeted with his thoughts. Holding out on Sarah, his own flesh and blood, was quickly turning into a hill too high. He had to have a chat with her sooner rather than later, but not now. He needed to choose his words wisely so she would understand.

"Grandpa, there's more I haven't told you."

Please don't tell me there's more.

"The milkman stopped by earlier. He was showing off a letter he got from the thief, or should I say one of the thieves, the one who's trying to come clean? And according to Tryg, Wil is the main boy Chief Stout's been trying to implicate. I assured him Chief Stout was sniffing around the wrong tree, but I happened to notice that the letters have your fingerprints stamped all over them. Want to know how I can tell?"

Ole reached down and retied a perfectly tied shoe as Sarah continued her one-sided conversation.

"I'll tell you how. The thief doesn't bother to apologize or simply say 'I'm sorry.' No, instead he takes his remorse a step farther. He asks for forgiveness. That's kind of unusual, don't you think? Reminds me of when I was a kid. Whenever I stepped out of line, you refused to settle for 'I'm sorry' or 'I apologize.' No, I had to ask for your forgiveness."

Having difficulty raising his aging eyes to meet hers, Ole said innocently, "What's on the menu for supper tonight?"

"Grandpa? You haven't heard a word I've said, have you? Why not?"

"All I want to know is what we're having for supper. I think I'm in the mood for a little fish. How about you?"

"Grandpa?"

Ole reached down and retied his other perfectly tied shoe thinking about the boy who had been victimized one too many times by the trappings of a hellish existence he was strapped with calling his life—a life marginally void of direction and caring, but a life that was, nonetheless, in the process of amazing change.

Sarah rested a warm hand on Ole's shoulder. "No matter what," she said softly, "I want you to know I believe in you. I always have, and I always will."

As a teary-eyed Sarah turned and walked away, Ole let out a puff of breath. *My dear, dear Sarah.*

CHAPTER THIRTY-ONE

J o sent Brue to the Tomlinson's with a brown paper sack filled with buttered popcorn and a promise she'd pick her up no later than eleven. Feeling as if she were back in high school, she stood on tiptoes primping in the mirror above the kitchen sink. She wedged a bobby pin into a wiry wave to hold it securely then carefully scrutinized her lips. Why hadn't she tried out her new tube of lipstick before throwing the old one away? Even cherries weren't this bright.

Unable to stop fretting, she glanced at the minute hand on the grandfather clock as it crawled toward the zero hour, her nerves pulling tighter than finely tuned strings on a harp. Already she was wishing the night away. *Why do this to myself?* After nudging the minute hand forward by five minutes, her nerves calmed, but not enough.

At six o'clock sharp a light knock took away what little was left of her breath. Frank Breck looked even more handsome than he had at the shivaree. A generous shock of camel-colored hair lazily blanketed his forehead—there had to be a telltale farmer tan under there somewhere. His fine features and snowy white teeth set off an intoxicating smile. He was tall enough that Jo had to look up to gaze into his striking emerald eyes. She glanced at her watch, tempted to move the hour hand ahead to eleven, anything to make it easier to relax in his presence. Could he be feeling this uneasy, too?

But when she got into his Hudson, she grinned full on. You could take the farmer off the farm, but you couldn't take the pig smell out of his car.

At the corner of Charles Street and River Lane, Frank gave Jo a shy glance. "Thought we'd go to Stables Supper Club for a leisurely bite and then head over to the Rivoli Theatre afterward. *The Valley of Decision* is playing with Greer Garson and Gregory Peck. Sounds like a decent picture show. Are you okay with that?"

"That would be wonderful," Jo said. Any further words escaped her. The harder she tried to relax, the tenser she became. Houses passed by on the tree-lined streets as she searched for something interesting to say, only to keep hitting a dry well. Halfway through their supper of roast beef, baked potatoes, and scalloped corn, Frank's fork hit the floor with a loud clink, drawing curious gazes from surrounding tables. He blushed. It was then that their walls crumbled, and Jo finally relaxed enough to enjoy his masculine presence.

The first time they touched elbows during the movie, Jo thought it was an accident. The second time she knew better. She felt beguiled, giddy with Frank's magnetism and engaging smile. How long had it been since she'd enjoyed herself this much? No longer was she wishing the night away. Eleven o'clock was closing in far too fast.

As they stepped out of the theatre, Jo gazed up into the star-studded sky thinking it wasn't possible for this evening to go any better.

"It's still early," Frank said. "What do you say? Want to stop by the Canton Café for a soda before I take you home?"

For the next half hour they sipped fountain drinks and gazed into one another's eyes, swapping stories about their childhoods, both the good and the not so good, and shared dreams they'd dreamed way back when and how differently their lives had unfolded. So much about Frank felt wonderfully right.

"From what I understand, you've never been married," Jo ventured.

"That's right." He smiled. "I'm still looking."

"From the way you interacted with Brue at the shivaree, you appear to be very fond of children."

"Who isn't? I'd like to have a nest full some day."

Unable to hold back a grin, Jo shook her head.

"What?"

Her cheeks grew warm. "Oh, I don't know," she said. "With all the attractive young women around, I can't understand for the life of me how you've escaped marital bliss."

Jo could tell his ego hit the ceiling with that observation.

"I'm definitely looking for bliss, but it's awfully hard to find," he said forthrightly then busied himself wiping a few drops of condensation from the glass and tabletop. "Came close once, but not close enough."

Jo asked why with her eyes.

"She was married," he said then slipped a straw into the glass and stirred the cola.

"You must have been devastated when you found out."

"I was, but I had a hunch she was married long before we got involved. To be honest, deep inside I didn't want to believe it. I rushed to judgment that it wasn't true when she subtly pursued me," he said, anchoring his gaze on Jo's. "She had a couple of towheaded kids, too."

Jo looked away. "But what about her husband? Weren't you concerned about him?"

Frank looked straight ahead, his expression unreadable. Clearly this conversation was not getting better. The wall that had tumbled down earlier in the evening worked its ornery way back up.

A short while later, he walked her to her door and leaned down to give her a quick kiss good night. She turned slightly, giving him her cheek. As he descended the porch steps, he said, "I'll give you a call again soon."

Jo stood dazed as Frank's taillights disappeared over the crest of the hill.

At the close of this their very first date, something felt sadly broken.

CHAPTER THIRTY-TWO

Big Ole rolled over in bed like a walrus flopping over on a slippery rock bank. He rubbed his weary eyes and assessed the day. Clearly the sun wasn't doing its job. Fog swirled outside the second-story window like steam spewing from a cast-iron kettle. At least the weather looked mildly intriguing.

He took a shower then lathered his face, his razor merely scratching the stubble. It wasn't doing its job either. He replaced the blade, finished shaving, and lumbered downstairs to enjoy a bowl of oatmeal, a glass of fresh-squeezed orange juice, side of bacon, and a cup of coffee perked strong enough to walk on. Bernie's coffee never disappointed.

Ole loved his early morning routine. He sauntered to the great room, glossed over the highlights in the morning paper, then retreated to his office and lit a pipe. An hour later, he sensed movement and peered up. "What's that?"

Sarah carried in a stack of paper half a foot high. "It's the morning's mail."

"That's not exactly what I meant," Ole said. "What I meant was why's there so much of it?"

"I think the mailman likes you."

"I like him, too. Now let's get the man fired."

Sarah laughed. "Now, Grandpa."

Ole eased back and smoothed the arms of the chair. "How about if in the future you start sorting the mail first. Pitch the unimportant stuff before bringing it in."

"I already did that," she said confidently.

Ole slowly shook his head. "I'm getting a sneaky feeling this is going to be a very, very, very bad day."

He pulled out the company checkbook then foraged through the mail, plucking out first the bills that needed to be paid, which were anything but hard to find. He wrote checks until his hand cramped. This wasn't working well. Deciding it might be more productive to wheedle the stack down a few papers at a time, he set the rest of the mail aside and headed for the kitchen. Time for a break.

As he passed the registration desk, Sarah looked up. "Where are you going?"

"Out to the park."

"What for?"

"Why to feed the squirrels, of course," Ole said, his tone incredulous.

"In the fog?"

"It'll lift." He walked on, but beneath his breath he muttered, "sometime."

Ole riffled through the pantry. "Bernie, what in the world did you do with that sack of peanuts?" he said shy of a shout.

Bernie glanced back. "They should be right where they always are."

"Which is?"

"On the floor right inside the doorway there."

Ole squatted and nosed around some more. "Well, they aren't here."

"What?" Bernie joined Ole in the pantry and pulled on the light string. "That's odd. There was a full sack and it was here yesterday. I swear to it." He turned to Ole and tugged on the light string again switching off the light. "You don't think ..."

Ole didn't know what to think, but he did know what he didn't want to think. He cuffed the back of his neck. Massaging it, he stopped by the registration desk. "Sarah, have you noticed anything disappear during the past few weeks?"

"Nothing other than that fifty dollars you haven't returned to the cash box yet, why?"

"You mean the fifty dollars I borrowed when I was short on cash for a taxi?"

"That's right."

"I stopped by the bank on my way home that day and put the money back in the cash box myself."

"Grandpa, it's not there. I checked the box again this morning."

Ole returned to his office and continued cleaning up the mail, but found concentration far too difficult. He plucked a cigar from his desk drawer, but tossed it aside. At the moment, it didn't smell appealing. Not knowing what to do with himself or how to get away from his unsettled thoughts, he sauntered to the park in the billowing fog. He had been sitting there for about three or four minutes when a squirrel scampered down the trunk of a tree. It stopped at the base and looked up at Ole expectantly, its eyes darting to and fro.

"I'm sorry little fella," he said, "but I'm plum out of nuts today. We'll get more by tomorrow. That's a promise."

Disappointment rattled Ole. No one had ever stolen anything from the boarding house before. And Wil was the only one he knew who had had a problem with sticky fingers. Stealing peanuts made no sense. But why would he be so brazen as to steal money from the cash box? He'd seemed eager and honest about paying back his debts. Or had he been? The boy needed confronting, but what if he wasn't guilty?

An unsettling pain tore through Ole's heart.

But what if he was?

CHAPTER THIRTY-THREE

Ole whittled away at the pile of bills again for the better part of an hour before giving up. The sun finally broke through the clouds and streamed through the office windows. He wandered to the kitchen, stopped at its entry, peered at the wall where Wil had lobbed the ruler-straight row of biscuits, then glanced back at the pantry, still torn. Wil wouldn't have stolen the peanuts, and he wouldn't have stolen the money. If he had, though, why? There could never be an acceptable reason for blatant thievery.

Ole thrummed the counter.

Bernie was kneading bread dough. He punched it a few times with the heel of his hand, folded it against itself, sifted on a smattering of flour, then kneaded it and folded it and kneaded it again. "Something on your mind, boss?"

"I guess you might say that. When Wil gets in today, would you ask him to bring me a fresh bag of peanuts? Don't say anything about our not being able to find them, okay? Let's hear what the boy has to say."

Bernie looked as disappointed as Ole felt. "Be happy to, Mr. Harrington."

At four o'clock, Ole made every effort to sit at his desk looking natural. That was a tough assignment, but he forced himself to do it. If only Wil would step through his door and bear good news.

He arrived at precisely five past four with a wide grin. To Ole's amazement, he didn't bear good news—he delivered it. "Hi, Mr. H! Bernie said you wanted a bag of peanuts. Will this be enough, sir?"

A shocked look escaped before Ole could contain it. "I think that should do it."

"What're they for?" Wil said, suddenly eyeing Ole suspiciously the way he would if he'd gotten a whiff of some foul-smelling fish. "Ain't it kinda' late to go feedin' the little squirrelies? I mean, it's gettin' awful close to nighttime. Besides, we're startin' to fix supper."

"Thought I'd—"

"Mystery solved," Sarah said from the doorway then glanced at Wil. "Sorry to interrupt you, Wil. I'll only be a second. Grandpa, I thought thought you'd want to know that I found that money in the cash box. It wasn't missing after all. I didn't realize you stuffed that fifty dollar bill under the tray."

For the first time since Ole could remember, he felt disingenuous, like a kid with his fingers caught in a piggy bank and here he was talking to a kid. "What was I saying?" he asked, warmth flooding his cheeks. "Oh, yes. Thought I'd have the peanuts ready for in the morning."

"Did you try to find 'em earlier today?" Although Wil's tone was leery, Ole's nod was every bit as reluctant.

Wil stepped back as if he felt a need to distance himself, his smile fading like old worn-out trousers. "You don't trust me."

Ole's heart thumped in his throat. "I'm sorry, son. It's just that we've never had anything disappear from the boarding house before."

"And I got sticky fingers, right?"

"You had sticky fingers. Life is tough for all of us, son."

"I'm not your son."

"We're all trying to find our way," Ole said. "And you and me, we haven't totally earned one another's trust yet ... now have we?"

Wil's stunned gaze quickly met with the floor.

"That's going to take a while," Ole continued. "I need to prove myself to you and you to me. It's all these little incidents and all these little tests that will determine if we'll be successful in building or breaking that trust. Do you understand what I'm trying to say?"

Wil nodded hesitantly, his face hardened with disappointment. "I understand."

"Fine." Ole forced a confident grin. "I believe I hear the kitchen calling. You know, your work isn't going to get done all by itself ... and Wil?"

Wil stopped at the door and glanced back.

"Will you forgive me ... for even beginning to question you?"

Later that evening after Wil left for the day, Bernie walked in with a full on grin. "About the peanuts, Mr. Harrington. The boy told me he was worried about the bag getting wet when the cleaning lady scrubbed the pantry floor. He said he moved them to a higher shelf, but felt he had to put them toward the back so I'd be able to get to all of my canned goods."

Ole let out a roomful of stale breath. "What's the matter with me, Bernie? I should have believed in him." He crushed a fresh piece of notepaper and hurled it, missing the trashcan by a city block. *But I didn't.*

CHAPTER THIRTY-FOUR

A satisfied grin cut into Ole's cheeks. Hank's update validated his hopes for Wil. Several stormy days excluded, the boy had stopped by to play horseshoes an hour every morning precisely as promised. He proved a formidable player, too. According to Hank, Wil's ability to concentrate was an opponent's worst nightmare, and he exhibited an eagerness to keep coming back for more.

At a few minutes before eleven, Ole stood in the hallway peering through Hank's door. As if viewing a pose for a Norman Rockwell painting, he observed the old man and young boy interacting. Hank's fingers were poised on the radio knob while Wil stood hunched over with an ear to the speaker. They both appeared absorbed as Hank turned the dial from right to left and back again, stopping between stretches of noisy static.

Hank switched off the radio and turned to Wil. With a smile in his raspy voice, he said, "I'm pleased to hear you like baseball. Too bad we couldn't find a good game to listen to. So tell me, who's your favorite team?"

Ole stepped into the room and their surprised heads snapped back when he answered for Wil. "I'll bet that would be the Senators."

Hank wheeled his chair around, and his face lit up. "Well, come on in, you ugly old buzzard. Wil and I finished playing a mean game of horseshoes a few minutes ago. We were hoping to top the morning off with an inning or two of baseball, but that wasn't to be."

"Who won, might I ask?"

"Horseshoes or the ballgame?" Hank said flatly.

Wil smiled at the tease.

"Who do you think won? This boy here is unstoppable."

Wil looked up at Ole, his puppy dog eyes begging for approval, and Ole complied. He roughed Wil's hair affectionately then plopped down in a wing chair near the window. "The way he pitches a biscuit, I'm not at all surprised, but don't let me interrupt you gentlemen. I believe you were talking baseball."

"That's right, we were." Hank interweaved his spindly fingers and gazed up at Wil. "You wouldn't happen to know who Bucky Harris is, would you, boy?"

"Aww, course I do. Any dummy knows that. He managed the Senators and then the Phillies a couple a years ago."

Breaking a grin, Ole pushed forward on the chair and twiddled his thumbs. "Hank, here, is a good friend of Bucky's. I'll bet you didn't know that, did you?"

Wil's eyes swelled to the size of plums, his head spinning from Ole to Hank. "No foolin'?"

"No foolin'."

"Do you play ball?" Ole asked.

Wil nodded.

"Then why haven't I seen you out in the park?"

He rolled his eyes, tapped a shoe anxiously against the rug, and frowned. "Cuz no one wants to play with me."

"Now why would that be? Judging by your aim and the way you've been whipping Hank playing horseshoes, that makes no sense whatsoever."

Wil's defenses kicked in. "Cuz the stupid knuckleheads don't like losin' all their balls in Amber Leaf Lake, that's why."

After Ole and Hank traded surprised looks, Ole said, "You mean to tell me you can hit a ball that hard?"

"Aw, that ain't nothin."

"You're right about that," Ole said. "Near as I can figure, you don't have good control at long distances or the balls wouldn't go flying into the lake. You'd know how to place them."

Wil stopped tapping the rug and stared Ole down, his puckish eyes filled with conviction. "I know how to place balls just fine."

"If that's the case, why do they end up in the lake?"

"You ain't listenin," Wil insisted. "I place them there."

"Respect, son. Respect," Ole cautioned. "Now why would you do that? It makes no sense, not if it's keeping you out of the game."

"Who cares?" Wil shot back unfazed. "Those kids ain't good enough to play with anyways."

"Well, son, if what you say is true, one of these days you're going to have to show me your stuff."

"Oh, yeah? Why?"

"Respect, son," Ole repeated.

Hank cleared his throat and wheeled his chair forward. "Because I might be able to find a decent baseball team around here that could use a good arm."

Wil looked at Hank as if he couldn't pull it off.

As they were about to say good-bye, Hank spun over to a large cabinet at the far wall. "There's something you might want to take a look at before you leave," he said as he pulled open its doors.

Wil's eyes instantly glommed onto crowded baseball paraphernalia nearly tipping off its shelves. "Wow! Where'd you get all this stuff?"

"Guess I'm a bit of a collector," Hank said understatedly. "Used to play a little ball back in my younger years."

Ole leaned in and said, "Don't let him fool you, Wil. Not only does Hank know Bucky Harris, Hank used to play pro. Played with several of the big teams. Didn't you, Hank?"

Wil stood with his mouth agape until Ole seized his shoulder. The boy looked as if he could ogle Hank's treasures for the better part of a day.

"We've got to get going," Ole said. "I hear our taxi driver blowing the horn."

Tripping over his own feet as if he were hobbling around in shoes a size too big, Wil kept turning back to sneak a glimpse of Hank's bedroom window all the way out to the street.

CHAPTER THIRTY-FIVE

Wondering whether or not she was doing the right thing, Jo headed into the country. Brue was sitting at the edge of the seat peering out the windshield.

"Mom? How come ditches are so deep?"

"It's not so much that ditches are deep as it is the roads are high."

"Why?" Brue asked.

"I'm sure to lower chances for a washout when it rains and probably when it's windy to help keep snowdrifts from accumulating, too."

"Do cows ever break through those wire fences?"

Grateful for the questions diverting her attention, Jo smiled. "Could, I guess. I doubt it, though. They look content to stay right where they are, chewing their cud."

Swirling dust. Warm sun on a cloudless sky. In many respects, a tailor-made Fourth of July.

"Mom?"

"Yes, dear?"

"Why are you rubbing the steering wheel like that?"

Jo chuckled. "Guess I'm a little nervous."

"Why?"

"Because the last minute invitation from Frank bothers me. I don't know if I should have accepted or not. Besides, there's a chance we could be disappointed when we see his farm."

"Will anyone else be there?"

"I don't think so. Just Frank, you, and me."

Her words barely out of her mouth, the Chevy shimmied hard. Jo quickly engaged the clutch and brake. "Hang on, sweetie."

"Wow!" Brue said, her voice vibrating. "Feels like we're riding on a washboard, like it's gonna shake the car apart or somethin'."

Jo eased the car over the rough patch and drove on. Another half-mile down the road, she stomped on the foot-feed and soared over a low hill, the heavy car rising and lowering like a ship on the high seas.

"Wee!" Brue cried with glee.

Jo glanced at her notes. Look for a weathervane on the roof of a barn and a mailbox jutting out of a creamery can at the end of a long narrow driveway. "There it is." As she turned, a thickset collie appeared out of nowhere, tail wagging and barking alongside the car until she pulled into the farmyard.

Frank hurried out to meet them with a sparkle in his eyes, and her heart fluttered. She had made the right decision after all.

"I see you found the place okay." He opened Jo's door, and she stepped out into the balmy summer's day and looked distractedly at the charming farm and its buildings, slowly taking it all in. "I wasn't expecting this. I feel like we're strolling into heaven."

Frank guided them through a side door, entering the house through a mudroom. Although it smelled of barn, cows, and pigs, it was scrubbed clean. "Oh, my," Jo said. "A mud scraper, clothes tree, milk pails, rubber boots all in a row, a Parsons bench, hook rack. How quaint."

Although the appliances in the kitchen appeared up to date, a cast iron pump stood aside the sink like a sentry, adding more charm to the farmhouse. Brue gaped at it. "Does that thing work?"

Frank plucked her up and set her high on the counter. "Why don't you give it a few pumps and find out?"

Clear water gushed out after several hard pumps. "It's ice cold," Brue exclaimed.

A long moment of pure joy later, Frank helped her down and led them into the living room.

"There are signs of your mother everywhere," Jo said approvingly.

Frank nudged a sewing basket closer to the sofa. "She loved to cook, and read, and crochet. I left her doilies on the end tables and sofa, and *The Saturday Evening Post* on the coffee table where she put them. Makes it feel like she's still here."

Frank had adored his mother. That was good.

Jo gazed at the windowsills lined with pots of red geraniums. "She loved flowers, too, I see."

Warm pictures of happy times hung on the walls with care, and a spindle staircase ran along the side of the living room wall opening onto a catwalk that ran the length of the entire room with doors leading into three upstairs bedrooms. "I like the feel of this place," Jo said.

"It's where I grew up." Frank pointed at the upper right-hand door. "That was my bedroom when I was a kid."

Jo stood for a wonderful moment breathing in the sights and sounds about her and felt struck by a sense of longing. Brue and she were happy where they lived, but their home could never give them a sense of warmth and spaciousness, not like this. "I'm surprised to hear myself saying this, but I find myself envying you."

Frank smiled, appearing pleased with Jo's admiration.

"Hungry? How about a bite?" He stepped back for Jo and Brue to lead the way. His eyes held Jo's for a long moment, the glint in them giving her a pleasant shiver. He appeared as content having her in his world as she felt being there.

Frank snatched a few items from the refrigerator and placed them on the pre-set table. "I baked a ham last night and threw together some potato salad so we wouldn't have to heat up the place. It's plenty warm out. Why make it hot in here, too, right? Thought we'd drink milk instead of coffee, and for dessert," he grinned, "I thought Brue wouldn't mind cutting into an ice-cold watermelon."

Brue's face lit up.

"You're going to spoil us," Jo said.

He pulled out Jo's chair and then gallantly stepped around the table and pulled out a chair for Brue. "Are you going to be able to reach your food okay?" he asked. "I can find a cushion if that would help."

"I'm okay."

Frank turned on his heel. "Ho-oh! I forgot the bread."

"Ho-oh!" Brue echoed.

"What's the matter?" Jo asked.

"There's lipstick on my milk glass."

Frank set a basket of rolls on the table and reached across. "Let me take a look."

Jo's eyes swept from Brue to Frank. She found it impossible to read the guarded expression on his face, and that troubled her.

"I guess there is at that." He went to the kitchen cabinet and, without further explanation, gave Brue a clean glass.

Sounds from the farm broke into their dinnertime banter—a distressed cow bawling in the distance, an occasional hen clucking excitedly, birds squawking overhead. "I love it out here," Jo said. "It's so pastoral and serene."

"It's home. Unless I can I get anything else for you, I'd say it's time to tour the rest of the farm." He turned to Brue. "And for you, young lady, I have a big surprise."

Her face lit up.

They stopped at an artesian well. Frank reached for a metal dipper and they each took a sip of its icy water, tasting of a hint of rust and iron. "My mom never needed an ice box," Frank said, looking deep into the well. "She put everything in Mason jars. Butter. Milk. Cheese. Jello. Then she'd drop it in the well here. The water kept spinning them, keeping them cold."

"Didn't they ever freeze?" Brue asked. "Not even in the winter time?"

"No. The jars kept tumbling from the speed of the water. I don't recall the well ever freezing over."

They took a quick pass through the chicken coop where Brue gathered a couple of eggs, then past the hog pen. When they reached the barn, Frank picked up Brue again so she could see the empty stalls over the top half of the Dutch door. "Sorry, little girl," Frank said, "but there's not a whole lot to look at in here today. The cows are all out to pasture."

Jo eyed the hay bails, pitchforks, push brooms, corn brooms, shovels, milking cans, and the rest of the paraphernalia lining the far wall. "You have a lot of work here."

He nodded. "I've cut back on the number of animals I have. Most of my work is out in the fields these days, and speaking of fields, I think it's time for the surprise." He led the way to the back of the barn where a horse stood tethered to a buckwagon.

Brue's eyes lit up again. "Do we get to go on a hayride?"

He grinned. "Hop on board. I think you're going to like this."

Brue scampered up onto the back of the wagon while Frank helped Jo onto the buckboard. He grabbed the reins and after releasing a "tck, tck, tck," the horse snorted, lunged forward, and they were off—through the barnyard, down the long driveway, and out onto the gravel road with the collie running along behind. Frank pulled at the reins, guiding his horse into and alongside the cornfield then onto a tree-lined meadow where they stopped beneath the shade in a grove of tall oaks.

Jo's heart sang at the beauty of Frank's idyllic world, a world she would have no difficulty coming to love. They sat for an engaging moment to appreciate the breeze rustling the leaves, an occasional fly buzzing past, and the sun filtering through the leaves.

Frank reached for Jo's hand. "You up for a little serenade?" They stepped over the seat and onto the back of the wagon where he drew a large case from beneath the hay and pulled out a guitar. As the birds chirped and the soft winds blew, Frank sang western tunes of long ago, beautiful tunes—*Cool Waters, Tumbleweed, Home on the Range, Cattle Call*. Even Brue sat mesmerized as he plucked at the strings. Sounding like Bing Crosby, he was lost in the lyrics, lost in the melody, and Jo lost more of herself to the intriguing world of Frank Breck.

The day slipped past too quickly. He grilled steaks for supper and they ate corn on the cob and barbecued beans. But as day faded into night and they were about to leave, Frank frowned unexpectedly when Brue picked up a porcelain figurine sitting on a cabinet in a far corner of the living room. It was elegant, of a man and woman who were dancing.

"I think you'd better put that down, sweetie," Jo said.

"I'm sorry, Mom."

"It's all right," she said softly, while Frank merely appeared relieved.

In the deepening twilight, he walked Jo and Brue to the car. "What a shame this day has to end," he said. "It's been absolutely perfect. I've thoroughly enjoyed every minute of it."

Jo's heart fluttered at his words. "So have I."

"Look," he said, draping his muscular arm over Jo's open door, "I'll be heading out of town in a few days, but I'll give you a call again when I get back."

Billows of dust chased Jo's Chevy down the winding country roads toward home.

"Mom?"

"Yes, dear?"

"Why didn't Mr. Breck tell you where he was going this weekend?"

Jo gave Brue a brief glance. "We've only started seeing each other, sweetie. He's free to do whatever he wants."

"I know, but why wouldn't he just tell you?"

CHAPTER THIRTY-SIX

O le kicked back in the chair and eased his well-shined shoes on the far end of the desk.

The high school coach had gotten wind of a good arm from Ole's old friend Hank. Time to cash in on a friendship. After ten minutes of small talk and another five of arm-twisting after revealing who had the arm, Ole promised to have the boy there tomorrow at half past ten and assured the coach he would find their visit well worth his while.

The next morning Ole hailed another cab and headed over to Fountain Street. He couldn't wait to get there. "Son," he said, "Hank and I are excusing you from your morning duties. You and I have an appointment to keep, and we don't have much time to get there."

"Where are we goin'?"

"To the high school. Thanks to Hank here, the coach is waiting for us."

Hank's grin quickly vanished when Wil took a decent-sized step back.

"Oh, no," Wil said adamantly. "I ain't gonna go there. You ain't gonna make me."

"Why not?" Ole was riddled with disbelief. "I would think a young whippersnapper like you would jump at the chance."

"Nope!"

Hank wheeled his chair closer to Wil, lines of concern wrinkling his paper-thin forehead. "What's the matter, boy? You love to play ball too much to pass up a chance like this."

Wil fell back into scuffling mode, kicking a foot against the paisley carpet.

"Wil?" Hank said softly. "What's going on? Why won't you tell us?"

Wil kept his gaze glued to the floor. "The coach don't like me."

Wil was right. Ole had already gotten an earful when he spoke to the unhappy coach, but he wanted to hear Wil's side, not that it mattered. The coach wasn't equipped, nor did it appear he had the desire, to bother with a troubled kid. What did you do?" Ole asked.

"Nothin."

"People don't dislike people without good reason."

Wil looked up. "We had a run-in, okay? He stuck up for a kid who was bein' a jerk every time the coach wasn't lookin'. When I got blamed for doin' somethin' I didn't do, I had to raise my voice cuz the coach wouldn't listen, an' he threw me outa sports just like that."

"Apparently that's no longer an issue with him."

"Well, it is with me," Wil insisted.

Ole looked down at his own arm, "I would toss the ball to you myself, but I've got limitations. It's called rheumatism. Come with me, son. Be a man, okay?"

After a concerned good-bye to Hank, Ole walked the several blocks to Amber Leaf High with Wil in tow, reluctant all the way.

The instant they entered the field, Ole sensed something was up. The coach, who was sitting on a bench in street clothes, rose and extended a hand to Ole and then to Wil. Wil stared at the grass avoiding eye contact, but immediately grimaced at the coach's powerful shake. Ole's heart sank. If Wil only knew how hard he had to work to get the coach to give the boy a chance.

Then Ole eyed a young man crouching at the pitcher's mound. A pinch of snuff packed in his lip and all decked out in full dress uniform, he was digging through a bucket of balls.

"Who's that?" Ole asked.

"Moe. My son. He's home on furlough. Thought he'd get a kick out of pitching a few balls. Plays the minors. Has quite an arm."

Wil's going to get clobbered.

After a few pleasantries, the coach called his son over and made introductions. Moe, who appeared indifferent, returned to the pitcher's mound and Wil to home plate.

"Okay," the coach called out from the bench, "let's start with a few slower pitches. Then we'll evaluate how well you handle the ball."

Slower?

"Any place in perticular you wannit to go?" Wil asked, his tone soused in sarcasm.

The coach pointed a burly finger, his mocking chuckle grating on Ole. "Right field," he said.

The tension between the coach and Wil was anything but difficult to miss and Moe's bored and arrogant sneer wasn't helping matters.

"Amazing timing," Ole said.

"My son being home, you mean?"

"That's what I mean."

Again the mocking chuckle. "If Wil is as good as you say, what are you worried about?"

Ole shook his head. Wil was half Moe's size and hadn't had a chance to practice. With any luck at all, he might be able to nail one ball.

Wil's eye stayed riveted on the pitcher's hand as he wound up his muscular arm and hurled a ball. If that was a slowball, what would his fastballs be like? Ole wondered. But to his surprise, Wil connected with a clean hit into right field.

The coach raised a disbelieving brow. "That was lucky."

Wil did it. He hit the first ball. Ole was beginning to enjoy this.

"Let's try another one." The coach smiled too confidently as he gave the nod to his son who released another pitch, throwing it low and outside the plate.

Wil stretched and whacked the ball into the outfield again.

Ole let out a gleeful chuckle. Wil was two for two, and Ole had a front-row seat. Two strong minds colliding, one of which was destined to gain some long overdue respect. The coach should never have thrown Wil away in the first place.

The coach cleared his throat. "You got any power, boy?"

Seizing the bat at both ends, Wil stretched it high above his shoulders and glancing back at the coach, he shot off a smug grin. "How much power you want?"

"Oh, I don't know." The coach flashed his son a you'd-better-nail-this-kid-with-all-the-power-you-got nod then said to Wil, "Think you have it in you to put one out of the park?"

Wil didn't flinch. "Think your boy can pitch one I can't hit outa the park?"

The coach bristled and so did Ole. Wil was asking for it, but it didn't matter. He had the courage to take on Moe, making Ole feel prouder than he had in years.

Moe stopped chewing, knitted his brows, gave the bill of his cap a quick tug, and then unleashed a blazing fastball.

Wil nailed it. Completely nailed it, shattering the bat. The ball soared, whistling clean out of the park and leaving the coach and Moe with their mouths agape.

"Is that good enough for ya?" Wil asked understatedly.

When the coach finally got his senses back, he said, "I think that should do it for today."

CHAPTER THIRTY-SEVEN

May I come in?"

Big Ole looked up and mashed the cigar into the ash-tray. To his unhappy surprise, Henrietta Braddingly was entering the office without an appointment or invitation. Her gray hair sticking out all over the place, skin dried up like a fig, and her generous body balancing on under-sized shoes, she doddered toward his desk carrying a generous bouquet. With Wil getting on board with the Packers, her sudden presence unnerved him. Taking another beating seemed preferable to having a conversation with the woman, but Ole stood just the same, being careful not to show the slightest hint of pain.

"You look far better than I had expected, Mr. Harrington," she said, her words pouring out like syrup.

Ole grinned inwardly. *That makes one of us.* "Oh, I don't know. When I saw my reflection during my morning shave, I thought I looked rather handsome. The black bruises beautifully offset the pupils in my eyes. I rather miss them."

Henrietta batted her thinning eyelashes. "You are such a witty and charming gentleman." She plunked the floral arrangement on the corner of the desk and looked around. "I meant to bring these flowers earlier. I think they look rather lovely right here, don't you?" She suddenly glowered at him. "Aren't you going to thank me for them?"

I'd rather not. You're welcome to take them back home with you. "If I must. But it really wasn't necessary for you to bring them."

"Mr. Harrington, you are utterly impossible," she teased.

Big Ole rocked back and grinned. "You'll have to forgive my bad manners, Mrs. Braddingly."

"Oh, please. It's not necessary to be so formal. Feel free to call me Hen—"

"I've had my moments of feeling a bit on edge. Heard a lot of chatter recently that tends to play havoc with my mood at times. I do hope you have no intention of joining that chorus." *Or dare I say I've heard you're the one leading it?*

"What sort of chatter?" she asked innocently.

"Maybe you'd like to tell me. It appears there are those who feel they understand what's going on in my world better than I do these days. What's worse? They've been taking liberties with my reputation as well as the reputation of our exemplary chief of police. That wouldn't be why you're here, would it?"

"I'm afraid we don't see things quite the same way," she said, helping herself to a chair. "How do I say this delicately? It seems the entire town continues to be unhappy with you and not without good reason. We feel badly about your getting roughed up, but we don't feel it's right for you to sit back and allow those hoodlums to harm anyone else."

"What hoodlums?"

For an instant her eyes opened, and he wished they hadn't for in them he saw all that he opposed—cold-hearted arrogance, self-righteousness, and half-baked pity disguised as caring, eager to be unleashed.

"Please don't be coy, Mr. Harrington. It doesn't become you. Everyone knows what hap—"

Ole's fingers dug into the arms of the chair. "Was everyone there?"

Although her mouth opened, it took a while for "Well, no, of course, not" to finally ease out.

"Then how could everyone possibly know what happened?"

"Chief Stout said—"

"Chief Stout wasn't there either."

Mrs. Braddingly glowered again. "Why are you protecting that awful Thompson boy?"

"What makes you think he's so awful? Have you ever met him? Talked to him? Seen him up close? Taken the time to get to know him?"

"Everyone knows where he comes from."

"Which is?"

When Ole challenged her with a daring look, she met it head-on. "Riffraff. Is that the word you're looking for? Or do you prefer the word undesirable? Boys like him don't change, Mr. Harrington. Certainly you of all people should understand that."

What Ole did understand was that he had just invited an attack. He should have known better. He did all he could do to hold himself down, but his protective feelings of Wil had grown too intense, and the words kept coming. "From what I've heard, you came from a decent home, Mrs. Braddingly, and look what happened to you."

Her face puckered. "Well! That's no way to talk to a lady."

Ole looked about the room. "I didn't know there was a lady around."

She hopped up as fast as her heavy legs would lift her, gathered her bag, and in an apparent attempt at retaliation, she said, "I'm afraid you've made a serious mistake, Mr. Harrington, that you will live to regret."

Ole needed another smoke. He pulled out the desk drawer and plucked out a cigar. "May I?" he said.

"I'd rather you didn't."

He took his good old time lighting up and inhaled several short puffs. "I'll take that as a threat."

She lifted her ample nose.

"I do know what I'm doing," Ole assured her, "and have good reason for not coming forward. Although you of all people don't deserve as much, you and the entire town will understand in due time. Meanwhile, I'd appreciate it if you'd back off."

"I have no intention of backing off."

"Very well." Ole stood. He'd had enough. "You're welcome to leave now, and I'd be grateful if you took your manipulative flowers along with you."

Henrietta strutted off in a huff leaving the flowers behind. Her presence dampened Ole's room like a dark cloud snuffing out the sun. But this was one of those few times he could have cared less—until she stopped at the door and said, "I have feelings, too, you know."

Ole awakened in the middle of the night and stared at the ceiling, looking for answers—answers and relief. If only Henrietta hadn't stopped by, but, come to think of it, why had she bothered to come? To talk Big Ole into cooperating? She knew his reputation better than to try that. To prove to herself she was right? To relieve herself of guilt by dropping off flowers? Or to get information to strengthen her stance? What did it matter? In the greater scheme of things, Ole was no better than Wil or that Anders kid. There were more ways than one to diminish a person. Wil and Teddy had done it with their hands and feet, but Big Ole Harrington had done it with his tongue.

CHAPTER THIRTY-EIGHT

Big Ole smiled at the scene before him and felt no shame whatsoever about breaking it up. Hank was leaning forward in his wheelchair, spindly fingers interwoven, an ear within an inch of the radio. Wil stood at his side listening with rapt attention.

"Hank? Wil?"

With a subtle lift of a forefinger Hank signaled Ole to wait, and Wil whispered a thoughtful "Shhh!" They were listening to the final play. Bases loaded. Ball one. Ball two. Ball three. Strike out! Hank and Wil whooped in unison and after striking hands high in the air, they managed to give Ole the attention he sought.

"Washington Senators playing, I see," Ole said.

"That's right." Every feature on Wil's youthful face curved into a grin. "And they won, but barely. Ain't that right, Hank?"

"Too bad I didn't get here sooner," Ole said. "We could have chomped on these while listening to the game." Ole stuffed a huge hand into a brown paper bag and pulled out three hot dogs heaping with mustard, ketchup, and pickle relish along with forks, knives, and napkins, not that they would need them. He also pulled out three bottles of Coca-Cola and popped off the caps with a Swiss army knife.

"So what brings you out today? Besides wanting to stuff our bellies, that is," Hank said in his not-so-weak shut-in voice. "It's not like you to darken my door this often." He smiled at Wil. "Frankly, I'm beginning to feel a little crowded."

"Why, you ungrateful old buzzard. Got good news," Ole announced. "We got Wil here a position with the Packers."

"No!" Hank's voice gushed with glee. He pushed far forward in his wheelchair, nearly tipping it. "The local baseball team here?"

"That would be the one."

"By gummie!"

Confused by Wil's reluctance again, especially after astonishing the coach and his son with his skill, Ole said, "Cat got your tongue, boy? I told you you're on the Packers team, and you look as if I'd told you someone died."

Wil sneered. "Aww, that ain't nothin'."

Oh, yes, it is.

All expression drained from Hank's face. "What's the matter? Afraid you aren't man enough to play?"

"I ain't no such thing," Wil huffed.

Ole considered Wil's past, seasoned with out-of-reach opportunities. How many times had he been put down by a dad who didn't believe in his own abilities, let alone his son's? How many times had Wil shied away from trying because he felt he wasn't good enough? He'd never had a decent chance to build his confidence. He'd been brow beaten one too many times by the pitiful bloke he called Dad.

Ole lifted Wil's chin. "Then you'd better fix your attitude. The Packers are going for a Class AA championship in our Southern Minnesota League. They need talent, and you've got it. In spades. Show up for practice next week. That is, if you think you've got the guts."

Wil scowled. "I'll be there. I ain't no chicken."

Ole could count on Wil's being there, but on the chicken comment, he knew better. The boy had issues with fear. Significant issues. But who with a lick of sense could blame him?

CHAPTER THIRTY-NINE

Ole couldn't get to the kitchen fast enough. "Wil? We've got an amazing problem. Sybilrud just turned eighteen. Volunteered. Left yesterday for the Army. Star players like him are few and far between. The Packers are shy a good player. Coach asked if you'd mind stepping in at the last minute."

Wil blanched. "But I ain't even practiced with 'em yet."

"I know, I know, but they need you. The bleachers are going to be full. What do you say? Want to suit up?"

This wasn't just any game. This was Wil's first game with a serious team—the real thing, and Ole wanted to be there. The next day, he arrived early and found a satisfactory front-row seat. As the bleachers began to fill, he recalled his image during his early-morning shave. For being up in years, he'd healed well. Four weeks and there was little to nothing left of the fading scrapes and bruises, little to draw attention to himself. To his dismay, though, as he awaited the game, a pattern emerged. First came the surprised and apprehensive looks, followed by looks of pity and resentment. Big Ole Harrington. The double crosser who wouldn't cooperate with Chief Stout. He endured those nerve rankling looks for a too-long moment, then plastered on a pleasant smile and dutifully shook hands with anyone and everyone nearby until the tension evaporated.

Time for the game to begin. All suited up, the team filed onto the field with Wil straggling a couple of yards behind. Although Big Ole felt pride about to split his chest wide open, he couldn't miss the unfolding scuttlebutt. He didn't need to turn around. The finger pointing and scowls were unmistakable. Ole could swear they were making a point they wanted him to hear. Words like scum, scoundrel, and crazy came on the heels of roughed up Big Ole Harrington.

The audience cheered as the players ran out onto the field. Except for Wil. He ran out to a chorus of boos. At first Ole grimaced, but then his shoulders relaxed. As did the coach, this audience was about to receive the surprise of their lives. At Wil's first chance at bat, the audience booed again. Wil didn't look back. He stood at home plate, rigid. Was he cowering? From there the show only got worse. Ole riveted his eyes to the ground and tried not to let the groans get to him. He couldn't bear to watch Wil who struck at every wild pitch and couldn't seem to make a single hit.

Ole sat unsettled through the first three innings as zeros filled the scoreboard. Something was going on with the boy. He was going through the motions, but hadn't gotten into the game.

At the top of the fifth inning, Tryg and Sarah sidled in next to Ole with an overfilled bag of popcorn in hand.

Since confronting Ole about Wil and offering her support, Sarah hadn't breathed another word about it. Ole got the distinct impression she still didn't want to believe he was guilty.

"How's it going?" Tryg eyed the scoreboard, but then he did a double take. "Hey! What's going on? The Packers are down five to three? I thought we were having a good season."

"Both teams scored in the last two innings." Ole tapped his cane on hard soil. "I'm not sure what's going on with Wil, though. He's not on top of his game. I can't understand for the life of me why the coach doesn't let him pitch. We'd at least be able to keep the other team at bay."

"Maybe the coach is saving him up for relief pitcher," Tryg said.

At Wil's next at bat, Ole watched closely. Wil approached home plate with his right arm hugging his side. The boy also snatched up his bat too fast and held it palms in as if purposely shielding his wrist from view. Ole then peered at Wil's baseball jersey. No wonder. The short-sleeved jersey completely exposed his wrist.

"Something isn't right about his posture," Tryg said.

Ole nodded. "It does seem a bit wooden at that. Give him time. He'll loosen up."

"It's getting a little late for that, isn't it?" Tryg said. "We're already at the top of the sixth."

With each strike, the crowd jeered until Wil struck out. Ole looked up at the hecklers. "They don't understand," he said with no small amount of concern.

At the bottom of the sixth with no change in score, Ole stood, readying himself. "You're right about Wil," he said, "about his posture. The boy is self-conscious is all. I sensed it from the minute he walked on the field. He might be able to use a little help."

"What are you going to do?"

Ole heard the question, but ignored Tryg. At the announcement of the seventh inning stretch, he pulled a hanky out of a pocket and approached the players' bench as if it were part of his job. He gave Wil's teammates an acknowledging glance and then, quickly shaking the wrinkles out of the handkerchief, he grabbed Wil's forearm. "Son, it appears you've got quite the sprain here. This should help." Ole wrapped the hanky snugly around Wil's wrist, being careful not to further expose it. Wil didn't say anything. Ole doubted he could. But Ole did feel Wil's shame-filled gaze and the stares from his fellow players as he bandaged. When he was certain he'd completely hidden whatever Wil was hiding, he patted Wil on the shoulder and said, "I think that should do it. You'll do better now."

Ole returned to the bleachers and settled down, but not the jeers. He glanced up at the crowd again and felt the scorn of the spectators, a scorn that wasn't necessarily misplaced. Then when the game resumed and Wil stepped up to bat, he swung wildly at a ball that appeared deliberately tossed out of range. Although Wil's body had simmered down, his mind still didn't appear focused. "Stee-rike!" the umpire shouted.

Tryg lifted a hand and tented his eyes, as did Sarah. But not Ole. He sat at the edge of the bleachers, every muscle in his body feeling tighter than a corset. "Come on, son. You can do it."

The pitcher wound up his arm and pitched another ball, this one smack dab across home plate, and Wil took another powerful swing.

"Stee-rike!" the umpire shouted as the ball slammed into the catcher's mitt.

Come on, son. You can do it. Come on.

For the first time during the game, Wil glowered at the crowd behind him.

Good. He's getting up his courage.

Wil crouched into position. He took a couple of anxious strikes at the air. The pitcher wound his arm again and fired the ball directly over home plate. Wil struck a clean blow, hitting the ball hard enough to make third base, and the crowd finally cheered. But the next player struck out, and the next, and the Packers were unable to score.

At the bottom of the eighth inning, however, with two outs and bases loaded, it was Wil's turn at bat. He dusted his hands in the dirt and stood at the ready.

Ole grinned. The boy was in the game.

The pitcher threw a fastball. "Foul!" the umpire cried. The players on the bases remained edgy, rocking on their cleats, appearing impatient to run, while Tryg and Sarah and Ole sat in the bleachers holding their breath.

Wil dusted his hands again, clenched the bat and gave it a casual twirl, then dug his feet in and postured.

"Come on, son," Ole said. "Come on."

The pitcher released another ball. Wil pulled back and took a full-powered swing. The sharp crack of the bat, the whistle of the ball slicing the air as it spun clean out of the park. The crowd jumped to their feet and cheered without restraint, but not before Tryg, Sarah, and Ole. They flew to their feet and engaged in backslapping hugs. "He did it!" Ole cried. "Our boy finally went and did it!"

The excited players leaped up and surrounded Wil at home plate. But Wil? He craned over the jubilant display, his gleeful eyes appearing to seek Big Ole's.

Then Ole looked up, his prophetic words coming back full force. '... one day you will come up from behind and the kids who have everything now will be looking up to you. Not because you're any better than they are. You aren't. Not because God loves you more. He doesn't. He loves all of us. You will come up from behind simply because God promised it.' Ole backhanded the moisture threatening to gather at the sides of his eyes. Old men don't cry. Then he gazed at Wil who finally entered into the fray.

With momentum on the Packers' side and a raucous crowd thundering their feet against the bleachers, the Packers held back their opponents, holding their lead in the ninth inning, and winning the game seven-to-five.

Ole stood for a moment to collect himself then looked up at the thinning crowd. They still needed more time to grow their appreciation for Wil. As for Wil, he would need ample time to learn to value his skill. Ole shook his head. But would Chief Stout ever allow them that time?

CHAPTER FORTY

W hat took you so long, Jo?" Ardena's eyes darted about the tables and booths in the bustling Copper Kettle. "I was worried I was going to get thrown out of here."

Jo sank in the booth. "I'm sorry. Sarah stopped by when I was walking out the door. So why the distressed look?"

"We've got a problem," Ardena said.

A frazzled waitress scurried to their table and dropped off menus. When she turned on her heel, the front door swung open and in walked Tryg. And Sarah. Smart looking, happy looking, and absolutely lovely. Tryg removed his fedora and locked eyes with Jo.

Ardena glanced toward the door and did a double take. "You're jealous."

Jo plastered on a half smile, unsettled that it mattered. "Not jealous ... concerned."

"What about?"

Jo's shoulders sagged and her cheeks grew warm. "Sarah. And Charlie."

"I don't know about that. If you hadn't noticed, Sarah looks very happy with Tryg. Maybe contented is a better word."

"It does appear that way, doesn't it? But like I told you before, Charlie and Sarah are infatuated with each other. Big Ole's noticed it, too."

Ardena hopped up and hailed Tryg and Sarah to their booth.

"What are you doing?" Jo asked.

"Move over, my dear." Ardena got up and crawled in next to her. "We're about to get company."

Since Ardena wasn't, by nature, anywhere near aggressive, whatever was going on with her at the moment must be important.

"You might want to join us, Tryg," she said. "I overheard a conversation that concerns you."

Tryg suddenly appeared troubled as he and Sarah settled in. "What's going on?"

"First, let's see if we can get a little background here. Jo, you've been way too quiet about Big Ole. I get the feeling you're protecting him, aren't you? Would you mind letting us in on why?"

Jo drew in a breath, but refused to say anything.

"Jo?" Ardena's jaw tensed. "You're coming up against a strong headwind."

"What's that supposed to mean?"

Ardena lowered her voice. "Henrietta Braddingly just left."

Jo sloped forward. "*The* Henrietta Braddingly? The one who sues people and then sues her attorneys so she won't have to pay her legal bills?"

Ardena nodded. "That's precisely the one."

"Let me guess," Tryg said. "She's turning up the heat."

"That's right. While I was waiting, she sat in the booth behind me here talking so loud I overheard every word."

"And?"

"It's not what she said as much as what she's planning to do that's the problem."

Sarah's eyes widened. "What's that?"

"She's taken it upon herself to be a judge and jury of one. Mentioned something about having stopped by the O.M. Harrington one day last week to see your grandfather. He must have been unusually straightforward."

"I hesitate to ask why," Tryg said.

"As you should. Sorry, Sarah, but she said she thinks he should be sent to an insane asylum."

Sarah's eyebrows knitted together. "She said *that* about my grandfather?"

"It gets better. She wants to get a petition going to recall Chief Stout. Says he isn't doing enough to protect the citizens of Amber Leaf."

Tryg exchanged a concerned look with Sarah then said, "I was afraid of that."

"Let me tell you, it was ugly," Ardena continued. "If she keeps it up, she's going to start a riot."

Tryg unthinkingly tapped a menu against the tabletop. "But Wil just got on with the Packers. She needs to give Chief Stout time, saying nothing about Wil."

Jo folded creases into her napkin as she drifted off thinking about the problem that was not about to go away any time soon. Big Ole needed to ease the fear in peoples' troubled minds, but how could he if he refused to let them know what he was doing or why?

"That's not all," Ardena said.

Jo felt drawn out of a stupor. "Isn't that enough?"

Ardena shook her head. "Tryg, since you're an attorney, she wants you to draw up the petition."

Sarah let out a puff of breath. "What are we going to do, Tryg?"

He shook his head. "There's got to be a way we can handle this ourselves."

Jo looked nervously around the capacity-filled café. "How can we pull that off? If Madame Braddingly leaned toward reasonable, that would be one thing."

"But she isn't," Tryg said flatly.

Ardena took her turn folding and refolding her napkin, looking at it too intently one too many times. Feeling pricks of guilt, Jo decided to back down.

"I do know more about Big Ole," she said, "and make no mistake about it, I believe in him. He knows what he's doing, and he of all people doesn't do anything halfway. You wanted to know why I'm protecting him?"

"We all do," Tryg said.

"That's fair enough, I guess." Jo exhaled a breath. "When Case had his accident—"

Although Tryg looked away, knowing the importance of what she had to say, Jo barreled on. "... and I was left to fend for myself, my friend Evelyn asked around at the boarding house. Thought maybe they might have a job for me. But there weren't any openings. None. The next morning I get a call offering me work. I find out later that a man named Harrington had heard about me. Since the boarding house's laundry lady was in a family way, he'd asked if I could help out temporarily. That laundry lady never did come back. I heard she'd miraculously been offered a job at a laundry outfit uptown that was closer to her home, which I understand pleased her immensely. As for me, I got to stay on." Jo recalled the cold snaps that came every January when temperatures dropped so low they could break a thermometer and walking out on a porch was enough to freeze a body standing up. "I was thrilled to get a job close to home. With Brue to raise alone and the severe weather conditions we get at times, who wouldn't be?"

The door swung open and Jo looked up. A woman was maneuvering her small child to protect him from the closing door. The sad look in her eyes brought back memories of Jo's first days without Case. "I know this is hard for you, Tryg," she said, "but please bear with me. I have a point."

He nodded as if he understood.

"A year ago this past December, I was paralyzed with grief. Didn't have it in me to crawl out of bed. So depressed it took an effort to cook a meal. So tired it took a week to get up enough strength to even run to the grocer's with what pittance of money I had left. You can imagine how I felt when in the wee hours of that Christmas morning two crates of groceries magically appeared on our front steps—cheeses of all kinds. Canned fruits and vegetables. Flour. Butter. A small sack of sugar. Even a few gifts in red Christmas wrapping for Brue. I was beside myself. There was no note. No way to track the giver. But when I lugged those empty crates out back, one overturned and there burned into a bottom slat I stumbled across the words O.M. Harrington House."

Sarah's eyes glistened as Tryg reached for her hand. He offered her a comforting smile then turned back to Jo. "So what you're saying is—"

"Big Ole was there for me when I needed him. These past weeks being there for him has been my feeble way of beginning to repay him, not that that could ever be possible, and I can't stop. Not now."

Ardena wiggled uncomfortably on the bench seat. "I understand. But for as much as I respect your wishes, Jo, don't you think this is a teensy bit serious? What if someone else gets hurt because you refuse to talk? Because you choose to look the other way? Your conscience would strangle you."

Jo cast pleading eyes on Ardena. "Look. He has the right not to reveal anything on his part, only his need for me to keep silent. If anyone knows what he's doing, it's him."

"Problem is," Ardena said, "he has the grace to handle it. He knows what happened and, who knows, maybe even why. But you don't. You need to have his respect and trust, too."

Sarah offered a warm smile. "Jo? Thank you for believing in him."

Jo nodded. "There's got to be more we can do to help buy him time."

"Maybe there is," Tryg said. "I'd like to see Wil play a few more games. My gut tells me he's star quality, but he'll need time to prove himself. Ole's smart. He's noticed Wil's skill, too.

"As for Henrietta, we could wait her out for a few days. See if she does contact me. If and when she calls, you could stall the appointment for as long as possible. In the meantime, we need to do anything and everything we can to tamp down the rhetoric and neutralize her. We also need to find out why she has a burr in her saddle, and if we do, you can bet we'll find a way to pluck it out if we have to use a microscope and tweezers."

After picking up the tab, Tryg and Sarah walked off, leaving Ardena and Jo to themselves.

Jo reached for her purse then paused. "About what you said before."

Ardena smiled. "About your being jealous, you mean?"

Jo nodded. "I don't have the right."

"But infatuation is infatuation. I don't know how you can stop that."

"Too bad for me," Jo said matter-of-factly. "Tryg is a prince, and we do have a strong bond. So many years of division and pain make me feel a strange loyalty to him, but I've got to override it."

"That's a tough assignment, isn't it? How do you plan to do that?"

"It is tough. But between Frank and Sarah, maybe there's hope. I'm going to give Frank a chance. As for Sarah, maybe I'd do well to help her instead of fighting her. What do you think? And as for Charlie, he's not the same guy who couldn't wait to get overseas. Between the sound in his voice and the look in his eyes, he's hurting badly. Since Sarah lost her husband to the war, their common pain has to be a powerful magnet. Maybe she needs to be reminded of that."

"You could be right," Ardena said. "I don't know that there's much you can do about any of this other than let it play out."

"That's certainly easier said than done."

CHAPTER FORTY-ONE

Making corrections on a summary Tryg had been working on for the past half-hour, he scratched out a couple
of words, added a few more, stared at it, changed it, and
stared at it again. Although something still wasn't right, he found it difficult to concentrate. He tossed the pencil aside and massaged the bridge
of his nose. He was tired. He'd been working hard these past months.
Too hard. Now the words were sitting on the surface of the paper like a
blackbird perched on a picket fence—black on white just resting.

Was it Sarah? She was withdrawing again. He could feel it. Was it
this whole mess with her grandfather that had consumed her? Or was it
Charlie? Was he in pursuit?

Tryg stared out the window where sunshine glinted off the wind-
shields of an occasional passing car. He mindlessly flexed the bows on
his glasses and glanced at the calendar. Thursday. Sarah had Thursdays
off. He grabbed his sports coat and said, "see you in the morning," to a
couple of confounded ladies in the outer office.

Forty-five minutes and a mile later, Tryg ascended the steps of the
O.M. Harrington. To his pleasant surprise, Sarah quickly finger-combed
her hair away from her lovely face, a warm smile finding its way up
her cheeks. "This wouldn't be your first outing during business hours,
would it? Shame on you," she teased.

They stopped by Piggly Wiggly's and filled a picnic basket with salami, cheese, strawberries, grapes, and a couple of sodas and then drove north toward Edgewater Park. Beneath a trickle of slow-running water at a nearby drinking fountain they washed the fruit then found a shaded area near the water where they spread the blanket and took their joyous time eating their fill. Sarah looked contented and happy out in the great outdoors. The weather couldn't have been more balmy, the breeze more gentle, nor the company more pleasant.

"Why haven't you ever married?" she said seemingly out of the blue.

Before Charlie had come back to town, she had shied away from serious subjects. Why the change? Although Tryg balked, she prattled on. "I don't mean to pry. It's just that you have so much to offer. I find it hard to believe you're still running free."

"We don't want to spend a beautiful afternoon rehashing old loves," he said and meant it.

"Why not?" she challenged. "How will we ever get close, really close, if we don't learn the intricacies of one another's lives?"

Tryg smiled inwardly. *She wants to get close.* He plucked up a stray flat stone lying in the grass near the edge of their blanket and skipped it across the water. Ripples rolled out, growing larger and softer until they stilled, the way his hurt had grown more distant and softer with time. "I was engaged once," he said. "Her name was Elizabeth. She was a nurse at Naeve Hospital."

Sarah drew a bandana over the cheese and fruit at the bottom of the picnic basket. After shooing away a few annoying flies, she sat up straight and folded her legs beneath her. "I'm sorry. I had no idea. What happened—that is, if you don't mind my asking?"

Tryg did mind. He wanted the hurts of the past to die and stay dead, but he complied. "She joined the Red Cross. Made it out to the front lines. Suffice it to say, lawyers are no competition for Army doctors, especially during wartime."

"Oh, Tryg. I can't imagine how painful that must have been." Sarah's tone was soft and sympathetic. "Forgive me for asking. I didn't mean to be rude."

"There's nothing to forgive. How about you? I assume you've never been married since you still go by Harrington."

Her eyes hinted of forming tears. "Actually, that's not true."

"You don't need to tell me," he said, suddenly not wanting to know.

"I was married. My husband got killed. Operation Market Garden … in the Netherlands."

Tryg sat slack jawed. The emotional weight he'd been fleeing by coming on this outing yanked him down like a hard-pulling anchor. Learning about Sarah's troubled past brought back memories of Tryg's own tour of duty and suffering in its aftermath. He found it difficult to take a breath. "Now it's my turn to be sorry." He gathered up what was left of their food. "How about if we find us a boat to rent? It's too beautiful this afternoon not to enjoy it." He smiled. "What do you say? The gentle sway of the water? Or a nice long walk around the lake?"

Sarah must have realized the unintended weight of bringing up the past. "I recall seeing fishing tackle in the trunk of your car," she said with a grin. "If it's okay with you, I think I'd rather go fishing."

"Do you know how to fry walleye?"

"No, but Bernie does like you've never tasted them before."

Later that evening when they returned to the O.M. Harrington, Sarah led Tryg into the kitchen where he laid their catch on the counter. It was apparent Wil hadn't seen or heard them come in. He was too busy whistling *Swinging on a Star* as he dried supper dishes.

Sarah looked around. "Wil? Where's Bernie?"

When he turned, he nearly dropped a plate. "I didn't hear you come in," he said. He suddenly looked stripped of confidence, as if he didn't belong there. "Bernie's out back."

"Would you tell him we brought home some walleye?" Sarah grinned. "Tryg and I caught them ourselves." She then turned to Tryg. "Have you had a chance to meet Wil yet?"

"No, I don't believe I have, but I've seen you play ball. That's some talent you've got there." Tryg extended a hand. "Nice to meet you."

After a shy handshake, Wil quickly returned to the dishes.

Tryg stopped with Sarah at the registration desk. "So that's the kid who's been terrorizing the town? He looks different up close, doesn't he? Vulnerable in his own way." He shook his head. "No wonder Ole took him in. And to think that Henrietta Braddingly ...."

CHAPTER FORTY-TWO

Jo guided Brue to their usual pew, fourth row from the front, far right side. Papers rustling, feet shuffling on the hollow floor. Clearing throats. Whispers. Soft voices. Dust dancing on the beams of sunlight streaming through its tall and slender windows. When Tryg slipped up the far left aisle, gently guiding Sarah by the small of her back, Jo suffered a sudden bout of yearning. The sights and sounds lost clarity as she imagined for a brief moment how wonderful the feeling of being guided down a church aisle again early on a Sunday morning by the man of her dreams. Was it even possible to build that kind of relationship with a mystifying Frank Breck?

As for Sarah, did she have any inkling how fortunate she was to have Tryg?

Big Ole shuffled along behind them, and when the bells in the belfry stopped pealing, he led in the weekly a cappella singing of the *Doxology*. The church fell quiet, and Tryg approached the lectern, his confident gait arresting.

"Our scripture reading this morning is brief and can be found in the book of Jeremiah, the seventeenth chapter, beginning with verse nine," he began. "'The heart is deceitful above all things, and desperately wicked: who can know it? I the Lord search the heart, I try the reins, even to give every man according to his ways, and according to the fruit of his doings.'"

After several stanzas of *The Old Rugged Cross*, Calvin Doherty repeated a portion of the scriptures Tryg had already read. "The heart is deceitful above all things, and desperately wicked: who can know it?

"The problems our world faces today," he said, "are catastrophic, no thanks to a few in high places who have desperately wicked hearts, hearts that have been allowed to go unchecked. Consider if you will the current leadership our brave soldiers are fighting against, leadership that sees itself as superior, its race as superior. Coupled with that self-deceived attitude is a mindset of unprincipled authority, shameless authority that is insistent on taking over and leading nations it deems inferior like an unscrupulous kid taking control over a sandbox."

Wicked hearts that have been allowed to go unchecked. Stung by the power of the scripture, Jo questioned herself. She gave Sarah a quick glance. Although on a far smaller scale, would God consider their hearts wicked? Sarah's for undoubtedly being duplicitous in her affection for Tryg? Jo's for being suspicious and judgmental about it? What concerned her even more was a subtle niggling she felt deep inside. A niggling she did not want to own—that niggling that smacked of jealousy.

Although it baited her, it was Tryg's responsibility to learn about Charlie's interest in Sarah. He certainly must have gotten an inkling about it by now. And although Jo had knowledge of Ole's assault, she owed it to him to look the other way. But looking the other way on both fronts came with a price. Calvin's words about hearts being allowed to go unchecked troubled her.

Jo's mind wandered during the bulk of Calvin's sermon. She stole another peek at Sarah who was eyeing the floor. Poor Tryg. Would he be left again by another love interest?

She stole a peek at Big Ole, too. If she allowed herself to be honest, his overt protection of a wayward boy that hadn't hesitated to endanger his life both warmed and unnerved her.

But when Calvin wrapped up his sermon with another scripture from the book of Proverbs, Jo sat up and took notice. "Trust in the Lord with all thine heart and lean not unto thine own understanding," he said. "In all thy ways acknowledge him and He shall direct thy paths. That's hard to do sometimes, isn't it?"

Calvin was right about that. It could be utterly impossible to do.

"But if we trust and acknowledge Him," Calvin continued, "our weakness gains strength, because our focus is on Him, on His power and His might. For what we find impossible now appears possible. Meditate on this throughout the coming week. Look for the Lord in your most trying circumstances."

The instant Calvin finished the benediction and they stood to leave, Brue tugged at Jo's sleeve. "Look, Mom. There's that Wil guy."

"Where?"

"Right there behind the back row. He's standing next to Charlie."

Jo followed the point of Brue's small finger as Tryg and Sarah made their way down the far aisle. They stopped long enough for Tryg to shake hands first with Charlie and then with Wil. Charlie appeared to look at Sarah longingly, yet Tryg, Sarah, Charlie, and Wil were all grinning with not a hint of displeasure.

Jo turned and looked back at Calvin. 'For what we find impossible now appears possible.'

CHAPTER FORTY-THREE

On Friday evening, Jo absently dried the dishes and stacked them in the cupboard.

Still no word from Frank, and after how many days now? Where did he go? Is he even back from his trip yet?

Was that his strategy? To keep her wondering? Or was he a klutz? *Drat!* Either way, it was working. Like a moth to a glittering flame, he was drawing her in. She didn't want to be drawn in, and yet deep inside she did. Why dwell on it? She needed to get her mind on something she could do something about. But what? She still hadn't had that chat with Big Ole about Henrietta Braddingly's threat to draw up a petition. Before Jo talked to him, though, there had to be more she could do to help block the attacks than wait the woman out. Jo considered Tryg's suggestion that they do anything and everything to tamp down the rhetoric. Was there a concrete way to accomplish that? What was Henrietta's biggest concern? Safety, wasn't that it? Or at least that's what she wanted everyone to believe. What kind of power did that woman exercise over the residents of Amber Leaf? Fear, right?

Time to erase a problem. Although leery of the Anders kid and not positive the burglaries weren't coming from yet another source, after meeting Wil, Jo felt confident he wasn't the threat everyone thought. Calming the neighbors' concern could be a powerful way to siphon power from Henrietta Braddingly. An hour later, Jo's home buzzed with a standing room only crowd of anxious neighbors.

"Like I told you when I called," Jo said, "Chief Stout could use a little help."

A wellspring of protests bubbled up.

"No, wait a minute," she said firmly. "I need everyone's attention. Please. According to Chief Stout, the fact that there hasn't been any robberies or assaults since Big Ole's isn't necessarily good news. We don't know if whoever has done these things is cowardly or is purposely holding off to catch us unawares a few months from now after we've let our guard down. With the war going on, most of us here in Amber Leaf are vulnerable. Women. Children. Older men who aren't as strong as you once were. I'm not proposing we stir up trouble or take on a problem that belongs to the chief. But I am proposing that we become a force in our own right. I don't know about the rest of you, but I don't particularly like going to bed at night feeling afraid."

"But what are we gonna do?"

"Yeah. We're no match for hoodlums."

"We are if we have a plan," Jo said.

Again the chorus of protests.

"They break into our homes."

"They steal."

"Didn't you see what they did to Big Ole?"

"Of course, I saw it," she said. "But think about it. They were sneaky, weren't they? Did their dirtiest work after dark when no one was around. It's nighttime that I'm most concerned about. We need to find a way to protect ourselves."

"How can we possibly do that?" someone said. "We aren't armed."

Jo smiled. "I beg to differ. We *are* armed. We won't need guns or even knives if we band together. The way I've got it figured, safety in numbers is our best strategy."

"Safety in numbers?" someone said.

"That's right. We feel most vulnerable when we're alone, don't we? So what I'm suggesting is that if you hear anything threatening, all you have to do is run to the phone and start calling the rest of us. Scream. Yell. Bang pots and pans. Do whatever you can to make a racket."

"That's right," someone else said. "Then we can grab our flashlights and all tear out into the streets and to the rescue. That thought alone makes me feel safer."

Sam Wilder broke in with a grin. "Jo's right. C'mon, everybody. Let's not roll over and play dead. I haven't pulled out my bugle in years. Used to play a decent reveille, if I do say so myself. Let's have some fun. If Jo's plan works in our neighborhood, it won't be long before the whole town is singing our tune."

Within the hour, her neighbors left looking far more confident than when they first arrived. When the last of them disappeared down the back steps, Jo peered through the screen door and smiled. Chalk up a first chink in Henrietta's armor.

Jo felt better, lighter, as she looked up into the night sky until a cat screeched in the distance and a chill ran up her spine. Suddenly looking up into that same sky seemed akin to looking into the black belly of a coalmine, and she cringed.

Jo slipped a whistle under her pillow then tucked Brue snugly into bed before beginning her nightly routine. The back porch dark as pitch, she double-checked the latch on the screen door then pulled the skeleton key from her apron pocket, locked the door and double-checked it. She flipped on the light switch and closed the kitchen door far enough to dimly illuminate their home. What burglar in his right mind would be drawn to light? She checked each window to make sure all were closed. Although the screens were flimsy, the noise they would make if anyone messed with them would also be a deterrent. Her home closed tighter than a bank safe, she fretted about what she would do when a sweltering heat wave came. How could she possibly shut her windows in ninety-plus-degree weather with humidity soaring higher than the day's hottest temperature?

Jo followed the same routine on the front porch, double locking doors and double-checking windows. She set the phone on the floor and stretched the cord, positioning it as close to her bedroom as possible.

Brue was still reading when Jo turned on the fan and crawled into bed beside her.

"How long do I get to sleep with you, Mom?"

Jo shuddered at the thought of her daughter sleeping alone on the far side of the house, even if their home was small. She remembered what life was like when Case was around. She never gave safety a thought. Never had to. Now she lived and breathed it. She had a little girl to protect and refused to do so in a state of fear. Big Ole definitely knew what he was doing, but how long could Anders' dad rein in his wayward son? Jo recalled Ole's haunting words and what they had implied. 'That Anders kid is a mean one. He's hiding behind Wil's reputation to preserve his own hide.'

She smoothed a lock of Brue's soft hair away from her forehead. "I think it might be best if we continue to double up until the burglars are caught, sweetie. I feel more comfortable having you close where I can keep an eye on you."

"Oh, goodie! I hope they don't get caught. It's fun sleeping with you."

Oh, the innocence of a child.

After tucking the covers tighter around Brue's shoulders and kissing her lightly on the forehead, Jo nestled under the sheets, but her unsettled thoughts kept her from drifting off. She had to do more than call a neighborhood meeting and secure the house.

"Say, Brue," she whispered. "Are you sleeping?"

"Hunh-uh. Why? What's the matter, Mom?"

"Nothing much. I was wondering if you've ever heard anything about a boy they call Wil Thompson."

"Uh-huh. Everybody knows about him. His dad is real mean and gets drunk all the time. I don't think he has a mom either. And he always gets in trouble."

Jo seized the edges of the top sheet, pulled it up slightly, and then through the dark she stared at the shadowed ceiling, frowns pulling at her forehead. "What kind of trouble?"

"I don't know. I guess stealing and stuff like that."

"Do you know if he gets into any fights?"

"I dunno." Brue rolled over on her back, pulled her side of the sheet up slightly, and stared at the ceiling just like Jo. "I don't think so. At least I've never seen or heard anything about it."

"Does he scare the kids? Are you afraid of him, Brue?"

"Hunh-uh. Everybody's kinda scared of Teddy Anders, though. That's the guy Wil hangs around with."

"The businessman's son from uptown?"

"Uh-huh. I think so."

"I've heard about him, too. Punkin, if you ever hear anything you think I should know about, tell me, okay?"

"Why, Mom?"

"Because if you ever feel threatened by anyone, I want you to know how to deal with it. I don't want you walking around afraid or holding stuff in, not that I think you're going to have any problems, of course." Jo tenderly patted Brue's arm. "Now get some sleep."

Jo resumed gaping at the ceiling. She listened closely to sounds in the night, grateful she could hear little over the whining blades of the fan. After a forever moment of no relief from her troubling thoughts, she smoothed her pillowcase, punched the pillow a few times, then smoothed it again. Other than Chief Stout's concerned, though casual, take on Teddy, no one was talking about the Anders kid. Why? Because he came from a better home? That wasn't right. At least Ole knew better. That Anders kid is a mean one, he'd said. But was the kid really mean or was he downright ruthless?

CHAPTER FORTY-FOUR

Jo eased onto the secretarial chair, not sure she wanted to sit. Not only was Ardena standing at the side of Jo's desk with arms folded firmly across her ivory blouse, her expression was unreadable. "We've got trouble, Jo," she said. "Henrietta called while you were at the courthouse."

"And?"

"I couldn't put her off, so I asked Tryg what to do. It grieves me to admit this," Ardena said looking genuinely concerned, "but she sounded reasonable, and she had an excellent point."

"Go on."

"Since Big Ole still refuses to talk, and Chief Stout hasn't gotten to the bottom of his beating or the robberies yet, she's now in a dither about getting that petition going to get him out of office. We're not going to be able to hold her off like we had hoped. She's too determined."

"But it's wartime, Ardena, and it's not his fault. Besides, who could possibly take his place? He's a big man, he's smart, and as far as I'm concerned, he's doing an outstanding job."

Exasperated, Jo raked her fingers through her hair and accidentally jabbed a fingernail at a bad angle into a bobby pin. "Ouch! What did Tryg say?"

"I'm not at all surprised." He stepped out of his office and strolled toward her desk. "Henrietta hasn't missed a town council meeting yet.

We know what she's like. She's not going to back down. I told Ardena to go ahead and set up an appointment sooner rather than later."

"Then what are you going to do?"

"Hear her out. See if I can calm her down. There's got to be a way to find out her real purpose for doing this. She jumped on it way too fast not to have an angle. I wonder if something happened between her and Big Ole and she's out to get revenge."

"But why make Chief Stout the sacrificial lamb?" Jo asked.

"To get at Ole. Either that, or Chief Stout is her intended target and she's using Ole. Unfortunately, Ardena is right. Now that more time has passed, Henrietta has a valid point. Someone's got to be brought to justice or this thing is never going away. I hope she doesn't bring a posse along with her." Tryg hesitated. "Jo? Do we know anything about her family? Husband? Children? Any other close relatives?"

"She's a widow, I do know that, and I think I heard she has a son."

"She does," Ardena said. "He lives in Chicago."

"Any idea what he does for a living?" Tryg asked.

Ardena shook her head.

At half past two, the door swung open and Henrietta Braddingly stormed in. Fortunately, she came alone. Unfortunately, she came scowling. "I'm here to see Mr. Howland," she said, her tone and look condescending.

Jo stood. "Good afternoon."

As Jo glanced at Ardena who sat poker-faced, Tryg appeared at his door. After a quick greeting and invitation into his office, he said, "that's a lovely dress you're wearing. It brings out the rich blue in your striking cobalt eyes," then closed the door behind them.

Jo grinned at Tryg's brilliant move.

She then buried her nose in an accounts payable ledger, while Ardena resumed typing. Until the shouting started. Jo jumped, and Ardena's Corona fell silent.

"I want that petition drawn up immediately," Henrietta huffed.

Although Tryg's response was muffled, Jo and Ardena stared at the closed door, listening intently. After a few more loud demands, the room fell quiet.

And the clock ticked on.

Half an hour later Mrs. Braddingly emerged, marched through the office, heels clicking loudly, nose held high, gaze straight ahead, and not so much as a word of good-bye.

Ardena arched a brow. "I get the distinct feeling somebody just got combat fatigue, and I can't tell if it was Henrietta or Tryg."

"There's only one way to find out," Jo said.

She tapped lightly on Tryg's door with Ardena breathing down her neck. Curious as to what they were about to find, Jo slowly opened it. Tryg was facing the window. With feet elevated, only the tops of his oxfords and the tip of his elbow resting on the desktop were visible. She and Ardena moseyed forward until they rounded his desk where he sat stone-faced.

"How did it go?" Jo asked.

"I began with the petition," he said. "Told her I was sure she'd worked the numbers and knew she could get enough signatures. When I went on to say that Chief Stout had a great reputation around town, she let me know in no uncertain terms that he wouldn't for long. That's when I saw red. I asked her who she intended to get to replace him. One thing led to another. She wouldn't give any names. So when I pressed and told her how difficult removing him from office would be, she finally coughed a name up. And only one."

"Which was?" Jo said.

"Try Shermie. She caught herself and said, 'I mean Sherman.' When I asked for his last name, she got indignant. 'I said his name is Sherman,' she repeated. So I asked her what this Sherman guy did for a living. Was he local? And she said, 'He's a police officer. And, no, he isn't local. He lives in Chicago.'"

"Her son," Jo and Ardena said in unison, their jaws dropping.

Tryg nodded. "When I asked if he would be interested, she said 'absolutely.'"

"Then we have something to work with," Jo said.

"Had. I caught her in the crosshairs and fired. Told her we knew Shermie was her son."

"What did she say to that?"

"Nothing. She sat stone faced. Then I went on to tell her that I doubted the town council would be pleased to hear she set up our revered chief of police, saying nothing about Big Ole Harrington to get her son an important job. For the first time since I've had the bad fortune of knowing that woman, she was at a loss for words. Hopefully the town will begin to quiet down now."

"Congratulations, Tryg," Ardena said. "You did it."

Jo sighed. "But what if she gets something else up her sleeve?"

CHAPTER FORTY-FIVE

How was your day at school?" Jo asked.

"Good, I guess." Brue scrunched up her nose. "I don't like practicing writing ovals, though."

"Why not? When I was in school, I thought it was fun."

"Makes me feel guilty. Miss Peterson says 'o-val, o-val,' way too slow so I sneak in a whole bunch more. Is that cheating?"

"If it is, it sounds like an awfully good kind of cheating to me."

Jo held her fork in midair while Brue carried out her nightly routine. She mashed a potato with her fork, formed it into a round mound, pressed a hole into the center, spooned in a small measure of mustard, then filled the rest of the hole with a ladle of hamburger gravy and stirred it together as if she were whipping up batter for a cake.

"Mom?" Brue said mechanically. "When Poke and I were coming home from school today, d'you know who we saw?"

"I have no idea. Who?"

"That Wil guy."

Jo chased a forkful of potatoes and gravy down with a quick swig of water. "Was he behaving himself?"

"He had to," Brue said innocently, her attention still fixed on the potato mixture.

"Why did he have to?"

"He and Teddy Anders—" Brue looked up. "That guy looks a whole lot meaner than Wil does."

"What about them, Brue? What about Wil and Teddy?"

"They were talking to Chief Stout. He must have told Teddy to get rid of his cigarette, cuz Teddy tossed it on the ground like his fingers caught on fire or something. The next thing we knew, the chief was holding open the back door of the police car and he made the two guys climb in."

"You're positive it was them?"

"Course, I am. We saw them real good when Chief Stout drove away. They didn't look very happy, though."

Later that night after tucking Brue in bed, Jo picked up the phone to call the O.M. Harrington House. Big Ole would definitely want to know Wil had been hauled in. But then, she cradled the receiver. If Ole hadn't heard about Wil yet, she wasn't up to hearing the disappointment in his voice. Besides, he deserved to hear about it in person.

CHAPTER FORTY-SIX

Tryg dropped a generous tip on the counter and headed out of the Copper Kettle in a daze. What was Jo thinking?

A handful of steps down the sidewalk later, he pulled open the door and looked around. "Where's Ardena?"

"She'll be late this morning," Jo said. "Had a dental appointment. You look worried."

Tryg plunked on a chair, his voice bouncing off the anything but sleepy office walls. "Thought you'd appreciate knowing that I had a very interesting chat over breakfast, and you'll never guess who with."

"Okay. I'll take the bait. Who?"

"The clerk from Skinners."

Jo appeared to flinch then too quickly buried her nose in a pile of work.

"Do you have any idea what we talked about?"

She shrugged with what appeared to be feigned indifference.

"He said everyone's talking about my new office worker. Said the women are jealous and the men are smitten." Tryg tapped a finger on Jo's desk. "Jo Bremley, if I didn't know any better, I'd say you're blushing."

She didn't look up.

"Problem is, I understand some gal stopped by his store one afternoon about a month ago," he continued. "A mystery woman. From her description, he thought she might have been you. But then he said she bought a bunch of boys' clothes, so he knew it had to be someone else. Jo? Why aren't you looking at me? Yoo-hoo! Jo?" Tryg groaned. "Oh, no! I knew you were holding back, but this crosses a line. You've got to be careful, Jo. The squeeze is on."

"Hopefully not any more."

"Why do you say that?"

"The boys got hauled in yesterday," she said, her gaze finally meeting his. "And I'm not what you'd call mildly involved. At least now maybe word will get out and I won't have to protect Big Ole anymore."

The hairs on the back of Tryg's neck sprung up like a porcupine. "Your loyalty to Big Ole aside, you should never have gotten caught up in this in the first place. That man is courting disaster." Tryg let out a puff of air. "You aren't afraid to make tough choices, I'm going to give you that one. Remember Ardena's warning? What if something happens to someone else and you could have helped prevent it? I mean, how could you of all people live with yourself?"

"I know," she said, her voice barely audible.

"Well?"

"Why don't you ask Sarah? She's his granddaughter, not me, and you're dating her."

"With her, I'm one step removed," he said, "and I plan to keep it that way."

Jo appeared to balk. "What's that supposed to mean?"

Warmth rose up Tryg's cheeks and all the way to the tips of his ears. He'd unwittingly admitted something not only to Jo, but also to himself, and he felt exposed.

Quickly changing back the subject as if covering for him, Jo said, "I'm still not talking, Tryg. I can't violate him."

"I understand," Tryg said. "He has to know what he's doing. I have yet to see that man make a wrong call."

Jo broke what appeared to be a relieved smile. "I thought I'd stop by the O.M. Harrington House tonight and tell Big Ole about the boys. I've already told him so much, though. The more I say, the worse I feel about myself."

"He has a right to know, but as for you, you're going to have to pick a side. You need to have the courage to be hot or cold. You know the old saying."

"If we don't stand for something, we'll fall for anything, right?"

"That's right. You've already shown you're courageous, but you either need to align your allegiance with Chief Stout or align it with Big Ole. It's not wise to go middle-of-the-road here."

"I'm aligned with Big Ole."

Tryg nodded then got back to work, thinking of the irony of his own words. He certainly had the courage to stand for something, too. He was a fortress, refusing to allow himself to fall for anything—or anyone. Sarah included.

CHAPTER FORTY-SEVEN

A mber Leaf shimmered in the flaxen sunlight. The easy way people drifted across the streets and along sidewalks carrying packages, huddled in conversation, waving to one another, afforded a stark conrast to the far side of the world where war continued to rage.

Tryg headed south on Broadway. As he passed Skinner Chamberlain's, he caught a glimpse of a mannequin in the storefront window, a mannequin with blueberry eyes and flowing shoulder-length auburn hair—like Sarah's. What were the chances of noticing it immediately on the heels of his comment to Jo? 'With her, I'm one step removed, and I plan to keep it that way.' Where did that fool notion come from?

He wanted to find a quiet place where he could grab a private table and enjoy lunch alone. Too much had been happening lately. He needed to pull his thoughts together and sort things through. He hesitated when he reached Hotel Albert. They had a quiet dining room. Why not go in? Once inside, he saw a man's hand waving, pointing to an empty chair at his table. It was Charlie. He was eating alone. "Your timing is perfect," he said. "I was just about to order. Thought I'd stop by for a quick lunch then head back to the boarding house to catch up on a little reading."

Tryg pulled out a chair. "I'm feeling sheepish," he said. "We've been meaning to give you a welcome-home of some kind, a small fishing outing, maybe, but I'm afraid we've gotten a little too distracted with Big Ole. If anyone has earned a good reception, it's you. You deserve better."

"I'm not much for the limelight these days anyway, Tryg," Charlie said. "Don't give it a thought."

Tryg's concerns about Sarah aside, Ole's request to have a chat with the troubled soldier had weighed on him, too. Feeling he owed a fellow GI as much, he surveyed the restaurant. "How about grabbing a table over by the far wall? It'll be more private."

Charlie seized his coffee mug. "Sure thing."

Tryg and Charlie made small talk for the better part of five minutes, Tryg studying the man and identifying with his tired and half-empty look. "Having nightmares, are you?" he asked understatedly.

Charlie peered at Tryg for a split moment as if sizing him up and then released a slight nod. "As one soldier to another, I guess you might say that."

Tryg offered an understated accounting of his credentials. "Operation Husky. Italy."

"Operation Market Garden. The Netherlands," Charlie responded.

Tryg returned Charlie's slight nod. Two wounded soldiers. Two different skirmishes. Two afflicted men who without knowing one another's stories understood each other only too well. "As I recall, that's where Sarah lost her husband."

Rather than reacting, Charlie stared at his cup and twirled it around mechanically with a forefinger. That was interesting. Had Tryg been worrying needlessly? After ordering a light lunch, Charlie looked up and leveled his gaze on Tryg, his expression hopeful. "I assume you've had your share of nightmares, too."

Tryg nodded.

"Did you ever get past them?"

Tryg wished with all his being he could say yes, but he could not and, what was worse, he doubted he ever would. "Not completely, but they say we do in time. I didn't get mine from the war, though."

Charlie appeared unconvinced. "Do you mind expanding on that?"

"After taking a hit and spending a few months in the hospital, a buddy of mine picked me up at the train depot in the Cities." Tryg felt miserable rehashing his past, but if anyone looked as if he had a need to know, it was Charlie. "We had a snowstorm of epic proportions that day and tried to outrun it. On our way home, a deer leaped out in front of us. We swerved to miss it and hit the ditch head on. I guess it would be more accurate to say that I swerved to miss it. I was driving. My buddy was killed instantly. You may have heard of the guy. Case Bremley?"

Tryg's words must have found their target, because in the flickering of an eye, realization appeared to batter Charlie's senses. "Not Jo's husband?"

Tryg nodded, a stab of hurt searing his vulnerable heart all over again. "That's something you never get over." It was Tryg's turn to mechanically trace a circle on the table with the bottom of his porcelain cup. "How about you?"

"Oh, I dunno. In some sick way I guess maybe I was luckier than you, but not by a whole lot. Got shot down. I was flying too low to the ground when I took a hit. Maybe the word hit is a little underplayed. By the time the Jerrys got done with me, my plane looked like it made a hard pass through a threshing machine before it caught fire. Fortunately between high humidity and the ground being saturated after a week of nonstop rain, the fire fizzled out."

"Get hurt bad, did you?"

"Na'ah. Just a slight concussion was all."

Tryg held back his words. There was a lot more to Charlie's story. He sensed it. He felt at one with him at the moment, the way he used to feel around Case. No pretense. Just two good buddies sharing in a deep and meaningful way the misery that had battered their lives.

Charlie inhaled what appeared to be a sizable breath of restaurant air. "I came to before the Germans could get hold of my hide. My head hurt something awful. Everything was one big blur at first. But then I saw what looked like an abandoned barn at the far end of a field. I staggered through tall grass up to my knees only to find it wasn't abandoned after all. About choked when I found myself staring eyeball to eyeball with a wild-eyed Kraut. It was either him or me. Shooting from a plane is impersonal. I could handle that any day of the week. But arm-to-arm combat? Now that's something altogether different. Dying up close is ugly, but then you already knew that. Staring into shocked and horror-filled eyes. Hearing the groans and the gurgling. Smelling sweat and fresh blood. I won the struggle all right. But when the Jerry's body went lifeless, his hand fell open and it was what dropped to the ground that nearly destroyed me."

Charlie hesitated, undoubtedly to collect his emotions. "He was clutching a picture," he choked on. "Didn't take a lot of figuring to realize it was a picture of his wife and kids. He was just a soldier, Tryg, like you and me. Poor guy was scared to death. He was weak. Didn't stand a chance." Charlie shook his head, his eyes shadowed in despair. "And that was only the first one."

Tryg didn't want to know how many more there were. He only wished the old Charlie could be back, the Charlie that had been so excited about life before he headed overseas only to learn firsthand what war was really all about. And yet Tryg knew that never could happen. Not now. Charlie's scars were the kind that would last a lifetime. "Are you home on leave, or have you turned in your uniform?"

"Neither. Got double vision from the head injury."

"How bad is it?"

"Bad enough to keep me out of the sky, at least for the time being anyway. If I get lucky and shake out of it, I'll probably head for the Pacific. This time I'll know what I'm getting myself into."

Tryg found his lunch with Charlie surprisingly meaningful. The guy had substance. They talked more about the war, got into a little politics, and even touched on sports.

But then Charlie's countenance changed. He slipped from animated to sad. "Say, Tryg. There's something we should probably talk about." Suddenly he stopped mid-sentence. Tryg pivoted to see what had captured his attention.

Jo stood in the doorway, searching the room. Seeing them, she hurried to their table.

"Hi, Charlie," she said impassively. "Sorry to bother you, Tryg. I had a hard time finding you. We got a call from the courthouse about an hour ago. They need you there at two this afternoon instead of three."

Tryg glanced at his watch. A quarter to the hour already. Where had the time gone? He quickly got up and thanked Jo, then tossed a few dollars on the table. "I've got it," he said, but as he started to say good-bye, he cringed at a contemptuous look on the young soldier's face. What was that all about?

CHAPTER FORTY-EIGHT

s Jo reached for the handle, the door of the O.M. Harrington swung open, and she gazed into Sarah's surprised blueberry eyes.

"Wait a second. I forgot my wallet," a familiar male voice behind her said.

Charlie again.

Jo plastered on an impassive, neutral look, as if that was possible. "Is your grandfather in?"

Big Ole sat near the hearth probing his teeth with a toothpick. "You were looking for me?"

"Yes, sir. Can we have a private word somewhere?"

"My office private enough?"

"I think that will do."

Although they crossed paths in the hallway with Charlie, who said a quick hello, Jo was more concerned about Big Ole. His breathing appeared labored.

"I certainly don't mean to complain," she said after Ole settled in his chair, the pitiable thing squawking beneath his generous weight, "but I'm beginning to feel like the town gossip."

"Your conscience is having a heyday with you, I see. Take heart, my dear," Ole said with a mischievous grin. "Why, Mrs. Bremley, you may have become the town gossip, but you've got to be the loveliest gossip ever to set foot in Amber Leaf."

"You're impossible, and to think I've been sticking my neck out for you."

"It's my pleasure. Now what has you so distressed?"

"Chief Stout is closing in on Wil," she said as she lightly closed the door behind them.

Ole hesitated. Disappointment and concern clouded his face. "How so?"

"The chief hauled him in yesterday along with that Anders kid."

Ole dropped his weight hard onto the chair and, gripping its arms, he leaned back. "That's odd. Wil didn't mention a word about it. Mind if I ask how you found out?"

"Brue. She and her friend, Poke, saw them on their way home from school yesterday."

"I see," Ole said thoughtfully. "No wonder he was late getting to work."

"It's only a matter of time before something is done." Jo's heart was breaking for Ole and for Wil. "Things couldn't look more bleak. What are you going to do now?"

Ole peered out the window, giving Jo his back, but he talked just the same. "That's a fair question, I guess." He swiveled back. "It's not the boy's fault, Jo."

"But he did it."

"I know. You will be discreet?"

"Absolutely. You have my word."

"Do you remember how I told you before that Teddy Anders was a mean one?"

Jo nodded. How could she forget?

"He wouldn't have hesitated to do me in completely, but like I also told you, Wil was the one who stopped his incessant kicking. Teddy ..." Ole gave his head a bitter shake. "Animal would have been a much more appropriate name for the kid." Ole picked up a piece of notepaper and fidgeted with its edges the way he always did. "I've only told you a few things about what happened that night. Truth is, after doing their dirty work, they tore off together, the two of them, leaving me alone to fend for myself. While I lay there trying to even get a finger to move, Wil came back. He was alone. Cradled my head in his arms. He'd reach up every now and then to backhand his tears, but they were gushing like a spigot. Every time he cradled my head again, I got a new washing. He pleaded over and over again, 'please, mister, please don't die.' I was conscious enough to hear the terror in the boy's voice. He was broken. And when he told me he was going to get my cane, I heard your car and was vaguely aware of your headlights coming over the hill. Wil tore off like a bat out of Hades. I heard rustling in the shrubs nearby and was positive he'd found a place to hide in Evelyn Tomlinson's lilac bushes."

"So he was there," Jo said. "I knew I'd heard something, too, but didn't want to believe it. Looked around, but didn't see anything."

"That was probably him. He had to have been hiding there the entire time, watching everything unfold." Ole hesitated. "You know, that boy was merely passing on what he knew, Jo—what had happened to him. I'm not a psychiatrist, but it doesn't take a whole lot to see that he was filled with anger and vulnerability and was crying out for help. He didn't know what to do with all the confusion he'd been carrying around."

"The day I drove by and saw you walking to his house," Jo said, "did you see him or his dad?"

"Both."

"And?"

"Bad parenting. Neglect," Ole said thoughtfully. "I knew a boy years ago. His dad beat him up all the time. He didn't stand a chance. Ended up in prison and never was able to turn his life around. I don't want that to happen to Wil. I've seen something in him. I've thought all along that if I could be instrumental in turning his life around, all the grief I've endured would have been well worth it." Ole glanced at the calendar.

"All of our days are numbered, and mine are closing in on me. I want to help that boy if it's the last thing I do. My old buddy Hank and I already got him on the Packers' team. That boy has raw talent the likes of which I've never seen before."

Jo smiled reassuringly. "I understand. You've got my support."

Just then, swift foot drops pounded out in the hallway.

"Thanks," Ole said, glancing distractedly toward the twirling door-knob. "I just might need it."

CHAPTER FORTY-NINE

C hief Stout barreled into the office, leaving no question in Ole's mind he was there to get answers. Answers Ole was hard-pressed to give. Answers that would expedite Wil's one-way trip to Red Wing. That wasn't about to happen, not if Ole could help it.

"Rare and unexpected appearances make me a trifle nervous," Ole said flatly.

"Relax," the chief replied. "There's no need for this to be unpleasant. I merely stopped by to deliver some important news."

Jo stood. "I think I'd better leave the two of you alone."

"No need to leave on my account," Ole said.

"He's right, Jo. What I have to say isn't private. Besides, if you can talk some sense into this revered old man's head, it might be better if you did stay."

Chief Stout, without invitation, pulled up a black leather chair and plopped down like he owned the place.

Ole waited until he was well seated and quipped, "Please, have a seat."

The chief hesitated then cracked a smirk. "After our last conversation," he said, "I took a hint. Pumping information out of you is like sucking blood out of a rutabaga."

"That's not about to change."

"And this one's just as bad. She's been covering for you. Haven't you?"

Jo shrugged, her expression innocent.

"I tried to corner her a few weeks ago," the chief continued, "but she wouldn't cave."

She wouldn't? Ole smiled.

"Said I should talk to you myself. Didn't you, Mrs. Bremley? Since I couldn't get anywhere with the two of you, I've been exploring every avenue imaginable. And then, of course, we have Madame Braddingly's paranoid sense of urgency that certainly lit a blaze under my size thirteen's."

"Your point?" Ole said.

"Wil Thompson belongs in reform school. Even you have to admit that, or should I say especially you?"

"No, I don't."

"Under the circumstances," he continued, "I think you might want to start cooperating."

"Under what circumstances might those be?"

"I've hauled the boys in for questioning."

Ole's hand tightened into a fist. "I believe I heard something about that. So that's the important news you came to tell me?"

The chief nodded. "What happened that night, Ole? Why aren't you talking? Why are you protecting those hoodlums? And why, for heavens' sakes, would you bring one of them under your own roof? Doesn't make a lick of sense. What about the safety of your guests here? Don't they have a right to be protected? What about your granddaughter? I can't for the life of me understand your thinking."

"I thought you said you hauled the boys in for questioning. If that's the case, I assume they've told you all you need to know."

"No. I only have part of the story. I came hoping to get the rest."

"You're wasting your time. I have no memory of that evening," Ole said and then getting up, he walked around the desk and reached for the chief's hand, his gaze toward the door an invitation. "Thanks for stopping by. If and when I get my memory back, you'll be among the first to know."

"Oh, no." Chief Stout pushed back, his fingers squeezing hard into leather. "That's not going to work, Ole. Not with me." The chief stared Ole down hard. "The Anders kid confessed."

Ole's old heart fluttered. He turned toward the windows and looked over the park to calm himself then said, "He did, did he?"

"That's right. Wil's pal sang prettier than a little robin redbreast. Said the whole episode was Thompson's idea. Of course, that came as no surprise."

Ole simmered with contempt. "Some pal. Why didn't you tell me this before?"

"I just did."

"Help me understand this," Ole said. "The Anders kid threw the whole beating on Wil Thompson's shoulders, and you believed him?"

"That's right. I did."

"What makes you so certain Teddy has his story right?" Ole asked assertively. "What makes you think poor little Teddy wasn't the instigator?"

"The Thompson kid refuses to talk. If he was innocent, he would save his hide. And then there's the fact that he has a truancy record stretching from here to the Canadian border, saying nothing about that incorrigible old man of his."

Jo looked at Ole thoughtfully then turned to the chief. "I don't understand. What makes you think the Anders boy is squeaky clean?"

"I don't know that I'd go that far," he said. "Came from a good home, though, doesn't have a record, and at least he's talking. It's amazing what a little threat of reform school will do. We've got more than enough evidence now for a hearing."

Big Ole smacked the heel of his hand on the desk. "I told you I wanted to handle my own business."

"That's the problem. It never was your business. The locals have been looking to me to handle this maddening affair all along. That's a bit odd, don't you think? People wanting me to do the job I'm being paid to do? To protect them?"

"They don't need protecting."

"You beat all," Chief Stout scoffed. "Where'd you ever come up with a fool notion like that? The boy is going to get sent up, Ole, and there's not a thing you or I can do to stop it. Now why don't you tell me why you're defending him?"

"A better question would be, why are you out to get him, and what's your hurry?"

Chief Stout scowled. "I saw you at the hospital, remember? How can you be so forgiving? Wil is one bad apple. He nearly took you to within an inch of your life for crying out loud."

Ole slipped his thumbs behind his suspenders and stretched them. "Maybe you hadn't noticed, but I'm still here. In fact, I'm doing fine. As for the boy, have you ever taken a hard look at him? Seen how vulnerable he is?" Ole hesitated, an unpleasant realization playing with him. "You aren't taking this out on him because of his drunken dad, are you?"

"Absolutely not." With an ankle crossed over a knee, the chief plucked at a pant cuff. "If you spill the beans, maybe we can get him a lighter sentence."

That was a surprise. "You would do that?"

"I would."

Ole pondered the chief's words, shook his head, looked about the room while trying to find a place to begin then said, "Okay then. You know as well as I do that that boy was bent on destruction, but not any more. You've been to his house. Know his dad. No wonder the poor kid was such a mess. He was acting out, that's all. Didn't have it in him to harm me."

"You can't be serious," the chief scoffed. "What were those bandages and bruises all about? Those boys weren't playing doctors and nurses, that's for sure."

"If you will remember, I was there, Chief. Believe me, he didn't have it in him. You been to any of the Packers' games lately?"

"The Packers' games?"

"That's right. My buddy Hank and I got Wil into baseball. His talent is phenomenal. Mark my word, in no time at all, that boy will be the heart and soul of the team."

"He already is," Jo interjected.

Ole nodded his agreement. "And now, Chief, you're taking that away from him. You're taking that away from our entire community, too." Ole lifted his chin and said, "Can't you at least wait until after the playoffs?"

"Those games don't have a thing to do with this." The chief set his jaw. "The boy made his choice. Now he's going to have to live with the consequences."

"I'm not testifying against him," Ole stated flatly.

"That would have been helpful, but it isn't critical. We've got enough dirt on Willie boy to send him to Red Wing for a mighty long time, and you can bet your frilly pantaloons that will happen sooner rather than later."

"When you say a mighty long time, how long are you talking?"

"He has a prior and he's sixteen now so it could be a couple of years."

"What do you mean, a prior? For what?"

"Ran away from home a few years back."

"He got up sent up for that?" Jo asked sounding incredulous. "Why?"

"He and his dad got into it bad one day and Wil took off. Was gone about a week before we could find him."

"Who was the bad guy, Chief?" Ole asked. "Wil for running away or his dad for abusing him?"

"Or did his dad have cause, Ole? He was at the end of his rope. It's not easy dealing with a rebellious adolescent."

Ole pulled out a desk drawer and plucked out a cigar then carefully removed the cellophane casing. He struck a match against the bottom of his shoe, and held the flame to his cigar, drawing it in with quick, short breaths. "I don't know that it's possible to escape a toxic environment without having it rub off on you like a common cold or the flu."

The chief sighed. "So you're blaming his dad? Those boys are dangerous, Ole, and you're not a professional."

"So what you're saying is that I should look at this from a position of weakness rather than strength, is that right? What's more important here, Chief? My pride? Or turning a young boy's life around?"

"I've noticed you're only talking about Wil," the chief said. "Why's that? What about that Anders kid?"

"Because near as I can tell, it won't take much to steer Wil in the right direction. The other kid I have my doubts about. Little Teddy doesn't have an excuse."

"But Wil took the lead in nearly destroying you."

"No, he did not. If he had, we wouldn't be having this conversation."

"If what you say is true, why doesn't he stick up for himself? Why is he shouldering the blame?"

Ole thought for a moment. "Because he's a good boy. It appears we're all being tested in life, aren't we? We all have a purpose for being here. Every last one of us. That includes Wil. I can't do anything to change the assault. I'll admit it was humiliating and painful, but it happened. It's done, and it's been a fast track to humility. Being humble never did come easy for me. But this boy ..." Ole paused and thoughtfully emitted a small puff of smoke, "he's had a tough go in life. He's confused, and he's suffering. Doesn't know which way to turn. Neither does he have an anchor, so I'm trying to help give him one."

Ole tapped the cigar against the ashtray, a small amount of ash breaking off and sliding in. "He's suffered more abuse than we can imagine. Learned all the wrong lessons from his lost and miserable dad. He doesn't have anyone to believe in him, only people who don't hesitate to put him down. People who curse him, fight him, and take advantage of him."

"So what you're saying is— "

"What I'm saying is I've seen something in Wil, something vulnerable and good. He needs a little help is all."

"But working with him is like—"

"That's what I thought, too. But I couldn't have been more wrong. He's hungry for attention and even hungrier to learn."

"What made you so all fired-up sure you were the right one to help him in the first place?" the chief challenged.

"It was what I learned about him."

"Which was?"

"I'd rather not say."

"Then I can't get on board with your line of thinking."

Ole let out an exasperated sigh.

"All right, have it your way," Ole said. "But keep this under your hat." He then reluctantly shared bits and pieces of what he'd seen and heard that fateful night and the first few days following, careful to leave out the most vulnerable parts that would further strip the boy of his dignity.

"Why didn't you tell me this before?" the chief asked.

"If you will recall, your mind was made up. You weren't looking for why, you were looking for who."

"Does anyone else know about this?"

Ole nodded at Jo. "Her. The only other person who has an inkling is Tryg. He only knows a small amount, and I prefer to keep it that way. Oh, and then there's Sarah. She's figured it out on her own."

Chief Stout ran a finger over the stubbly growth on his chin. "I see," he said finally. "We've got a problem then. The State's already called for a hearing. You, me, or anyone else for that matter has no more say at this point. The only thing we can do is beg for leniency."

Ole drummed his fingers on the desk. "How soon will this transpire?"

"Usually takes a couple of months at most, but with Wil's record, he was quietly placed on the docket. I'm afraid they've made his hearing a priority. It could happen any day now."

CHAPTER FIFTY

T he floral truck pulled up in front of the office again with the delivery of another large bouquet. This time the driver carried in a dozen red roses, which were even lovelier than the first arrangement, and presented them to Jo. She sniffed several of the flowers, feeling lightheaded from their sweet fragrance. With them came a note that read, *Thank you for the most wonderful Fourth of July of my life. Frank.*

The instant the deliveryman closed the door behind him, Ardena descended on Jo's desk like a cat on a mouse. "Why the unhappy face? If I got flowers like that from Calvin, I'd be hooting and hollering. You wouldn't be able to hold me back."

Jo mindlessly rubbed her thin fingers along the sharp edges of the delicate card. "It's the sentiment, I guess. You have no idea how much I want to believe his words."

"Why wouldn't you believe them?" Ardena said, sounding surprised.

"Because his words and actions don't match, that's why." Jo glanced at the calendar. "The Fourth of July was two weeks ago today. Why did he wait so long to send them, and why hasn't he called me yet for another date? Besides, there's more."

"I'm waiting."

"Brue found lipstick on her milk glass when we were out at his place."

"And?"

"He gave her a different glass, but didn't offer an explanation."

Ardena fingered the petal of a flower. "Did he look guilt-ridden?"

"No."

"Does he have a sister?"

"I don't know."

"You know, even old women have been known to wear lipstick. It could have come from an elderly neighbor."

"I hadn't thought about that," Jo said. "But he makes me feel needy. The space between dates makes me feel shut out. How can you ever build a real relationship on mystery?"

"Please don't tell me you're shielding your heart from love. Come on, Jo. Give the man a chance. Did it ever dawn on you that he might be consistently slow with everything he does? If you pull out a magnifying glass, you'll find problems with every guy you go out with."

Ardena could very well be right. Maybe Jo was being too self-protective, too uncomfortable in the world she was caught up in—a beautiful world, yet a world sprinkled with feelings of distrust, confusion, and fear. She already feared losing who she really was, and she barely knew the man.

Jo fingered the note. "But he's lived long enough to have an orchard full of beautiful Fourth of Julys."

"You're doing it again. You're looking for problems. From where I stand, it looks like you might be his walking fantasy."

"I don't want to be anyone's walking fantasy, Ardena. I want reality."

Ardena fingered a ruffle on her satin blouse. "I dunno," she said. "I think I'd take the compliment and run."

"What about you? Did you feel comfortable when you started dating Calvin? Did you wonder if he'd ever call you again, or how long he'd stick around? I don't remember feeling that way with Case. Of course, we were kids when we dated."

"You are definitely suffering from cold feet," Ardena said. "Don't worry. I was apprehensive, too, when Calvin first started asking me out. Dating him felt like I was sleepwalking through a dream that was too good to be true. I was terrified of waking up one day and not finding him there. It's normal to feel that way at the beginning. It's like buying something new and valuable and fearing you're going to lose it or scratch it or break it before it has a chance to become just another possession. This, too, shall pass."

"I guess I'm asking a deeper question," Jo said thoughtfully. "Did you trust who he was?"

"You know Calvin. How could I not?"

Jo's heart sank. "That's what I thought."

Frank was a temptation, a magnet drawing her leaden heart toward him, rescuing her from a world of loneliness. How Jo hoped Ardena was right. Maybe it was cold feet. To a degree, the roses made her feel special, but then she remembered Frank's past love. That married lady. The woman with a husband and two towheaded children. Jo didn't have the right to judge Frank, but she did have a right to understand him. There had to have been a good reason why he got caught up in a relationship with her. Maybe she was a love from his youth, someone coerced into a marriage she didn't want. Maybe her husband was abusive and Frank merely wanted to rescue her. Jo would never find out what was behind his secrecy unless she asked, but it was too soon in their relationship for her to probe that deeply. That needed to come with time.

Later that evening, the phone rang and Jo's heart leaped. The welcome sound of Frank's virile voice filled her once again with warmth and hope. But after a pleasant chat and a promise for another date, she couldn't shed the uneasy feeling that it was a stubborn hope, a hope gift-wrapped in uncertainty.

CHAPTER FIFTY-ONE

The door flew open, smacking against the wall of the great room and rattling its windows. Startled, Ole looked up. He mechanically folded the evening paper and placed it on the counter while Harry Thompson, red faced and fuming, marched toward him.

"What have you done?" he spat, his pointing finger waggling accusingly to within an inch of Ole's nose. "Tomorrow will be just another day for you, but not for my boy."

Ole studied the man who appeared desperate to relieve himself of anger before he exploded completely. Ole then looked around the room, taken aback by fear radiating in the eyes of the guests. Yet he waited the man out.

"You ruined him. Who do you think you are anyway? The great O.M. Harrington—a cut above the rest of us, right?"

Sarah flew around the registration desk, cheeks flaming, eyes widening. "You leave my grandfather alone."

Ole held a hand out open-palmed to quiet her. "It's okay, Sarah," he said calmly. "This man needs to talk, and he's certainly earned the right." Ole then nodded to Harry. "You go ahead, sir."

"Sir?" Harry fumed. "Sir?" he repeated. "What a joke! Look, I may not be the best dad in the world, but I did everything I could to toughen up my boy. You undercut me. Gave him things I could never give him, not in a million years and filled his head with a bunch a' malarkey. Made him soft and now he's the one payin' the price. Do you have any idea what you've done?"

Ole stood quietly, hearing the man out. "Go ahead."

"You reduced my son to an experiment—that's what you've done. Now that experiment's due in court tomorrow and we both know how that's going to turn out. He doesn't stand a prayer. They're going to haul him off to a place where he could be destroyed. How can a kid like him ever stand up to a bunch of bullies at reform school? I hope you feel real good about yourself, Harrington," he said mockingly. "For every torturous night my boy spends in bed shivering with fear, I hope you lay in your bed shivering, too. Shivering with shame and regret. That is, if you have the decency to feel any guilt over your selfish actions." Slapping a hand at the air, Harry Thompson spun around. "Oh, what's the use?" he complained as he marched out of the boarding house faster than he'd come in.

Sarah watched the door close behind him. "How could you let him talk to you like that, Grandpa? You didn't deserve it."

"How could I?" Ole said thoughtfully.

With a tremendous amount of work and determination forged with steel, Big Ole Harrington had known a dizzying amount of success during his lifetime, only to discover the bitter taste of failure in his advancing years. He gazed at the clock that relentlessly ticked more minutes off his well-seasoned life.

"Because I fear the man may have been right."

CHAPTER FIFTY-TWO

J o cradled the receiver, tears stinging her eyes. "That was my neighbor." More loss. Another widow. This time, a widow without a child let alone children. This was one of the more tragic stories—a future shattered before memories of happily-ever-after could unfold.

"Oh, no," Ardena said, her understanding unmistakable. "What happened?"

"Ned Wilder's plane hit the Pacific on his first flight out."

Before Jo could collect herself, Tryg breezed in the office at a fast clip. "We've got a problem, Jo," he said.

Any problems they had were golden. They were still breathing.

Jo could still see Ned at the shivaree standing atop that hay wagon proudly saluting his friends, he and his bride in that beat up old Model T with rusty cans clanking behind them as they drove off down that long stretch of country road.

"There's something you need to know." As Jo reluctantly shared the bad news, Tryg squeezed his eyes closed and slowly shook his head. "I'm sorry to hear that," he said. After a respectable few moments of silence, his expression was less anxious, but also more resigned.

"What's this problem you were talking about?" Jo asked. "Sounds serious."

"When I was at the courthouse earlier today, I checked out this afternoon's calendar."

"And?"

"Wil's hearing is on the slate."

Emotionally richocheting from Ned to Wil, Jo felt whipsawed. "Can't be. Not that fast."

"We all knew Chief Stout was gunning for him and has been for some time. It's no surprise the incident with Ole rattled a few big cages. When a space opened up, looks like they jumped on it."

"Are you going?"

"I have to. Big Ole needs my support. There's no way that boy can skate through this thing on his own, and even then it's going to be a problem."

Jo didn't know who she felt sorrier for, Wil or Big Ole. The judge, himself, would be hard pressed to protect Wil from the cold cells of Red Wing. She thought about the effect doing time would have on Wil. The isolation. Harsh treatment. Lack of freedom. She could always send a letter or a care package every now and then to let him know someone cared, but that was little consolation.

When Tryg left for the courthouse, Jo slouched in her chair. All Big Ole had tried to accomplish these past weeks—was it about to swirl down the drain? If he were younger, it wouldn't matter as much. But he no longer had the luxury of holding out hope. She considered the exorbitant price he'd paid for an assault he could no longer hope to cash in on. Would he be able to gather himself and pick up the pieces? But for now, she needed to pick up Brue from the Wilder's.

CHAPTER FIFTY-THREE

ig Ole pulled out his pocket watch and chain. One minute since
he'd last checked the time. "What could possibly be taking that
blasted taxi so long?" he muttered beneath his breath. Even his
feet were beginning to smart from pacing.

"Grandfather?" Sarah said. "Do you want me to make another call?
See when the taxi will get here?"

Ole nodded. "Would you do that?"

A restless moment later, Sarah said, "Something must have happened with the first driver. They're sending another cab."

"That's going to take too long. I can get there faster if I walk. Would
you mind canceling it?"

The hill on Charles Street seemed higher for some strange reason,
harder to climb. The sun hotter, and Ole felt feverish. Then there was
the pain—a crushing pain. He couldn't find his breath. Fought for it,
but it wouldn't come. The sky twirled round and round. Barely able to
stand, he anchored himself on the bend of his cane. He wanted to lay
down. Oh, how he wanted to lay down and rest a while. Make it all go
away. But he didn't have the luxury. He needed to snap out of it and get
to the courthouse.

CHAPTER FIFTY-FOUR

After having stopped by to quickly give her condolences to the Wilders and dropping off Brue at Evelyn's, Jo stepped out into the balmy August afternoon and once again motored up the hill at full throttle. But at the crest of Charles Street, she slammed on the brakes. Big Ole stood in the middle of the sidewalk leaning his full weight on his cane, looking as if he was fighting for breath. Jo bolted out of her car and hollered as she ran, "Are you okay?"

Ole shook his head. "I fear my ticker is having a fit of temper."

"We've got to get you an ambulance!"

"No, Jo."

"Come on! I'm driving you to the hospital myself then. But you are going to the hospital."

She helped maneuver his heavy weight into the front seat. He slumped over, groaning with pain.

Jo hit the accelerator. The car lurched then died. She adjusted the throttle and tried again. The engine roared, and she headed up Newton, the road grumbling beneath her tires.

She glanced across at Big Ole every few seconds. "Hang on, Mr. Harrington. We're getting closer."

"It's Big Ole to you, remember?" he said, gasping and straining.

Some people have said that when they had a close-call, they saw their lives passing before them. Jo had never understood what that meant. But now in this brief close-call moment, her memories of Big Ole's life clipped past her faster than the stores ticking by.

Their first major encounter involved a mishap Ole had had with Brue when he had raised his cane and inadvertently ripped her dress. When Jo confronted him in the not-so-private Copper Kettle, he cautioned her to get her facts straight.

Also at The Copper Kettle, there was that picture he dropped on the floor—the picture of his bride and the raw pain Jo saw in his eyes when she retrieved it. He only wanted to be left alone to grieve for his cherished wife.

His gruff demeanor.

Their strained encounters at the O.M. Harrington.

The many times she watched him strutting along the sidewalks as if he owned them.

He offered Jo a job when she needed it most. When she moved on to greener pastures, only to find she'd made a horrid mistake, she was mortified when he flatly refused to give her her job back, but not without first challenging her to quit running away from Tryg.

She smiled at the day she caught him examining that snowman standing at the side of the road, the snowman that looked as if it were hitching a ride. Ole glanced around then slipped his hat atop it when he thought no one was looking. Twirling his cane, he glanced back admiringly, and with a spring in his step he walked on.

Then there was the night he left a Cinderella watch and glass slipper on Jo's doorstep with a note that read *Merry Christmas to Brue*.

She recalled his high standards and how she'd learned from them—how she and Tryg and Sarah violated him by coming to his aid when he didn't need or want anyone's help, behind his back nonetheless.

Beaten to within an inch of his life, he stood up to an entire community. Why? Because he knew what he was doing. Big Ole saw gold that no one else could see and was there when no one believed a troubled young teen could change.

And now the man with the greatest integrity she'd ever known sat beside her doubled over, writhing in pain, and gasping for breath.

Looking swiftly to the left and then to the right, she ran the stop sign at Broadway and Clark.

Big Ole Harrington reached across the wide seat and lightly touched her arm.

Jo turned again and looked into large, warm, and sparkling steel-gray eyes, jolted by how well and peaceful all looked with the dear man's soul.

"You don't have to drive so fast, Jo," he said, his choke a whisper. "I'll be with Jesus soon."

CHAPTER FIFTY-FIVE

The dog days of summer in full swing, the night air was oppressive, but far more oppressive was what Tryg feared was awaiting him in Ole's hospital room. How many more episodes could that dear man take?

Jo and Sarah were sitting at Ole's bedside paralyzed with grief. Praying. Weeping. Praying some more. Tryg stood quietly near the door to respect their privacy. In doing so, he noticed something curious. After a long while, he didn't hesitate to walk into the room. Not only did Jo look up, she appeared both surprised to see him and horror stricken at his full-on grin. "How can you be so calloused?" she asked. "Big Ole's barely holding on. We could lose him."

"Because while you were busy wiping your eyes, he's been sneaking peeks at you."

Sarah's head sprung back. "Grandpa? Is it true? Can you hear us? Talk to me, Grandpa."

His voice inaudible, his lips barely moving, Sarah leaned an ear closer and listened intently. "What? I can't hear you. Tell me that again."

Suddenly bursting into laughter, she wheeled around. "Jo? He said to tell you you're a slow learner, but you're coming around."

"I am?"

"You finally called him Big Ole in his presence."

All the fear Jo had been holding in rushed out with a whoosh. "You tell him—"

Sarah stepped aside. "Go ahead. He's all yours."

Just then a doctor walked in. "What's the verdict?" Sarah asked. "What happened? Is he going to be okay?"

"Unfortunately, he's had a mild heart attack, but he's tough. After a little rest, yes, I think he'll be fine."

Ole lifted a finger. "Tryg," he whispered.

"He's right here," Sarah said. "Do you want to talk to him?"

After Ole gave a slight nod, Tryg leaned in close and rested a warm hand on Big Ole's arm. "I'm here, Ole. What can I do for you? What? Wil?"

Tryg looked to Sarah then Jo for help. "He wants to know about Wil. How the hearing went."

"Go ahead," Sarah said. "He can handle it. He was prepared for the worst before he left for the hearing today."

Tryg reluctantly shared the basics. The verdict. Redwing until age eighteen. Chief Stout escorting Wil away. But Tryg held back the Teddy Anders briefing until Big Ole was stronger and his fragile heart could handle it.

CHAPTER FIFTY-SIX

J o timed Sunday's meal so it would be out of the oven a half hour after Frank arrived. At one o'clock she busied herself setting the table and putting the finishing touches on the meal, while keeping an ear out for his car. At a quarter past one, no Frank. At half past one, the lonely and steady tick, tick, tick of the clock reverberated off the walls. She sauntered into the living room and looked up the road. Still no Frank.

This was the second time in less than twenty-four hours that he had put her off, having canceled last night's date at the last minute. She hoped he hadn't heard the disappointment in her voice when he told her he was on his way out to do chores for a neighboring farmer whose boy had fallen out of a hayloft. Frank said the boy had made a soft landing on hay and didn't appear to have any broken bones, but he did get a decent-sized gash on his forehead and needed stitches.

Although Frank insisted he'd much rather spend time with Jo, he also insisted farmers needed to help one another, which Jo understood. So Frank took over the chores—milking cows, separating milk, slopping hogs, that sort of thing. Unfortunately that took a while. In his next breath, he had asked if he could stop by around one o'clock this afternoon, so Jo invited him for dinner.

Was this a repeat of last night?

At a quarter to two, she drew Brue into her arms. Holding back the hurt in her heart, she rested her chin on Brue's head and said, "Maybe we should think about eating."

Brue looked up with disappointment-filled eyes. "Why, Mom? I thought Mr. Breck was coming."

"I know. So did I, but something else must have come up."

Just then she heard tires on gravel and the killing of an engine. She didn't know if she should run to the door or avoid it altogether. What she did know was that she felt pure and utter relief.

She waited for the knock then sauntered casually to greet him. Frank stood on the steps with a smudge on his cheek, dirt on his trousers, two packages wrapped with brown paper and string, and a tin that appeared to be a container of candy.

"I'm sorry, Jo," he said. "I would have been here in plenty of time, but an elderly couple was stranded out in the middle of nowhere about a mile down the road from my place. Their tires were threadbare and one of them gave out. I had to give them my spare and put it on for them. Everything takes time."

She exhaled a relieved breath. He did have a good reason. "We're glad you made it."

"You might want to put this in the refrigerator," he said as he handed her the brown packages. "One's a chuck roast, the other's a couple of steaks." He then turned to Brue. "And this one's for you."

Brue popped the lid on the tin. "Peppermints! Oh, goodie. Thanks, Mr. Breck."

Jo placed the roast, potatoes, gravy, and string beans on the table. "We were getting ready to sit down. By the way, how did it go last night?"

He sniffed the food. "Smells good. How did what go?"

His unexpected response caught her by surprise. "The boy, silly. Is he okay?"

"Oh, that. Yeah, he's fine."

"What time did you get home?"

"I don't know. Around ten or so, I guess. Thought I should wait for them to get back from the hospital and then they offered me a cup of coffee. We don't get to talk much, so I stuck around for a while."

After dinner, Brue ran out to the park to play with friends while Frank and Jo sat on the front steps sipping iced tea. She thought about the persistent waiting on Frank and how it wasn't getting easier. After a few minutes of thoughtful silence, she said, "You had me worried, you know. First last night, then this afternoon. It looked like—"

"Like what?" He smiled ruefully. "Like I was going to stand you up?"

Jo nodded.

"No. I couldn't do that. Not to you." He reached over and gently brushed a lock of hair from her forehead, the tenderness in his eyes warming her and renewing hope. "You are without a doubt the most beautiful woman in all of the Upper Midwest," he said sincerely. "I'm not sure I'm worthy of you."

CHAPTER FIFTY-SEVEN

T hanks for agreeing to meet with me," Ole said. "I know it's last minute and you have plenty to keep you busy during business hours."

Tryg smiled. "Never too busy for a friend. How are you feeling?"

"Fit as a fiddle, thank you."

"I see you've gotten your color back."

Glancing up at the waitress, Ole paused. "I don't think we'll be needing menus, do you, Tryg? I'll have a lemonade."

"I'll have the same."

As the waitress walked away, Ole said, "My color, my spirits, my strength. Got them all back. The doc is a tough taskmaster, though. To say he has me exercising is an understatement. You'd think I'd just made varsity and we were practicing up for our first game. Wants me to cut back on tobacco, too, but I don't know. A man's got to enjoy life."

"You had us scared."

Ole nodded. "Sorry to do that to you … Tryg?"

"Yes?"

"What happened at the hearing? I've been anxious to hear about it."

Tryg hesitated. "I don't want to stress you, Ole."

"Nothing removes stress faster than dealing with a problem straight up. So tell me everything. I'm sure Wil was upset."

Tryg nodded. "The minute he laid eyes on me, he flew into a rage. Tried to elbow free, but the chief tightened his grip on him. Wil let me know in his own words that I was one of 'em and he never should have trusted any of us."

Ole opened his mouth, but the words got stuck. His fragile heart was ripping.

"It was hard to see him handcuffed," Tryg said. "Watching Chief Stout haul him away. It was probably best you weren't there."

"Did the boy even stand a chance?"

Tryg shook his head. "It was the most puzzling thing. I don't know why, but he refused to stand up for himself. He was resigned. Looked defeated. Chief Stout spoke in his defense. They let me say a few words, too, but there was no breaking through the system's concrete wall."

"How long was his sentence, did they say?"

"'Til he's eighteen."

Ole's shoulders slumped. "That's right. You did mention that in the hospital, didn't you? Eighteen!"

Tryg's tone took on a disgusted edge. "Seeing the mocking way that Anders kid walked out of the courtroom, I wanted to give him a left hook that would have sent him flying into Mower County. He looked as if he'd pulled one over on everyone, which he had."

"Over on everyone with the exception of you and me."

Tryg nodded. "He showed no remorse whatsoever over Wil either."

"Is that a fact? I think it's about time to have a long overdue chat with that lad. And speaking of Teddy, isn't that him walking across the street there?"

Tryg glanced over his shoulder. "Looks like he might be headed to his dad's office."

Ole stood. "Excuse me, Tryg. I need to see a very nasty boy about an unpleasant situation."

Ole stepped out onto East William and called across the street. "Anders? Wait up." Ole hurried across and gripped Teddy's elbow hard enough to draw a yelp then said through clenched teeth, "We're on our way to your father's office *now* and if you so much as whimper, you'll be behind bars before sundown."

"Leave me—"

"Let me be more clear. Your days of being protected have come to an abrupt end. Now let's get moving. I don't have all day."

Ole scooted Teddy briskly up Broadway holding a firm grip on the boy's elbow, half dragging him. When they reached the far end of the block, an officer pulled up and eased out of his patrol car.

"Police, police!" Teddy yelped. "I'm being kidnapped."

The officer bounded toward them. "Mr. Harrington," he acknowledged.

"Officer Dunhope, how nice to see you again."

Teddy's face scrunched into a scowl. Obviously this hadn't gone the way he had hoped.

"Where are you taking the boy?"

"Thought we'd have a nice little chat with his daddy."

"Looks like you could use an escort." Officer Dunhope seized Teddy's free arm. Between the two of them scooting the boy off hard and fast, Teddy's feet barely touched the ground.

When they reached the senior Anders' office, the officer backed off. "Let us know if you have any more problems, Mr. Harrington, and good luck with the boy's dad."

"Is Mr. Anders in?" Ole said to a startled middle-aged woman who hovered over a desk.

Anders appeared in an inner-office doorway, a scowl tacking another ten years onto his middle-aged face. "What's going on here? What are you doing with my boy?"

"We can talk about it out here where the whole world can hear," Ole said matter-of-factly, "or we can step into the privacy of your office. The choice is up to you."

Ole sensed his presence was unusually intimidating. Severe anger and self-righteousness will do that to a man, and at the moment he owned them both and could not have cared less.

The door closing behind them, Anders glared at Ole. "Do you mind telling me what this is all about? I reimbursed you for your hospital expenses, and Teddy's been walking the straight and narrow ever since."

"You make it sound as if you've been doing the town a favor. Well, I've got news for you. I've been protecting your son long enough. Gave him a chance. But your impertinent little weasel implicated his pal, Wil Thompson, and Wil was carted off to reform school. If that wasn't bad enough, I understand your son walked out of the courtroom looking a little too puffed up."

"Like I said, I paid you for any misdeeds so what's your problem now? From what I've heard, Wil deserves reform school," Mr. Anders said in a daring tone. "Everyone around town knows that boy's reputation, and I for one don't appreciate his negative influence on my son."

"Is that a fact?" Ole gave Teddy a severe frown then said, "Well, Anders, let me set the record straight. Your wayward son took advantage of Wil's reputation. Your son is the ruthless one, but it appears you don't care to see that. Teddy is the one who drove his bike into me, tore my cane away, threw it across the road into the grass, drug me across the gravel, and lodged enough kicks against my chest to nearly do me in. *Your* son, Anders," Ole spat. He was livid. "It was Wil Thompson who was in tears and made little Teddy boy here stop. It was Wil Thompson who came back to see if I was okay."

"Wait a minute," Anders said, looking like a drowning victim gasping for a last breath. "Something doesn't add up. If what you say is true, why would you let Wil take the heat for it? Why wouldn't he speak up for himself?"

"I asked him to, but he was more drawn to honor. That's something your son doesn't appear to understand. Wil decided he wanted to take his lumps for the rest of his trespasses. I saw something in that boy I knew I could work with. Working with your son, however, is an entirely different matter. He has ice coursing through his veins and I suggest you find a way to melt it."

Anders appeared to gulp at Teddy's smug grin.

"Wil told me your son will be old enough to join the Army next month," Ole continued, ignoring the brazen punk, "and that he wants to sign up. If he has a record, you know as well as I do there's no way on this troubled earth they'll take him. I've been planning to have a word with you since that nightmare happened, but other than the note I sent and your financial response, I wanted to see how things played out first. I have to tell you," Ole said shifting his gaze to Teddy, "seeing this heartless monster of yours send Wil up the river without giving it a second thought sends me over the edge."

Anders' already pale face turned a cooler shade of white.

"You will handle your son immediately if not sooner," Ole said, "or I will turn him in to Chief Stout without hesitation. I'll give you twenty-four hours to make a plan and not one second more. Let me know what you decide and why I should believe you. If I'm not satisfied, I promise you I'll have that chat with the chief twenty-four hours and one minute from now. Do I make myself clear?"

CHAPTER FIFTY-EIGHT

Ole poked around in the shed looking for a file. It didn't take long to find one. Labels lined the doors of all the cabinets. Everything in its place. Even the walls had special hooks and painted outlines for shovels, brooms, and saws. He filed a knife until sharp to the touch then plucked a small chunk of pine from the wood-pile and meandered to the front porch. He rocked, he whittled, and the rocking chair creaked.

With the exception of the war, Amber Leaf was at peace again. No more fretting about that wayward Thompson kid. Even Henrietta Braddingly appeared calmer, at least from a distance.

As for Ole, he was doing what he'd been doing day after day for the past three weeks—fretting about Wil, the boy's broken spirit, the tough new friends he was making at Red Wing, and how hard he would try to fit in. He worried about the harsh treatment that could destroy Wil's fragile existence. Ole relived over and over in his mind the warm, rich memories the two of them had built over the past few months. Wil was being molded into a decent, responsible young man, but now hope was dimmed and all because of the dismal new life he was forced to endure inside cold, dark, and dank prison walls.

The boy could have been lost to the war as easily, but at least there would have been honor that way. Harry Thompson was right about one thing. In an effort to make Wil's world better, Ole had reduced him to a failed experiment. When Wil needed him most, Ole could not deliver. Couldn't even make it to the courthouse.

Ole stopped whittling long enough to flick a wooden shaving from his shirtsleeve and then stopped altogether. Staring off, he relived that day in the kitchen, the day he had learned why Wil was so obsessed with hiding his wrist.

Ole had been studying him, trying to think of a way to ease his troubled soul. "You know, you never did tell me why you only roll up one sleeve," Ole had said nonchalantly, but the instant he reached for Wil's arm, Wil jerked it back, his eyes spewing shock and defensiveness.

"I'm asking you again. What's this all about, son? What are you hiding? You're among friends here. You know that."

Wil rubbed his arm and strolled to the other side of the kitchen, but then he turned back. He peered at Ole, the hurt in his eyes glaring.

Ole said nothing further. He stood quietly and waited.

"After ma died," Wil said finally, his gaze dropping to the floor as if he were reading from the pages of a book down there, "Pop took to the bottle. Went out all the time, you know, to get hammered. He kept leavin' me alone in that cold stinkin' house. I musta' been four or five back when this happened," he said with a quick glance at his wrist. "Don't remember if I was in school yet or not. I remember bein' scared to death every time he left, though. Don't know if I was afraid of losin' him, too, or scared of bein' alone." Wil hesitated as if thinking his words through and continued. "Anyways, one night he left to go out on another drunken binge. When I looked out the window and saw him headin' to his car, I don't why, but I panicked. I started poundin' on the window and hit it so hard my fist went straight through it. Glass shattered all over the place. I messed up my wrist real bad, but there wasn't no serious cuts to my veins or nothin'. Boy, did he get mad. It was in the wintertime, so instead a' goin' out on a drunk, he had to go out an' buy a brand new window and put it in. Yelled at me the whole time he was fixin' it. Said it was my fault he was a drunk. Said it was my fault my ma died. Said she would be ashamed of me for bein' such a baby."

"He blamed you for your mother's death?"

Wil nodded. "I hear about it all the time."

"You do know that's not your fault, right?"

Wil shrugged.

"Don't you go carrying that guilt around. It will eat you alive. It's not your fault. It just happened. Now about your wrist. Did you have any stitches?"

"Na'ah. It didn't bleed bad enough so I didn't need to go to no hospital or nothin'. I wrapped a cloth around it. Made sure it was tight."

"*You* wrapped a cloth around it? Where was your dad?"

"I told you. He was busy chewing me out the whole time he fixed the window. Called me a sissy."

Ole gently reached out his hand. "Let me take a look at it, son."

Wil jerked his arm back. "No."

"Son," Ole said, "I'd like to take a look at your arm. Be grateful if you'd hike up your sleeve."

Wil stood motionless for the longest while, then dutifully unbuttoned the sleeve, rolled it up to his elbow, and shoved out his wrist. "You wanna' see it? There it is!" he scoffed. "Now are ya happy?"

Ole could feel Wil's apprehensive yet surprised gaze as he lightly touched the scars on the boy's mutilated wrist. "It's not that bad. If I were you, do you know what I would do?"

"No, what would you do?" The edge was unmistakable in the boy's pained voice.

Ole smiled. "I think I'd be mighty proud of myself. No, come to think of it, I don't think I'd be proud—I know I would be. I'd show the entire world what a tough little shaver I'd been and how at that young age I was smart enough and cared enough about myself to bandage my own wound. That's what I would do, son. Yup! Without a doubt."

Ole's heart hurt at the memory. He set his chair back to rocking and gazed longingly at the bench out in the park where he and Wil had had their first encounter. He would give anything to see Wil ride his noisy bike along the paths again.

CHAPTER FIFTY-NINE

Ole unfolded the newspaper and spread it across the counter. "What's this world coming to, Sarah?" he asked. "Listen to this. 'Special to The New York Times ... Washington, Aug. 6 – The White House and War Department announced today that an atomic bomb, possessing more power than 20,000 tons of TNT, a destructive force equal to the load of 2,000 B-29's and more than 2,000 times the blast power of what previously was the world's most devastating bomb, had been dropped on Japan ... the 'age of atomic energy,' which can be a tremendous force for the advancement of civilization as well as for destruction, was at hand. At 10:45 o'clock this morning, a statement by the President was issued at the White House that sixteen hours earlier- about the time that citizens on the Eastern seaboard were sitting down to their Sunday suppers, an American plane had dropped the single atomic bomb on the Japanese city of Hiroshima ... The War Department said it 'as yet was unable to make an accurate report' because 'an impenetrable cloud of dust and smoke' masked the target area from reconnaissance planes.'"

Ole shook his head. "I don't even want to imagine the horror. Here we thought we had problems in Amber Leaf."

Sarah looked stupefied as he refolded the paper and strolled to the cribbage table. The story in the newspaper further suppressed Big Ole's already dampened spirits. He chewed on the words the way he chewed on his cigar and he grieved them.

Several minutes later Doc took up residence in the chair across from him. "You ready to get beat?"

Ole nodded. He wanted to get beat. This past month was one of the hardest he'd endured in years. Even talk of the war appeared distant, that is, until he read today's paper.

Doc peered over his bifocals. "Cards shuffled?"

"Ready to go."

As Doc dealt the cards, Ole glanced out the window, where a boy rode past on a beat-up bicycle.

"Looks a lot like Wil, doesn't he?" Doc asked. "Same color hair. A little smaller, maybe."

"Hmm?" Ole said emptily.

"Still thinking about Wil, are you?"

"Can't get him out of my head."

Merely seeing a boy on a bike was enough to give Ole that miserable feeling all over again. It was as if he'd lost a treasured son. He picked up the cards and arranged them. "You know, Doc," he said, "I've been thinking. You still drive."

"Yeah?"

"I'd like to see Wil. If I rounded up a package of goodies of some sort, would you consider giving me a lift to Red Wing? I need to find out first what sorts of things are allowable. What d'you say? Game?"

"I'd be happy to, Ole. You know that. Um, don't forget it's your turn."

Ole studied the pegs on the cribbage board then looked up. Charlie was carrying a cup of steaming coffee to Sarah who was sitting at the registration desk. The look in her eyes and the tenderness in Charlie's voice as he handed her the cup were arresting. And then the phone rang.

"O.M. Harrington House, Sarah speaking." Suddenly her face contorted into a question mark. "Really?" she said. "When? Are you positive?

Uh-huh. Any idea where he is?" She looked at Charlie and then glanced at Ole. "Okay, thanks. I'll let him know right away."

"Who was that?" Ole inquired from the far side of the room.

"Tryg."

"What did he want?"

Sarah wrung her hands. "He heard a rumor over supper."

Ole was apprehensive. Rumors were nothing more than speculation. "What kind of rumor would that be?"

"Wil escaped."

Big Ole caught his breath and shot up as if he'd instantly lost a hundred pounds. "Our Wil? He did what? But that can't be. When? From what I hear, the walls at Red Wing are sky high."

Sarah shook her head. "I have no idea, Grandpa. By the sound of things, it must have been about three weeks ago."

"But he's only been at that place for three weeks. That doesn't make any sense. Must be a rumor. Chief Stout would have told us by now if that was true. Did Tryg say where the boy is?"

"Looks like no one knows."

"Well, for heaven's sake." Ole felt a genuine grin sprout on his cheeks for the first time since Wil left.

"Grandpa, why are you smiling? When Chief Stout catches him, he's going to be in bigger trouble than he was before."

Ole ignored her. *Where could that young lad be?*

CHAPTER SIXTY

Never wager a bet unless you control the stakes.

Big Ole had held a strong hand, but ran out of time. Would it be possible to play another hand with Wil?

He sat on the front porch and slathered more butter on his already buttered toast. Ole had come from a decent home and had a decent chance in life right out of the hopper. He couldn't imagine, nor did he want to imagine, having cards stacked against him the way they were stacked against Wil. His cards ran counter to life's natural rhythm. Parents take care of their children who grow up, in turn, to take care of their aging parents. But Wil was left to raise himself, his father an adversary rather than a role model. Even with Ole's failed attempt, though, who more than he cared enough to guide Wil along?

"I see you've decided to eat outside this morning," Bernie said, breaking into Ole's musing. He pulled at his collar and looked about. "Sure is warm and sticky today, isn't it?"

"That's right," Ole said. "It's going to be a stifling one."

"Care for more coffee?"

"No, thanks. I think that should do it."

"But you're not eating your eggs, sir. Anything the matter with them?"

Big Ole had no desire to finish eating his eggs, neither did he have time to lollygag. "They're fine, Bernie." He choked down one last gulp of coffee then bounded down the porch steps.

Ambling up River Lane, he eventually made his way down Frank Avenue. He thought about Tryg. Where had he gotten his information? Who leaked it? Ole needed to take a breather, get his expectations down. If Tryg was right, if Wil was on the loose, why hadn't the chief bothered to say anything? He had to have known. Besides, in all that time someone would have seen the boy roaming around. Where was he living? Where was he getting food?

Ole reached Wil's ill-cared-for home having a hunch he would be nowhere in sight. If he was, his dad would cover for him. After appraising the house for the better part of a minute, Ole lumbered toward the backyard not stopping until he stood beneath Wil's tree house. He looked up and said, "Son?"

The question went unanswered in a quiet as heavy as the early morning air. Though not a leaf rustled nor a breath could be heard, Big Ole persisted. "Son? You up there?"

As he spoke, a robin flapped its wings then soared toward the tree. Rather than landing on a branch, it batted its wings and pitched upward not that high above, yet immediately over, the path of the tree.

"That—"

Big Ole peered up at the tree house and chuckled. "The little birdie get you, son?"

"How many times do I have to tell you I'm not your son?"

The loud whisper widened Ole's cheeks into a full-on grin. A short moment later, a couple of spindly legs shot out and dangled over the side of the tree house. A couple of worn sneakers. Pant legs dirty and frayed. Hole-infested filthy socks. What a magnificent sight.

"An' keep your voice down," the demanding whisper came again. "Someone might hear ya."

Ole leaned back against the trunk of the oak and twirled his cane, mimicking the limber movements of youth. "You plan on living in a tree the rest of your life? You huddle up there during a thunderstorm and a lightning bolt's going to make charcoal out of you. Come on down, son."

"No."

"I said come down."

"I ain't comin' down. I hate you, ol' man. You hear that? I said I hate you, an' I ain't gonna get sent away again. You tricked me before, an' you'll do it again."

"I didn't trick you. I think you know that. You know for a fact I wasn't the one who squealed on you."

"Then why didn't you bother showin' up for the hearin'?"

Ole looked down, his double chin folding against his throat. "I was hoping you would forgive me for that. I planned to be there … to stand up for you, but I couldn't get there."

"Oh, yeah? Why not? If it was important to you, you woulda' made it."

"It was. Very important. Unfortunately, the taxi didn't come, so I took off walking. Afraid I got a little sidetracked, but I can't undo that any more than I can unring Big Ben. You have no idea how upset I was."

"I hate you," Wil said again, this time through a voice set deep with hurt. His legs drew up and Ole's heart hollowed at the sound of cramped steps inching around on the thin planks overhead.

"You don't hate me." For a drawn-out moment, Ole wished he could press out all the blunders and all the hurt and make their lives whole. "You're a good boy, Wil."

"Liar. Good boys don't get sent up."

Ole smiled at that. "So tell me, why did you come home?"

Wil peered down from above. He looked confounded, but didn't move.

"Let me guess, the Packers, right?" Ole said. "In wanting to get back with the team, you're now torn between two worlds—one that could fulfill you and another that could entrap you, but your need to get back on the team trumps your fear of getting caught, right?"

Ole rested the back of his head against the tree trunk. What could he possibly do to help the boy now? "Come down, son."

Wil reluctantly crawled out, his feet hitting the ground with a thump.

Ole ran his fingertips along the bark of the tree then studied it from various angles and looked up. "Perfect place for a tree house," he said. "Brilliant, really."

"That's what my dad said."

"He was right. Speaking of your dad, I'll bet he's thrilled to have you home again. I know I am."

The boy shrugged.

"Look, Wil, I know he hasn't been the best father, but I was amazed to see how much he loves you. Didn't know he had it in him."

Wil looked stunned. For a moment, hope appeared to form in his eyes, but then his shoulders slumped. "Does not."

"You don't think so? You should have seen him the night before Chief Stout hauled you off."

Wil looked up.

"He came storming into the boarding house," Ole went on, "and gave me a tongue lashing like I've never experienced before. Said he knew he'd made a lot of mistakes, but he'd worked hard to toughen you up so you'd know how to handle life when you grew up. He asked me who I thought I was to mess it all up just because I had money."

Wil shifted his gaze toward the house, his expression radiating unmitigated disbelief. "Pop said that?"

"You'd better believe it. Made me feel like a real low-life."

"You mean my dad really stuck up for me?"

"Of course, he did." Ole hesitated, giving the weight of his words a chance to sink in. "Don't tell me he's never told you how much you meant to him before."

Wil cringed. "Ooooh, ick! That's sissy stuff."

"Oh, my," Ole said with a shake of his head, shuddering to think what it would be like stumbling around through life never being told you were loved. "You've got me in a tight spot here, Wil."

"Why?"

"You're up to hearing it? Be forewarned. We're wading in deep water."

"I can handle it if you can."

"I'll take that challenge. Who's the sissy? The one who has the courage to say 'I love you' or the one who doesn't?"

Wil bristled.

"I thought you said you could handle it. Your dad was the one who started all this sissy nonsense, wasn't he? That's probably how you got all broken up inside in the first place. Can you even say the word, Wil?"

"The love word? Yeah, I can. I love prime rib."

Ole chuckled. "Can you say, I love my dad?"

"I l-l ..."

When it became excruciatingly apparent Wil had to fight to get the word out, Ole said, "Takes courage to say it the first time, doesn't it? Eventually we all get used to saying it, though. You'll get around to it one of these days. There's no need to rush." Ole shook his head at the boy's misfortune.

Wil stood quietly. "What am I gonna do now, Mr. H?"

Mr. H. Ole warmed at the endearment.

"I didn't give a hoot about gettin' sent up," Wil continued, "at least not til my first day on the team."

"You mean when you hit that homer and won the game?"

"Yup. Now I don't got nowhere to go. I dunno' what to do with myself."

"That is a problem." Ole thought for a moment. "Do you understand what character is, Wil?"

Looking as if he'd never heard the word before, Wil shook his head.

Ole directed his cane up toward the tall oak. "Character is like that tree house you built up there. But character isn't the house we build on the outside, it's the house we build inside ourselves, the one nobody else can see. The house we build on the inside is the place where all of our thoughts and decisions are made. We can build a mansion or we can build a shack. We can make that place strong and wonderful, or putrid and decrepit. The choice is up to us."

Wil was quiet for a long moment. "Mr. H?"

"Hmm?"

"I don't hate you, not really."

Big Ole looked down into the cow eyes that begged, 'please tell me you don't hate me, too.' "I know you don't."

Wil did his usual punching his hands in his pockets and kicked at the grass.

"You took a chance coming back to Amber Leaf, Wil. If I heard you're back in town, you can bet Chief Stout's heard by now, too. He's probably already on the hunt. You're a smart kid, though. I guess I didn't need to tell you that, did I?"

"Have you talked to him?"

"Yes, I did."

"How much did you tell 'im?" Wil asked, defensiveness evident in his tone.

Ole suddenly felt crushed with regret. He didn't have the heart to tell Wil, yet he had to. "Everything," he said softly.

"*Every*thing?" Wil shimmied back up into the tree. "Go away."

"Now, Wil. I was only trying to get him on your side. I thought if he saw the whole picture and understood—"

"Didn't you hear what I said? I said go away. I don't never wanna see you again."

"Hey, what're you doin'?" Harry yelled through an open window. "Get outa' here. Leave my boy alone."

"But—"

"Haven't you done enough? I said git."

Ole cringed. Being chastised smarted something awful. Shoulders slumping, he shuffled past the house and down the sidewalk feeling utterly defeated.

CHAPTER SIXTY-ONE

B rue swirled her mashed potatoes around and around on her plate, lost in the cares of her little-girl world. In the quiet, she appeared hesitant to take a bite.

"There wouldn't be something going on in the neighborhood that I should know about, would there be?" Jo asked.

Brue glanced up, appearing surprised by the question. "Why?"

"Because on my way home, I saw Big Ole sitting out in the middle of the park, looking every bit as dejected as you. If I didn't know better, I'd say whatever the two of you have is contagious."

Brue propped her fork up and curled her small fingers around the handle, standing its tines on the plate. She held it the way one would rest on a pitchfork for a tired moment. "Is it ever right to snitch, Mom?"

"What?"

Brue shrugged.

Jo thought about Brue's question for a transient moment. "Why are you asking?"

"If I tell you, then I might be snitching, and I don't wanna be a snitch."

"Has somebody done something wrong? Is that it?"

Brue lifted her shoulders and her eyes widened.

"When Big Ole got hurt, we called an ambulance, right? Our purpose wasn't to stir things up, or get attention. He needed help. But, if we're trying to hurt someone by spreading the word, now that would be wrong. Snitching sounds bad, like you're purposely trying to get someone into trouble. Did someone do something wrong?"

Brue shrugged again.

"I think you'd better let me know what's going on," Jo said matter-of-factly.

Brue dropped her forehead on her palm and studied the table. "I saw that Wil guy today."

"You what? That can't be. Are you sure it was him?"

"Yup." Brue peered through a shock of hair. "But I don't want to get him in any trouble."

"Oh, sweetie," Jo said. "Don't worry about that. I'm relieved it was you who saw him. Where was he?"

"Chasing that Teddy guy. Poke and I were coming home from school when we saw him, and did he ever look mad."

"Angry. Did he ever look angry, sweetie, not mad. Did he see you?"

"I don't think so. They were running around the corner on First Street, but they were heading the other way. It was kind of scary."

"I can only imagine." Jo poked a fork at her meatloaf and played with it. "Have you heard anything about Wil's being home from anyone else?"

"Nope."

"And you're absolutely certain it was him?"

"Uh-huh."

"Let's finish supper. I think we need to take a walk over to the O.M. Harrington and have a chat with Big Ole. He looked so sad when I saw him. Let's cheer him up. Who knows?" Jo cut a smile. "Big Ole might even be able to help Wil."

In the evening's diminishing light, Jo and Brue were strolling across

Harrington Park when suddenly the cry, "Olly Olly oxen free," broke above the crickets' trill. Brue's friend, Poke, shot out from behind a hedge as a handful of reluctant kids surfaced here and there.

"Hey, Brue," Poke cried. "Wanna come and play hide an' seek with us? These guys are all cheats. I need someone who's easy to catch."

Brue rolled her eyes. "Can I, Mom?"

Moments after the kids ran off, Jo paused at the entrance of Big Ole's office. "Mind if I come in?"

He looked up. "Not at all, Jo. Where's your little girl?"

"Out in the park playing with Poke and some other little friends."

"Evelyn's boy?"

Jo nodded and offered a warm smile. "Have you heard the news?"

"Afraid so."

"What do you mean, 'afraid so'? If I didn't know any better, I'd say you sound disappointed."

"I saw Wil this morning. The kid glared at me like I was poison. Says he hates me." Ole unthinkingly wrung his hands, as if he were attempting to wipe away his disappointment with a washcloth. "Can't say as I blame him. He has every right. Everything seemed to go okay until Wil asked about Chief Stout, about how much he knew."

"And?"

"I told him the truth, that I'd told the chief everything. Wil didn't even give me a chance to say why."

Jo reached out and straightened a crooked lampshade until it hung just so. "Everything?"

Big Ole nodded.

"Why would he have a problem with that?"

"What are you getting at?" Ole asked.

"I was here when you talked to the chief and heard every word you said. Remember? You never violated Wil."

Big Ole's eyebrows shot up. "Of course not. I'd never do that." But then as realization dawned on him, he slumped back in his chair. "Oh, my. What have I done?" Ole recalled Wil's wet pants and cringed. "There's something else that happened, something personal that I held back even from you. No wonder he thinks I've betrayed him to the one person who could put him behind bars again. How can I go back and change Wil's perception now?"

"You've got to have another talk with him. You've got to make this right."

"It's too late," Ole said. "I've already tried that and messed everything up."

Jo lifted her chin. "I'm not meaning to be unkind here, but it might be you who doesn't understand. What do you do when a horse throws you?"

"He's not a horse, and even if he were, he would have had every right to throw me. He thinks I've violated him not only with my actions, but with my words, too. Now he won't have anything to do with me."

"Neither will a horse that has thrown you."

"I wish it were that easy."

Jo strolled over to the window and gazed out across Harrington Park. "Would you mind coming here for a miute? I think you might want to take a look at this," she said.

Ole got up and joined her.

"See Brue and Poke and their friends out there playing?"

"Yes. What about it?"

"They look as if they don't have a care in the world, don't they? Now, compare them to Wil. Imagine what life must be like for him. The Pokes and the Brues and all the other kids in the neighborhood have mothers that bake cookies and bring them to school. Mothers that pack lunches with sandwiches and fruit, do their laundry, lay their clothes out for them to wear every day. Drive them to dancing lessons and ballgames and children's after-school parties. But Wil? He's never had any of that. Any healthy attention he's ever gotten must have been negligible." Jo led the way back to Ole's desk. "Why do you think Wil came home?"

"He misses the Packers. Didn't take much to figure that out."

"Do you think he's going to be content watching their games from behind tall bushes? How long is that going to last? He obviously can't play. He'd get caught and hauled back to Red Wing in a heartbeat. Where's he going to go? What's he going to do? He needs you."

"But what about Chief Stout? What happens when he finds out Wil's back?"

Jo grinned. "Do you honestly believe he doesn't know? If you and I found out Wil's back in town, he has to know by now, too. Think about it. Doesn't quite add up, does it? And why hasn't the chief told you or anyone else about Wil's escape? Why hasn't he come looking for him? If he's trying so hard to find him, you'd think he'd be pounding the sidewalks trying to get information."

Ole eased into his chair. "You know, I've been wondering the same thing. Feared it was wishful thinking on my part. But I've got to be careful, Jo. This could be a trick. That said, what can I do about this whole mess now? I crossed Wil."

"No. That's not true and you know it. Wil crossed himself, and if anything, Wil crossed you."

"But if he thinks I've been spreading personal stuff about—"

"What about the beating you took? Chief Stout only strong-armed you so he could send Wil up. You've done everything in your power to keep that from happening. Take a chance. Give Wil another try. Somehow I've got a strong feeling Chief Stout is purposely looking the other way." Jo paused. "And so do you."

CHAPTER SIXTY-TWO

A familiar, out-of-place voice droned from down the hallway What a curious time for an unannounced visitor.

"I need to have a word with Mr. Harrington," the man said, his tone uncertain.

Determined footsteps pounded up the hallway, and then a man stopped at Ole's door appearing utterly defeated. Unfortunately, he had arrived too late.

"Mind if I come in?"

Ole leaned an elbow on a chair arm. "And if I said yes?"

"Can't say as I blame you."

Mr. Anders removed his fedora. He stepped no more than a foot inside Ole's office and walked nervous fingers around the rim of his hat.

Why do people feel a need to manipulate with pathetic looks? Ole wondered. Why can't they have the decency to play fair? "Okay," he said with a resigned sigh. "Have a chair."

Anders hustled in looking as if he needed to take a seat before Ole changed his mind.

"Isn't it kind of late for a visit? If you've come pleading for your son, you've come too late. We had a deadline. You didn't meet it. I'm a stickler on deadlines, Anders," Ole said sharply.

"I understand."

"Have you heard anything about Wil?"

"You mean that he's home now?"

Ole looked at him blankly, searching him out.

"Yes," Anders admitted. "He and Teddy had words out on our back porch last night."

"Does anyone else know Wil's in town?"

"I have no idea."

"Well," Ole said, "about your son. Now that my head's screwed on straight again, I finally got around to calling Chief Stout this morning. Told him we needed to have a chat, that I was finally ready to come clean. He said he'd stop by first thing in the morning. You should know that with the exception of Wil's being home again, I plan to tell him everything. I'm not holding back. What your boy did to Wil Thompson was inexcusable."

Anders' eyes looked vacant. "No. It's worse than that. What my boy did to you was inexcusable." Looking as if he were viewing a crime scene rather than staring into the eyes of an unhappy old man, Anders' tone was contrite. "It's not necessary for you to talk with the chief."

"Oh, but I disagree. It couldn't be more necessary. Unfortunately, due to my miscalculations and my insatiable need to run the world my way, I'm also running ridiculously late."

Anders shook his head. "Let me finish. Please. It's taken me a while, but I've finally come to my senses." Anders' gaze scraped the floor. "It took my boy attacking his mother to shake me out of my blind stupor. Last night that little viper pinned her to the wall. I had to pull him off. My own son attacked his mother. I don't know what was the matter with me. Why couldn't I see it?"

"Want a smoke?" Ole said, pulling out a cigar box.

"Sure thing. Thanks."

Anders' words hit Ole hard in the gut. Needing time to absorb them, he held out the box then swiped a match against a thumbnail. When it burst into flame, he held the fire until Anders' cigar lit and then lit his own. He shook the match until the flame blew out, tossed it in an ashtray, and slowly eased back in the chair.

"I turned Teddy in earlier this afternoon," Anders said tightly. "Pulled out all the stops. Told Chief Stout everything."

"But what about the Army? Teddy will never get in with any kind of record."

Anders shook his head. "He doesn't deserve to get in. Besides, that wouldn't be fair to the Army."

Ole identified all too well with Anders' pain, having suffered the incarceration of his own son-in-law. He got up, sauntered to the far side of the desk, and clapped Anders on the shoulder. "I'm sorry. You have my sympathy, and if it means anything to you at all, you also have my respect."

Anders looked up. "How could this happen, Mr. Harrington? My kid comes from a good home. We give him everything he needs, everything including attention. Where did we go wrong?"

Ole stared at the humble and broken man sitting before him. He looked pale, gaunt, and crushed with grief. "Who's to say? You know, Mr. Anders, life can be strangely inconsistent. Bad parents have bad kids. Bad parents have good kids. Good parents have bad kids. Good parents have good kids. I doubt it's right for any of us to take credit for the good or the bad, but in your case, there may be hope yet."

For the first time anticipation revealed itself in Anders' defeated eyes.

"There's a man who visits prisons, preaches to inmates. He's had a pitiable walk in their shoes. Since he's been more than successful cleaning up his own life, the inmates respect him. He's been instrumental in helping turn a good number of their lives around. He has the heart for it. I'll put a bug in his ear to spend some time with Teddy. That's a promise."

"But how do you know the man will want to?"

"Oh, he'll want to all right." Ole smiled as he announced with great pride, "He's my son-in-law."

CHAPTER SIXTY-THREE

It was well after dark when someone huffed up Jo's front steps. Then no sound at all followed by a tentative knock, loud enough for her to hear.

"Who's there?"

"It's me," came a loud whisper. "Big Ole."

She opened the door only to have him push it back and lead the way into her living room. "I saw your lights on. Mind if I come in?"

Jo offered an armchair. Brue was already in bed. "You're uncharacteristically secretive. What's going on?"

"I'm cashing in on your offer."

"What offer is that?"

"The one about Wil."

A grin broke loose as Jo said hopefully, "You mean you've had another talk with him?"

"Yes, ma'am. In about a half hour or so, there'll be a knock on your back door. It will be Wil." Big Ole chuckled and said, "By the way, I invited myself to supper at Tryg's house tonight. That man needs a good woman, Jo. Can't cook for squat."

She laughed. "But what does that have to do with Wil?"

"Everything. Tryg agreed to take him in for a while. As soon as the boy arrives, would you mind giving us a lift to his house?"

Jo had no more than awakened Brue when Wil knocked on the back door. A short while later, they arrived at Tryg's home. Wil hadn't said a peep the entire time. He looked overwhelmed and uncomfortable, like a kid making his way up the steps on his first day of kindergarten.

Holding the door open, Tryg whisked them inside. That sickening feeling of aiding and abetting that Jo had been struggling with took a surprising twist. Exhilaration coursed through her as if she were working in the underground for a righteous cause.

After Tryg grabbed Wil's paltry belongings and showed him to his new room, they gathered around the table.

"You know, Wil," Big Ole said, "there's something you haven't told me yet. How'd you manage to escape?"

Wil studied Tryg, Jo, and then Brue.

"They're safe," Ole said with unusual warmth. "You can talk freely in front of them."

Wil didn't appear convinced, but then said, "Chief Stout took my handcuffs off when we got in the squad car. Said they would hurt too much to keep on for that long a ride. We had to stop in Faribault for gas, so when he told me he was gonna go into the station for a minute to pay for it an' that he expected me to be sittin' in the front seat of the patrol car when he got back out, I gave him the slip."

Ole looked first to Jo and then to Tryg as if seeking confirmation of what he'd heard. "What did you do for food?"

"A five-dollar bill was sittin' on the front seat." Wil suddenly looked conscience-stricken. "I took it."

That Chief Stout. He set Wil up.

Ole shook his head. "So where've you been all these weeks?"

"Down to Texas and back."

"Texas? But how did you get there?"

"Boxcars."

"Five dollars isn't going to buy a few weeks' worth of food," Tryg challenged.

"It didn't. I jumped off here and there and did a few odd-and-end jobs. Sent the chief the five bucks I owed him, too," Wil admitted and for the first time he cut a grin.

"He had to be pleased to get that," Ole said approvingingly.

Wil suddenly appeared disengaged.

"Son?" Ole prodded. "When you told me the reason you came back was because of the Packers, those few days on the team were probably the happiest days of your life, weren't they?"

Wil nodded.

"That being the case, I think you'd better show up for the game on Saturday, and suit up."

"But if Chief Stout—"

Ole chuckled. "He left you in the squad car at the gas station in Faribault while he went in to pay for gas, right?"

"Uh-huh."

"He happened to leave you there all by yourself. No handcuffs. In the front seat. Door unlocked."

Light flickered in Wil's blue eyes.

"And he just happened to leave a five dollar bill lying on the front seat—and he just happened to leave a five dollar bill," Ole repeated. "Somehow, I've got a feeling you're not going to have any problems with Chief Stout, but we do need to be careful until we understand what's going on here."

At a quarter past ten and after a few heartfelt goodnights, Ole paused. "Wil? You be sure to show up for work tomorrow now, too, you hear?"

CHAPTER SIXTY-FOUR

Night passed with sleep visiting in fitful waves, sheets coiling about Jo's legs, so she got up rooster early and headed out with Brue, leaving her to spend another warm summer's day with the Wilder's. Arriving at the office an hour early, she perked a smaller pot of coffee since Ardena was taking the day off.

When Tryg came whistling in a half hour late, Jo looked up. "How'd it go last night?"

"Good morning to you, too." He grinned. "Not too bad, I guess."

"Like having a roommate?"

"I do, but I think it's going to take a while for him to adjust." Tryg slipped his fedora over a hook on the coat rack and fussed with his necktie. "Being treated well must feel foreign to him. You should have seen his eyes light up when I brought home pecan rolls from the bakery this morning. At first he seemed reluctant to eat. Said he didn't have any money to pay for them. It didn't take much to convince him it was my treat. We had bacon and eggs and orange juice, too."

"Makes you wonder if he's ever had a decent breakfast in his life," Jo said.

"I was thinking the same thing. Some day when the coast is clear, I'd like to take him to the Hotel Albert for breakfast. And speaking of breakfast, is the coffee perked yet?" His voice faded as he disappeared into the back room.

Listening to the splash of liquid and the clink of the coffee pot against the hot plate, Jo projected her voice. "Tryg?"

"Hmm?"

"How long do you think Wil needs to stay with you?"

He peeked around the corner and winked.

Jo's heart skipped a beat. *How I wish he wouldn't do that.*

"Shouldn't be long. Just 'til Ole has a chance to clear things up with the chief."

"But what I don't get," Jo said, "is why Chief Stout didn't tell anyone Wil ran away in the first place."

Tryg reappeared holding his cup at the ready for a sip. "Gets you to wondering, doesn't it? We're going to have to keep the wrong authorities from getting wind of Wil's presence. They'll haul him back to Red Wing in a heartbeat. Speaking of hauling people places—"

"Yes?"

"I had a chat with Sarah a couple of days ago," Tryg said, lightly placing the cup on Jo's desk. "We're toying with the idea of a boating adventure. Having a little picnic, renting a boat, that sort of thing. We checked our calendars. The soonest we can do it would be three weeks from Sunday."

"That's nice," Jo said. "You'll have lots of fun."

"We definitely will. I thought it would be a good idea if we had a little company, too. Sarah agreed."

"Anyone I know?"

"As a matter of fact, yes. She was telling me she and Charlie entertained Brue while you were at the boarding house having a chat with Big Ole sometime back. They both adore her. One thing led to another. Next thing you know, we decided it would be fun if you and Brue could join us. I've already talked with Charlie. He's up for it, too."

Jo's breath caught. Charlie? Sarah? Jo? Brue? What on earth was

Tryg thinking? "Sarah's up for this? Why would she want a mother and a young girl tagging along? Wouldn't it be more fun to go with another couple?"

"No, not at all. Sarah seemed thrilled with the idea. What's the matter? Don't you want to come?"

Absolutely not. "Of course. Sounds like an adventure."

"Great. Three weeks from this Sunday it is, at one o'clock," Tryg said and then he headed into his office. Whistling again.

She watched his door close. For being so smart, that man wasn't thinking. To invite Jo and Brue was one thing, but Charlie, too?

CHAPTER SIXTY-FIVE

Tryg ran a pencil along the straight edge and stopped long enough to watch Wil come in. "How was work?"

Wil took short, deliberate steps across the kitchen, his expression stone sober, eyes gathering moisture.

Tryg straightened. "What's the matter?"

"How come nobody told me about Big Ole?"

"You mean about his heart attack?"

Wil nodded.

Tryg tapped the tip of the pencil on the table a few times. "That's right," he said thoughtfully. "You couldn't have known. It happened when you were at your hearing. I'm sorry, Wil. To us, it's already old business, and Big Ole is doing great."

Wil's expression was crestfallen. "But—"

"But what? Did he have the heart attack because of you?"

Wil nodded reluctantly.

"Don't put that on yourself. There were a lot of contributing factors. Age. Exercise. Weight. Stress. But he's doing fine now, so don't give it another thought, okay?"

"But he said he was on the way to the courthouse when he got sidetracked."

"You didn't answer my question. How was work?"

A blush colored Wil's cheeks. "Bernie got all mushy on me."

"He did?"

Wil got sidetracked, too. That was a good thing.

"After he told me about Big Ole, he told me how much he missed me when I was gone. I never saw him get all teary-eyed before. He even threw a towel at me. Said the work wasn't gonna get done by itself. Then he looked away awful fast."

"Sounds like Bernie. He's an old softy if I've ever seen one."

Wil stepped closer to the table and crossed his arms over his tee shirt. He looked awkward, uncomfortable with himself. "What are you doing there?" he asked.

Tryg penciled in another line. "I'm drawing plans for a new house. Found a nice little piece of land east of town I've been thinking about buying."

"But you ain't married."

"No, not yet, but I hope to be some day."

Wil peered over Tryg's shoulder as he penciled out a few calculations. "Who you plannin' on marryin'?" he asked, sounding overly curious.

"I don't know yet."

"I think you should marry Jo Bremley."

The lead on Tryg's pencil snapped. He swiveled back. "Jo Bremley? Where'd that come from?"

Wil cracked a smile. "She's the most beautiful lady I ever laid eyes on. Mr. Harrington says she ain't only beautiful on the outside, she's beautiful on the inside, too."

"There's a couple of problems with that," Tryg said, leaning into the table. "For starters, Jo and I are friends and we can never be any more than that."

"Why not?"

"We can't, that's all. Besides, at the moment I'm seeing Sarah Harrington." Tryg wanted to add 'not that it's any of your business,' but he didn't want to be rude. He gave Wil a quick once over and then resumed drawing his plans. "Want anything to munch on? There's some fruit and cheese in the refrigerator."

"Thanks." Wil opened the door and buried his nose. "Can I have some a these instead?"

Tryg looked up. "Help yourself."

Wil strolled back to the table carrying a handful of oatmeal raisin cookies. "Ain't you afraid of Charlie? I mean, cutting into your territory and all?"

"Boy, you can be direct, can't you?"

"Well, ain't you?"

"Why would I be?"

"Cuz I see him and Miss Harrington talkin' to each other all the time."

"What's wrong with that? Jo talks to Big Ole all the time. Do you think they have anything going on?"

"Yeah, but that's different," Wil said, chucking a whole cookie in his mouth and chomping down.

"Why's that different?"

"Man, for being such a bright guy, you sure can be slow. Think I'll go an' sit out on the porch for a while. Inhale a little a' that clean night air before I turn in."

Tryg watched the closing door. A cool puff of air crossed the threshold, unusually cool for a late summer's evening.

CHAPTER SIXTY-SIX

With a hangdog look, Wil said, "Mind if I come in, sir?"

"Since when do you need an invitation? You look like you're carrying the weight of the world on your shoulders. Last I checked, you're not Atlas."

Wil looked around appearing to have difficulty facing Ole head on. He tried stuffing a hand in a pocket, but missed.

"Spit it out, son," Ole said.

"Bernie told me you had a-a heart attack. Why didn't you tell me? That's why you didn't make it to my hearing, ain't it?"

"What good would it have done to tell you, Wil? It's in the past. Little harm done. Looks like our Maker wasn't as ready for me as I'd thought he was. Besides, I'm back to my old self again." Ole smiled warmly. "But thank you for caring."

Wil nodded thoughtfully and looked around again. He inhaled a breath and quickly punched it out. "When I was ridin' the rails, I got a lotta time to think. There's somethin' you ain't never told me, somethin' that don't make no sense."

"What's that?"

Wil looked as if he preferred running away and hiding. "That night Teddy and me roughed you up, how could you go and forgive me for doing an awful thing like that to you?" he asked, his voice rough with feeling. "And then I go and sob like some kinda girl or something the whole time I'm trying to undo what we just done. And you saw what my dad did to me when he shoved me into the kitchen—you know, the first time you stopped by the house. It don't figure. When I thought he was gonna hit me, I started shaking all over the place and tried to run away. I didn't even stand up to him. It's not like I'm a little shaver or somethin'. I'm even taller than him," Wil said sheepishly, his eyes darting to the floor. "I couldn't stand to look at myself. I musta' gagged you, and you didn't even look embarrassed for me."

Ole smiled encouragingly. "That's because I wasn't."

"Why not? If you woulda' done that, it woulda' made me sick. But what did you do? After Teddy and I beat on you, you hunted me down and took me in. And when my dad grabbed my arm and tried to hit me again, you stopped him. You wasn't even scared."

"You know, Wil, the very things you were embarrassed about were the very things I found endearing."

"But why? That don't make no sense."

"Yes it does. Think about it. That's when I knew we had something to work with."

"But—"

"But nothing. Let those memories go, Wil. You're safe with me."

"But only sissies—"

"What? Cry? Want to bet? You'll gain courage as you get older. It's all a part of life, boy."

Wil paced nervously. "But there's somethin' else, too. I wanted to say," he hesitated then looked down, "I'm sorry, really sorry, for everything. You never did nothing to deserve what Teddy and me done to you, and you never deserved … what I'm tryin' to say is … "

"Is?" Ole said.

Wil's lips twitched as he choked out a broken, "Forgive me. Please, forgive me."

Wil disappeared into the hallway, his head hanging. Ole should have felt elated and grateful with the way he'd tried to make things right, but he didn't. Wil was the better man, and here he was just a boy. After all these weeks he courageously asked for forgiveness for taking part in Ole's beating and for cowering when he felt he should have stood up to his dad like a man. Although reluctant, Wil had had the courage and humility to ask forgiveness from each and every person he had violated when he indulged in his selfish acts of theft, too. He hadn't done it verbally where only those he'd violated were a witness. He wrote his requests with his own hand where the world could read it for years to come.

Now Ole was caught in a miserable place, a place where he had participated in something that wasn't bad enough to come clean about, but too bad to forget. What right did Ole have to require more of Wil than he required of himself? Ole had unfinished business, too, and if he wanted to take pride in the face that stared at him in the mirror every morning, noon, and night, he needed to reclaim his own respect as well. He picked up the phone and dialed. After the third ring, a female voice answered. An elderly female voice.

"Is Mrs. Braddingly in?"

"This is Henrietta Braddingly."

"Mrs. Braddingly, this is Big Ole Harrington."

Listening hard, he thought he heard shallow breathing at the far end of the line, but nothing more. "Mrs. Braddingly? Mrs. Braddingly, are you there? Do we need to call you an ambulance?"

After a long and protracted moment, the vacant words, "I'm here," worked their way through the wires.

"I have something to say, but I would prefer saying it in person. I was wondering if—"

"That won't be possible, Mr. Harrington. Anything you have to say to me I'm afraid you're going to have to say over the phone."

Digestive juices shot up into Ole's throat like pistons up a cylinder. Perspiration soaked his palms. "Very well." He took a sizable breath and forced out the words, "I've called to ask for your forgiveness." There. He'd done it. The words were out and could not be retrieved.

"Go on."

With what? Ole suddenly feared how far the woman was capable of pushing him at this rare and exceedingly vulnerable moment. Although she could be a bully, that didn't give Ole the right to be a bully, too. "You came bringing flowers," he said. "Instead of expressing my gratitude, I was harsh with my words and overtly disrespectful, and for that I am truly sorry."

"Very well," she said. A click followed and then dead silence.

That smarted.

He smiled in spite of her rebuff for he once again felt free. *And while I'm at it, I might as well get all of this sappy stuff out of the way.* He picked up the phone again and when he heard unpleasant muttering on the other end of the line, he grinned into the receiver. "Me and my taxi, we'll stop by and pick you up Saturday at a quarter to one."

"Why?" Harry Thompson asked, irritation percolating through his tone.

"Because you and me, we have a date to go to the Packer's game. You be ready, and you'd better not be drunk. If I smell anything on you at all, it better not be any stronger than aftershave."

After an unhealthy moment of irksome quiet, Harry said, "What makes you think I even wanna go to that fool game, let alone with you?"

"You," Big Ole countered. "Your honor. I'm taking you at your word."

"What word's that?"

"Your son. You said you cared about him. I think it's high time you proved it."

Harry harrumphed and slammed down the phone, leaving Ole once again staring into a dead receiver.

A few minutes before closing time, the door swung open and Jo looked up. "Wil?"

"Hi, Mrs. Bremley," he said, appearing uncomfortable.

Jo turned to Ardena. "Have you had the privilege of meeting Wil Thompson yet?"

"No, I don't believe I have." Ardena got up and offered him her hand. "Nice to meet you. I've been hearing wonderful stories about your athletic abilities."

The tips of Wil's ears turned rosy red. "Thanks. Is Mr. Howland in? He asked me to stop by if I could take an hour or two off work so we could hit a few balls."

"He's in," Tryg said, coming up behind them, grinning like a proud father. "I see you've all gotten a chance to meet one another. Did you bring the bat, balls, and mitts along, Wil?"

"I tossed them in the back seat of your car this morning."

"Great. Then let's hit the road. Good night, ladies."

"You look love struck again, Jo," Ardena said after the door clinked shut.

Jo felt as if a glass of water hit her face.

"Try as you may, you still look contented as an old heifer whenever Tryg's around, especially so when he's all caught up in whatever it is he's doing."

"I'm merely pleased to see him watching out for Wil. That boy needs all the help he can get."

"Tell that to your eyes. They're not in tune with your heart."

Jo turned sharply on Ardena. "Tryg is in a relationship."

"Some relationship. Did you forget about Charlie already?"

"I know," Jo admitted. "But if it wasn't for him, Sarah would be ideal for Tryg."

"Right. Sarah would be ideal for Tryg," Ardena said, her tone uncharacteristically mocking. "I've been doing a lot of thinking about this. There's no question she's a wonderful person and a real beauty, but she could never be as perfect for Tryg as you would be. Forgive me for saying this, but now that Charlie is cutting in ..."

Jo stared at Ardena's moving lips. Pressure from the outside didn't seem to let up these days. Knowing Ardena meant well, Jo endured. Passively. Allowing the words to flow through one impervious ear and out the other without allowing them to take root in her heart.

"I'm not meaning to be unkind here, but Case is dead, Jo. When are you going to accept that?"

Except for those words. They touched off a land mine. "That's not the problem, and you know it."

Ardena's eyes radiated frustration. "Then what is the problem? Don't tell me things are getting serious with Frank."

"No. It's Case. He's dead because of Tryg."

"No," Ardena corrected, her tone resolute. "Case is dead because of a car accident."

Jo walked back to her desk as if she could walk away from the memory and be rid of it once and for all. "Tryg was driving with a bum leg."

"And he swerved to miss a deer, and during a blinding snowstorm as I recall."

Ardena had no idea how difficult she was making this for Jo. "Look, I can't get past this, okay? I could never give my heart to Tryg after he shaved decades off Case's life, and I couldn't do that to Case. Neither could Tryg. It wouldn't be right. Besides, I won't be around much longer, anyway."

"Why?"

"Brue and I are still planning on moving to New York."

"What about Frank?"

"I'm crazy about him, but my gut tells me that's not going to go anywhere."

Ardena sighed. "Any idea when you're planning on leaving?"

"A year or so. Sooner if I can swing it. My cousin lives there, and it would be good for Brue to be around family."

"Margaret?"

"No, Shirley. Margaret lives in the Cities."

CHAPTER SIXTY-SEVEN

Ole sat in the back seat, his thoughts a tangle of grumbles. Of all the ridiculous times for a taxi driver to be in a hurry, why did he have to choose today?

When the brakes screeched and the cab lurched in front of the Thompson home, Ole hesitated to look up. He feared what he might find. To his surprise, Harry stood waiting on the porch. Although scowling, he was clean-shaven with a clean tee shirt and slicked down hair.

Harry hopped in. "I hope you know what you're doin', Harrington."

"Don't worry about it," Ole said. "I believe I've sized up the chief right."

"But what if you didn't? My boy could be in real trouble showing up at the game."

"That's a risk I'm willing to take."

"What about the risk I'm willing to take? Like I said, you better know what you're doin.'"

Ten minutes later they made a beeline for the ball field. Ole balked at the crowd. The only seats left were either reserved or in the nosebleed region at the top of the jamb-packed bleachers. Why hadn't he thought to get to the game sooner?

"Well, would you take a gander at that," Harry mocked. "I see they're reserving seats for goody two-shoes at ball games nowadays. What's this world comin' to?"

"Hey, Mr. H! Pop!"

Ole swiveled around. "Wil," he said. "What are you doing out in the bleachers, boy? You've got a game to play."

Harry looked on, appearing shy around his own flesh and blood.

"The reserved seats here," he said with a point of a finger, "they're for you and Pop." He dashed back to the field, leaving Ole feeling grateful and Harry standing with a dropped jaw.

"He's a fine boy, Harry," Ole said.

Harry gave Ole a thoughtful nod, but then suddenly appeared distracted. He looked past Ole and frowned. "Well, looky who's comin' to ruin our day."

"Mr. Harrington." Chief Stout headed toward them at a fast clip with an outstretched hand that played havoc with Ole's gut feel. What if Ole was wrong? Needing the man on his side, Ole didn't hesitate to stand and vigorously shake hands with a grinning chief of police.

But not Harry.

"And if it isn't the great Harry Thompson." When Chief Stout reached out to him, Harry appeared reluctant to seize his powerful grip.

"Mind if I join you gentlemen?"

Ole slid over to make room. "Not at all. Happy to have you, Chief."

Harry sat up straight. Locking his gaze on the outfield, he crossed his arms tightly across his beer-bellied chest, his right heel digging compulsively into the dirt.

Chief Stout eyed the team. "Say, Harry ... I understand the coach has your boy pitching today. This is a game I couldn't bring myself to miss."

"Why?" Harry snapped. "So you can haul him off again? How'd he escape in the first place? You were right there. He couldn't a' gotten away on his own."

"I fear I was remiss," the chief said understatedly. "How it could have happened is beyond me."

Ole smiled at the overabundance of innocence in Chief Stout's tone.

"At the last minute," the chief said, "I saw I was low on gas. Someone must have forgotten to fill up the squad car. You know how hired help can be these days. Got to double-check everything yourself."

Harry raised a skeptical brow. "A squad car low on gas?"

"That's right. That's what I was thinking, too. But these things happen. When we got to Faribault, I went into the service station for a minute. When I came out, the boy was gone. Simple as that."

Harry looked at the chief accusingly. "I 'spose you're chompin' at the bit to haul him off to Red Wing again the minute the game's over."

"Somehow I've got a feeling I won't be able to see where he went the minute this game's over."

"How can you do that, Chief?" Ole questioned. "Authorities find out, they'll haul him off faster than you can sneeze."

"Words out the boy fled the state," Chief Stout said. "I'm leaving it at that."

"But what about when the powers that be learn the truth?" Harry snapped.

"Don't worry, Harry. I'll twist a few arms. That's a promise. Besides, the Packers need your boy."

Finally breaking a grin, Harry relaxed enough to stop grinding his heel.

And, thanks to Wil's great pitching arm, the Packers went on to win the game seven to two.

Tryg glanced at the neatly folded clothes stacked on Wil's single bed. The poor kid didn't even own a suitcase. Tryg peered out the window.

Wil should be home any minute now. Although a guest in his home for only a few short days, Tryg missed him already, and he wasn't even gone.

The backdoor rattling, Tryg headed for the kitchen. He reached out to Wil and clapped him on the shoulder. "That was quite some game you played today. Your pitching was remarkable. I couldn't be more proud of you. One of these days you're going to make the pros."

Wil blushed.

Tryg slipped a hand in a pocket and looked down. "Ole and your dad had a chat with Chief Stout. The coast is clear, so you're free to go home now," he said, but then he inhaled an uncomfortable breath. "I wasn't expecting this to happen so soon."

Looking anything but happy, Wil shrugged. "Me neither."

"Go get your clothes. They're on your bed. I'll give you a lift home."

When Tryg pulled up to the curb in front of the Thompson home, Will looked around. "Lawn's mowed," he said.

"You sound surprised."

"I am. Pop usually makes me do all the heavy stuff 'round here. Somethin' musta' got into him. Looks like he's finally takin' a little pride in the place."

"Ole had mentioned your home was run down, but you're right." Tryg looked at the house with its clean windows and drapes hanging straight. The front porch was exceptionally tidy with several hanging potted plants. "Looks like your dad got his pride back, and you're the one who did that for him. Are you going to be okay, Wil?"

"Yeah," he said, his tone indifferent.

"Don't be a stranger now. You need me for anything, anything at all, I'm only a phone call away." Tryg turned to get out of the car.

"What're you doin'?" Wil asked warily.

"Thought I'd see you to your door."

"Why?"

Tryg didn't answer. "Let's go."

They were still walking up the sidewalk when Harry stepped out with a grin as wide as the house was long. He scuttled down the steps with a hand extended. "Thanks for bringin' my boy home, Mr. Howland."

Harry's warm emphasis on the word *home* told Tryg all he needed to know. The man valued his son more than the smokes, more than the beer. Tryg clapped Wil on the shoulder one last time. "Remember what I said. You need me, you know where I am."

Lingering for a thoughtful moment, Tryg watched proud father and son disappear through their front door and couldn't help but wonder. Would it be possible for Wil to begin a brand new life?

CHAPTER SIXTY-EIGHT

Two Weeks Later ....

After finishing Saturday's noontime dishes, Jo gazed at the lake shimmering like diamonds in the mid-afternoon sun. She would give anything if she could have her days with Case back. Days of laughter and warmth. The numerous mornings, afternoons, and evenings they'd spent drinking in the view together. Hearing and watching the waves lap lazily against the thin shoreline. Nights were especially beautiful when a full moon backlit a grove of deciduous trees that reached high into the clear-night sky. Beautiful as a painting, the trees flourished on a small, uninhabited island jutting out of the water a stone's throw from shore. The only life there, other than an occasional bird, came during the dead of winter when neighborhood children trudged across the frozen lake, or in the summer when a rare boat would row to the small island. Jo hugged herself, thinking. What a shame to waste a perfectly blissful afternoon.

Suddenly, Brue's footsteps pattered up from behind. "Hey, Mom. Can I go up to Academy Park?"

Jo lifted Brue's chin. "I was thinking about going some place myself. What do you think about going to the Packers' game instead?"

Meanwhile, Ole grinned at the sky. The weather had cooperated beautifully. Much to his pleasure, when he arrived at the Thompson home, Harry again smelled lightly of aftershave. Was clean-shaven. What little hair he had left was washed and well combed. He wore another clean tee shirt. Who would have thought a few short weeks ago that Big Ole Harrington and Harry Thompson's lives would coalesce around a troubled young boy?

As Harry hopped into the taxi and the driver drove on, Harry looked at Ole skeptically. "Why are you doin' this? Why haul me along to my son's games? I ain't nothin' but a useless drunk. You know that. What I can't figure is how can you stand to be seen with me."

Ole gazed at Harry. "I'm ashamed to admit it," he said, "but there was a time not all that long ago when I would have found it next to impossible just to look at you. But that was before I got to know you and your boy, and I'm afraid that was my loss."

They arrived at the ballpark early. Ole was determined to get a good seat for today's game without any special reserved seats from anyone.

Jo and Brue arrived in plenty of time to get a good parking space. Brue pointed excitedly toward wide-open seating in the upper bleachers. They had been sitting for several minutes watching the crowd swell when Jo took notice. Sarah was ascending the bleachers—with Charlie. Hand-in-hand nonetheless. When her gaze met Jo's, she smiled innocently and waved.

Jo tried to find a smile, too, but couldn't. How could they do this to Tryg?

"Hey, Jo, mind if we join you?" Charlie and Sarah plunked down next to them before Jo had a chance to answer. After a few quick words and nods, Charlie and Brue headed off to the refreshment stand, leaving Jo alone to deal with Sarah.

Jo could think of a lot of places she'd rather be at the moment than sitting next to Sarah-the-duplicitous-double-crossing-Harrington. They looked straight ahead, the awkward silence between them screaming.

"Charlie is a great guy," Jo ventured after a seemingly endless moment.

Sarah propped her feet on the bleachers in front of them as if she needed extra support. "He is."

More awkward quiet. What did Jo have to lose? How could they ever get past what they both knew and weren't talking about if she didn't just blurt it out? She looked over the crowd and found herself feeling unexpectedly triumphant the instant the words, "I wonder if Tryg will be here today," passed from her lips. She'd broken through. Now they could talk.

The warmth in Sarah's blueberry eyes suddenly cooled. "Tryg?"

"That's right. Wouldn't he be crushed if he knew you and Charlie had something going on on the side? And tomorrow the five of us are going boating together. Now, how do you suggest we handle this? I'm feeling like a real weasel here."

Sarah's startled chuckle carried a hint of disbelief. "You aren't serious?"

Confused by Sarah's response, a tremor tore down Jo's spine. How could this warm and caring woman be so calloused? What had gotten into her?

"Let me set the record straight." Sarah said, sounding surprisingly confident. "Tryg and I were planning on coming to the game together this afternoon. He called at the last minute and canceled. Said he was buried under too much work at the office. Charlie overheard our conversation. The minute I hung up, Charlie asked if I would go with him."

"And you said yes."

"Of course, I did."

"You and Charlie were holding hands, Sarah."

She looked off dreamily and smiled. "I know. He grabbed my hand just before we made our way up the bleachers. I have to tell you, it really felt good. As for Tryg and me, we're just friends. I'm sorry to say there's nothing more to it than that."

Jo shook her head. The chasm of disconnection separating she and Sarah at the moment easily spanned the Grand Canyon. "Tell that to Tryg."

"I guess I'm going to have to."

"What about tomorrow?"

Sarah looked at Jo incredulously "What about it?"

"You can't be serious?"

Sarah grinned coyly. "Jo?"

"Yes?"

"About Tryg—"

Talk about the obvious. "Yes?"

"Don't worry. I'll cut my ties with him tonight."

Although Jo was sitting down, she still felt as if she were about to lose her balance. "You'll what? Why? I thought you cared about him."

Sarah kneaded the handle on her purse and stared at it glumly. "I think you know why."

Jo quickly looked away.

"I can't compete with you, Jo. Haven't been able to from the very beginning. No one could."

Her head snapping back, Jo looked Sarah directly in the eye. "What in the world are you talking about?"

"I'm talking about the way you and Tryg look at each other. I swear his pupils dilate whenever you walk into a room."

"But I'm dating Frank," Jo said emphatically. "How could you not know that?"

"Right. So now you understand my conundrum. You have an inter-est in Tryg and Frank, and I have a sincere interest in Charlie and Tryg.

It's uncomfortable and it's untimely, but it's also honest." Sarah hesitated. "Do you remember that red Parker pen you gave Tryg some time back?"

Sarah's question caught Jo by surprise. "How'd you know about that?"

"I borrowed it from him one day when we met for lunch at The Copper Kettle. That was back when we were trying to protect Grandpa from being blackmailed, if you will recall. When I finished using the pen, I wasn't thinking. I started to put it in my purse. Obviously, I would have given it back, but the expression on Tryg's face startled me. He nearly panicked. So I asked him where he'd gotten it. He looked away and muttered 'from a friend.' And do you know what I said to him? I said, 'that's quite some friend you've got there.' Somehow I knew that friend was you."

Jo wasn't about to allow threatening tears break loose. "That's not true. Look, he and I had some icy moments over that pen." Jo reconsidered her words. "No. It was worse than that. He was professional about it. Emotionless and professional."

"Emotional and professional? Or conflicted?"

Jo didn't care for the way Sarah's words came flying at her.

"When I do settle down," Sarah said, "I want a man who looks at me the way Tryg looks at you. I refuse to settle for less."

"But—"

"But, nothing. I deserve better and, believe me, that's not your fault. Neither is it Tryg's. You give me hope that it can happen to me one day, too." She glanced toward the refreshment stand with a grin that radiated pure joy. "As a matter of fact, I think that day might have already come."

"There's nothing between Tryg and me, Sarah," Jo insisted. "There can't be. Not now. Not ever."

"Really?" Sarah said disbelievingly. "Why's that?"

"Because my conscience won't allow it. I'm positive Tryg's conscience would never allow it either."

Sarah looked down at the filling bleachers then out across the ball field where the teams were beginning to warm up. "You look awfully sad for someone who implies they aren't carrying a torch."

Sarah's words cut Jo's heart like sharp shards of glass. "I didn't say I wasn't carrying a torch. I said there could never be anything between Tryg and me. There's a difference."

"Is there? What about that way the two of you look at each another? Your bond is deep, Jo."

Jo looked away. "Did it ever dawn on you that there might be far more to the look you've seen in our eyes? That it might not be love for each other so much as love for someone else?"

"You aren't making any sense."

Charlie and Brue, loaded down with hotdogs and cokes, were ascending the bleachers. "Look," Jo said, "I really don't want to get into this, but it's no secret that Tryg was driving the car the day my husband was killed. The only reason I'm working for him is to save up enough so Brue and I can move to New York and begin a new life. Hopefully, the memories won't be so fresh and hurtful there."

Sarah squeezed her eyes closed. "I had no idea, Jo. I couldn't be more sorry."

"Don't worry about it." Jo let out a pleading sigh. "Now what are we going to do about tomorrow?"

Sarah looked as if she wanted to slither under the bleachers and hide. "Like I said, I'm going to talk to Tryg tonight. This isn't going to be easy."

CHAPTER SIXTY-NINE

How do you like them apples, Harry? Looks like we got here in time to get our old seats back."

Before Harry could get in a word, Ole bristled when he heard an overly loud, "Yoo-hoo?"

Harry craned his neck. "Hey, Harrington. There's an old woman sitting a couple a rows up. The way she's waving her handkerchief, you'd think it was a flag. Is she a widow or somethin'?" he said with an unsubtle smirk.

"How could you tell?"

"Yoo-hoo? Mr. Harrington?"

Ole forced himself to look up and offered a reticent smile and a nod. "Nice to see you, Mrs. Braddingly. Nice to see you." He quickly turned away.

"That was a wooden smile if I ever saw one," Harry said flatly. "And I'm not talking about the grin planted on *her* face."

At the bottom of the third inning, Ole headed to the refreshment stand for hotdogs and rootbeer. At the top of the fourth, he returned. "Hope you like it loaded."

Harry reached for it absently. "Thanks."

Ole sensed something was up. "Say, what's going on out there?"

Harry craned his neck for a better look. "I been watchin' my boy. He does have an arm, doesn't he? Unless I'm missin' somethin', seems no one's made a hit off any of his pitches yet."

Ole gulped a sizeable chew and chased it down with a swig of root beer. "Now why does that not surprise me?"

By the bottom of the fifth inning, the crowd caught on. "Go, Wil! Go, Wil!" they shouted in unison as Wil approached the pitcher's mound. Then the crowd fell stone quiet. Wil pitched another perfect inning. No runs. No hits. No errors.

By the bottom of the seventh inning, poor old Harry was a nervous mess. He teared up and choked out the words, "You know what my boy said to me the other day, Harrington?"

"No, Harry, I haven't a clue."

"Told me he loved me. My boy said that. To me!"

At first, Ole's heart fluttered. He had to be careful, though. That could be dangerous. But after getting a handle on his heart and a better grip on his mind, he choked down the bile squeezing up into his throat. He could handle Harry's crusty comments, but sitting next to a sappy Harry Thompson was about as pleasant as sitting next to a skunk that sprayed.

Ole shook off the thought then looked out on the field once again overcome with pride. Wil not only spilled over with talent, he also had guts, and the boy was coming through. Ole's hard work had paid off after all.

But then at the bottom of the eighth inning, Harry got overly excited. He jumped up prematurely as Wil was about to release a fast pitch. The batter snuck in a hit. Wil's chances for a perfect game, scrubbed.

When the crowd groaned, Harry rotated faster than a roadrunner on roller skates and cut loose with a long line of expletives, the likes of which were enough to even make Big Ole blush.

Ole pushed to his feet and laid a light hand on Harry's shoulder. "Down, Harry. Down. Next time. The boy can give it a try again next time. He's a shoo-in for a perfect game. You know it. I know it. And so does everybody else sitting in these here bleachers."

CHAPTER SEVENTY

J o watched the game, but was oblivious to the cheers all around her, impervious to the vibration of feet pounding the bleachers, and she totally lost track of the score, let alone the time. Her world had suddenly become complicated and needed sorting. The instant the bleachers emptied, she said a guarded good-bye to Charlie and Sarah then gathered Brue and hurried home.

The door slammed behind Brue as she raced outside to join her friends in Harrington Park, leaving Jo alone with her troubled thoughts. In less than twenty-four hours she would be engaged in one awkward boating adventure.

Needing help, she dialed Calvin's number at the church office.

"Calvin Doherty."

At the soothing sound of his voice, she felt as if she'd grabbed hold of a lifeline. "Good. You're there. Would you have a few minutes to counsel a friend?"

"By the sound of your voice, I'd say this is serious. Want to stop by the church, or is this important enough that I need to make a house call?"

"I'll come there. How soon can we meet?"

It didn't take long for Jo's footsteps to clack up the center aisle of Village Church. She rounded the door into Calvin's office. Somehow the small house of worship appeared as dark and hollow as she felt.

Calvin glanced up. "You look even more troubled in person than you sounded over the phone. Please. Have a seat."

Jo lowered onto a chair. No words would come out. Her gaze shifted from the bookshelves behind him, to the ceiling that could use a fresh coat of paint, and then to a sparrow that flew dangerously close to the outside window. She was spinning her wheels, going nowhere.

Resting elbows on the wooden desk, Calvin steepled his fingers, lightly touching them to his chin. He remained silent.

"My words are stuck," she said after a too-long moment.

"Take your time."

"People don't understand," Jo admitted finally, her heart in her throat.

Calvin's forehead ratcheted up. "They don't understand what?"

"Sarah Harrington is breaking ties with Tryg. She said she can't compete with me. Said she wanted to find someone who looked at her the way Tryg looks at me. Can you believe she could say such a thing?"

"I assume her breakup with Tryg will be imminent," Calvin said matter-of-factly.

"Tonight."

"I see." Calvin didn't appear surprised. "Do you think she might be right about Tryg?"

"Thanks a lot. Nothing could ever become of Tryg and me. You know that. Besides, I've been seeing Frank Breck."

"The farmer?"

"That's right."

"Your guarded look. What's that about? Frank? Or Tryg?"

"Sarah can give Tryg something I could never give him."

"And what would that be?" Calvin said flatly.

"Her heart."

Calvin's expression grew dubious. "Isn't it a little late for that? By the looks of things, you've already given him that ... some time ago."

"It isn't possible for me to fall for Tryg."

"Like I said, Jo Bremley, I believe you already have. And he's obviously fallen for you, too."

Jo lurched to the edge of the chair. "Don't you understand? I don't want someone to care for me out of guilt, and even if I could, we can't do that to Case."

Calvin slowly shook his head. "How do we ever give ourselves permission to accept the past and move on?"

"You're the preacher," Jo said. "That's why I'm here. I thought you might have some ideas."

"What about Frank? How's it going with him?"

Jo's words got stuck again.

"Jo?" he said warmly.

"I don't know. I'm crazy about him, but I can't seem to get happy. Something's holding me back."

"What?"

"I dunno."

"Of course, you do. Give it a try."

Jo sighed. "Maybe you're right. For one thing, it's still early in our relationship."

"And?"

"I'm afraid to give him my heart," she conceded. "I keep trying, but it doesn't seem to get any better."

"Why's that?"

Jo grinned sheepishly. "Calvin Doherty, you're beginning to wear me out."

He laughed. "That's my job. Come on. Spit it out. Far be it from me to spoon your words back to you, but do you remember what you asked me some time back? Actually, let me make this easy for you. It was when I was struggling with my faith. I'll never forget how you nailed me. You asked me when my pain began. So let me ask you—when and where did this discomfort begin?"

"You mean with Frank?"

"That's right?"

"When and where?"

He nodded.

Jo thought for a split second and was surprised she did not need to reach deep. "Try on our first date, I guess. At first, I felt intimidated by him. He's a walking dream. As the night wore on, though, our walls came tumbling down. I loved how I felt being with him. After supper and a movie, we went over to the Canton for a cherry Coke and shared stories about our lives."

"And?"

"He told me about a serious relationship he'd had in the past."

"Past tense. That's good. And?"

"She was married."

"Oh, my," Calvin said, his entire demeanor registering surprise.

For a quick moment Jo relived the disappointment she'd felt that night, how it tore at her, but then she batted the memory aside. "The worst of it was, he had a gut feeling she was married, but he ignored it. Didn't ask her about it. And he didn't express any feeling at all for her husband, let alone her kids."

"So you're afraid that if he could close off his heart to the woman's family, he has the ability to close off his heart to you, too."

"That's right. But there's more. Little things keep happening. Lipstick on a glass, trips out of town, postponed and late dates."

"You're afraid to trust him."

Jo stared at Calvin's aging wooden desk. "I guess that sums it up."

Calvin shook his head, his warm eyes filled with sadness. "How are you feeling about yourself these days?"

"Under the circumstances, I guess I'd have to say not too good. I feel confused and torn. Can't seem to walk away from Frank. I'm too attracted to him, but I can't really enjoy him, either. What do I do about it? Right now I'm biding time, hoping one day he'll see the light and things will change."

"We're all deceived, Jo, every last one of us. It's part of our human condition. We all get tried and tested throughout life, and every time we pass a test, we get a little stronger."

"I'm stuck, Calvin. I can't change the way Frank thinks or change the things he does. I don't think he gets it. It's almost like it's foreign to him."

"That's true. You can't change him. He has to do that himself. But there is one thing you can do."

Jo looked at Calvin, finally feeling a hint of hope. "What's that?"

"You're flirting with the truth, Jo. In a way, you're no different than Frank. You aren't facing the truth and you aren't acting on it. The eighth chapter of John, verse thirty-two comes to mind. 'And ye shall know the truth, and the truth shall make you free.' Think about it. The truth. That's the only thing that's going to make you free and then only if you choose to act on it. Let me ask you a question. How would you advise Brue if the tables were turned?"

Jo thought about that for less than a fractured moment. "Well, I guess if you put it that way, it is easier to see, isn't it?"

Suddenly Calvin burst into laughter, taking Jo completely by surprise.

"I don't mean to make light of your situation," he said, "but I had the funniest thought. Think about Big Ole. Can you imagine that man taking a shine to a lovely elderly woman and being fearful he might lose her if he was honest about his misgivings?"

Jo bit her lower lip. "You're right, Calvin. It is simple. I know it is."

"Don't give me too much credit. I have feet of clay like everyone else."

Jo smoothed a finger over a button. "I wish I wasn't so afraid of hurting Frank with the truth. I'm afraid of how he will react. I mean, what if he doesn't want to hear it? Now that I feel again how wonderful it is to be in a relationship, even if it is flawed, I'm reluctant to take the risk. I wish I wasn't so terrified of losing the guy."

"That's understandable," Calvin said. "Whatever you do, don't expect this to be easy. The truth can be frightening and even ugly at times. Under the circumstances, I can't say as I blame you for how you feel. No one could. Your fear is well founded, and life is tough."

Jo felt a stab in her heart.

"I know it's easier said than done, but don't give in to your fear. If he's a good man, it will all fall into place."

"And if he's not ..."

"Look, back to this Tryg thing," Calvin said. "Why don't you give me some time to think about it? We can talk again later."

Nudging up closer to his desk, Jo leaned an elbow on it. "That's why I'm here in the first place. I don't have time. Sarah and Charlie showed up at the Packer's game this afternoon. They were holding hands. To make matters worse, the five of us are going boating tomorrow afternoon at Tryg's invitation—Tryg, Sarah, Charlie, Brue, and me."

Calvin expelled a weighty sigh. "That certainly sounds uncomfortable."

"So what do I do?"

"On the surface," Calvin said, "it would appear that this problem belongs to Sarah and Tryg. Maybe it would be best to let them hammer it out themselves."

Jo considered Calvin's words, then got up and turned toward the door. What else could she do? The one person who might have been able to make her life easier, couldn't. "I guess you're right. Thanks for your time."

"Jo?"

Jo turned on her heel. Something in his tone gave her the impression he might have changed his mind, that he'd suddenly gotten an idea. "Yes?"

"Would you mind talking with me for a few more minutes? I was polishing tomorrow's sermon when you came in. I've got a few thoughts I'd like to run past someone and since you're here anyway—"

Unfortunately, Jo had misread him. "Be happy to."

He picked up a pen and playfully walking it across his fingers, he said, "I want to preach about heaven and what it must be like there."

Jo didn't hesitate to return to the spindle chair. "That sounds fascinating."

"I thought so, too. First let me ask you, is there any negative thought in heaven?"

"Of course not."

"None?"

"No."

"How about hatred?

"No."

"Anger?"

Jo slowly shook her head, wondering where he was going with his questioning.

"Envy?" he continued. "Jealousy?"

"No. Of course, not."

"That's what I thought." Calvin stared upward as if it were possible to see heaven through an opening in the ceiling. Then as if he'd snapped out of a daze, he said, "Let me give your situation more thought. Be at church in the morning. I have an idea about how I might tailor my message so that it's pertinent to your situation."

CHAPTER SEVENTY-ONE

At half past four in the afternoon, the taxi's brakes screeched to the curb.

"What do you say, Harry?" Ole swiveled in the seat. "Saturday nights can get lonely when a man doesn't have a good woman around. Got any plans for the evening? When's the last time you've had a juicy T-bone?"

The expression on Harry's face registered unmitigated surprise. "You mean—"

"You play any cribbage?"

Harry nodded reluctantly.

"Well, how about it?"

The moment they stepped inside the O.M. Harrington, Harry's countenance took a turn down a dark and troubled road. He scratched his belly and said, "You wouldn't happen to have anything to drink, would ya?"

"That we do. Coffee or lemonade?"

"I was thinking of something a little stronger."

Ole grinned. "I'll make sure the lemonade is good and tart. While I'm at it, I'll tell Bernie to throw a couple of steaks on the grill, too."

When Ole returned to the great room with two cold glasses in hand, Harry was nowhere to be seen.

"What's the matter, Grandpa?" Sarah asked.

"Harry left?"

"I doubt it. I think I heard him walking around outside on the porch. You've got your hands full. I'll get him for you."

Big Ole didn't appreciate feeling uncomfortable in his own boarding house, and watching Harry meander toward the cribbage table wasn't helping. The man looked as if his insides were in desperate need of crawling out. "Lemonade's getting warm and the cards are getting cold," Ole said.

"Nice place. Good view." Harry plunked down opposite Ole. "Your cribbage board looks like it's had plenty of use, I see."

"You bet. Too many geezers around with too much time on our hands." Ole gathered up the deck and shuffled three times. "Let's draw for the deal. You go first. Ahh. Your deal."

"You never did tell me why you're doing this," Harry said as the cards hit the table with a smooth rhythm, "why you invited me into your life."

"Wil's eye and hand coordination are inherited, I see," Ole said. "Like father, like son."

Harry kept dealing. "Six each, right?"

"That's right."

Harry tapped the cards on the tabletop then fanned them out. "Well? I ain't exactly what you'd call good company, you know. My boy could attest to that."

"Guess it's my move, isn't it?" Ole said.

"So why you wastin' your time on me? Doesn't make sense."

"I prefer to call it investing."

"Investing?" Harry repeated. "That's a laugh. So let's get right to it. In case you hadn't noticed, I've got quite the reputation."

Ole discarded two cards into the crib. "You're being a little hard on yourself, aren't you?"

"Just honest." Harry looked strikingly more comfortable after owning his faults. "I'm a loser, Harrington, and everybody around town knows it."

Ole was pleased Harry felt comfortable expressing himself, but this wasn't what he had in mind for a relaxing Saturday evening. "I doubt that's your fault."

"What you talkin' about? I can't keep off the booze. Don't want to neither."

This guy really needs a drink. "Why is it so hard to keep off the stuff?"

"I like it too much."

Ole chuckled.

"What's so funny?" Harry asked.

"I was thinking about the booze, about how you're loyal to something that doesn't return the favor." Ole hesitated. "Your dad liked the sauce, too?"

Harry's eyes grew to twice their size. "How'd you know that?"

"And his dad, too, right?"

"I dunno," Harry said. "He died before I was even born. Say, what does that have to do with anything?"

Ole shrugged. "Reminds me of that old expression, the sins of the fathers."

"Aww, no. You ain't gonna go preachin' to me. Not to this guy."

Ole studied his cards. "Relax, Harry. I wouldn't think of it. You do know how to deal out a mean hand, I'll give you that."

"Some tough cards, huh?"

"Not that I would admit to."

Harry raised his cards, hiding his face. "This sins of the father thing, what d'ya mean by that?"

"I thought you didn't want me to preach?"

"I don't. I want to know why it has to happen that way, what it's all about."

"I don't know. Kind of makes sense, though, doesn't it?" Ole pulled his cards back, studying them. "I mean, we hear things, see things, and then we think about them. Seeds get planted, and they grow. Becomes a way of life. It's hard to shake what's become so familiar." Ole hesitated. "You look sad, Harry."

"Aww, it's nothin'."

"I take it you didn't have an easy time growing up."

He slowly shook his head.

"Happens more often than not, I guess."

Harry's face scrunched up. "If sins are passed down from generation to generation, how does a man ever fix it?"

"Let me think about that for a minute. Dad's can only pass on what they know, right? Your dad couldn't teach you what he was never taught any more than you can teach your boy what you were never taught."

Harry's eyebrows pulled together. "What kinda stuff?"

Sensing he was about to hit a nerve, Ole braced himself. "You can handle hearing it?"

"'Course, I can. Why wouldn't I?"

"Okay then." Ole raised a brow and suddenly finding himself eager to hear a response, he said, "Healthy and nurturing love."

Harry looked as if the big swig of lemonade he'd swallowed was about to launch back up and out. He collected himself and squared his shoulders. "So what you're saying is—"

Ole nodded. "You think you're a no-good-for-nothing dad. But the way I see it, you're every bit as much a victim as Wil."

"And?"

"The family any of us are born into is not our fault."

"But what *is* our fault is not rolling up our sleeves to break out of it, right?" Harry eased off his chair. "I gotta' get outside. Think I could use a smoke."

CHAPTER SEVENTY-TWO

Tryg and Sarah stepped out of the Rivoli Theatre. "That was quite some movie," he announced. He felt estranged for some reason, but couldn't put a finger on why. The lights of Broadway and laughter from a boisterous crowd up the street mocked the darkness. "Want to go to the Canton for a soda?"

"I don't think so," Sarah said. "Not tonight anyway. How about if we drive up to the lake instead?"

Tryg nodded and lightly guided her by an elbow toward the car. Okay. Whatever you say.

"No. On second thought," she said, pulling back, "let's not drive. How about if we walk down to the band shell instead?"

Why the resistance? Why the change of mind? Tryg would normally reach for Sarah's hand, but something told him not to. He listened to her breathing. It sounded labored. Maybe he was walking too fast. "Why the walk? And why the band shell?"

Stuffing her hands deep into her pockets, she shrugged.

The air felt as thick as their silence. Suspecting he was about to participate in an unpleasant conversation, Tryg picked up the pace and changed the venue. If nothing else, he needed to seize what little control he could. Might as well get this over with.

"I thought we were going to the band shell," Sarah said as they descended the hill.

"No. Let's go to the shoreline instead."

Clouds slid beneath the half moon, leaving them standing in near utter darkness. Tryg found it difficult to read the expression on Sarah's face. Maybe that was for the best. "I take it you want to get something off your mind."

"No, but I do need to," she said, her voice soft, yet hesitant, then she took a step back. "I think it might be a good idea if we gave some thought to canceling our boating adventure tomorrow."

"It's a little late for that, isn't it?"

She looked up at him. "Tryg? I think you should know that I have every intention of seeing Charlie now."

Tryg's breath caught, but then he smiled into the night. What was the matter with him? Was he in shock or something? He should feel sad or maybe even angry, but he only felt relief. "Charlie, huh?"

Sarah laid a hand on his arm as if he hadn't heard her correctly. "That's all you have to say? Charlie, huh?"

"What else do you want me to say?"

"This isn't Charlie's fault, and it's not mine either."

"I didn't say it was."

Sarah kept babbling. "You know, I never have seen me in your eyes, Tryg."

"Is that a fact? What have you seen?"

"Jo."

That word hit him like a fist. "That's not fair."

"Not fair? Not fair to you? Or not fair to me?"

He paused. Inhaled a breath. "I understand," he said softly, a ripple of remorse piercing him to the quick.

"Anyway, about Charlie," Sarah continued. "It all happened by accident. He's around the boarding house all the time, and we're about the same age, so we naturally gravitate toward one another. Seems we both have a lot to say."

"I don't doubt you do," Tryg agreed.

"Can't you hear what I'm saying?" Sarah's voice ripped with exasperation.

"I'm hearing you're seeing Charlie and tomorrow is off," Tryg said.

Sarah maintained silence for a moment, but then she burst into laughter. "To think I thought this would be so hard. My suspicions have been right all along, haven't they? I never did stand a chance with you. You're too in love with Jo."

Suddenly unable to catch even a thimbleful, Tryg fought for breath.

"Charlie noticed it, too," she continued, "or he would never have pursued me. He said as much."

"When?"

"That day you and Charlie ate together, the day you had lunch at the Hotel Albert. He told me all about it. Said that when Jo walked in to tell you some meeting time had changed at the courthouse, the way you looked at each other drew the air out of the room." Sarah hesitated and then went on. "He said that when he saw your raw love for Jo, he felt violated for me."

So that's what that look was all about.

CHAPTER SEVENTY-THREE

Frank pushed away from the table. "You're one fabulous cook, Jo Bremley. I don't remember the last time I tasted a hunk of beef that good."

Jo snickered. "It was your chuck roast. All I did was salt and pepper it, throw it in a frying pan, cover it, and cook it on low heat until it caramelized on both sides."

"So that's the secret. Now let me help with the dishes."

"You even do dishes?" Oh, dear! This guy was too much of a prize.

Frank rolled up his sleeves and headed toward the sink. He washed. She dried. After lightly bumping elbows a half dozen or so times, he gallantly slipped Jo's best bowl onto the top shelf in the cupboard. They then retreated to the living room where they enjoyed a fresh, though weak, cup of coffee, turned on the radio, and listened to *Philco Vance*, a detective show starring Jose Ferrer.

At half past eight, Evelyn dropped off Brue. Jo tucked her in bed, resisting the urge to fret about Frank and that conversation she promised herself she'd engage in, no matter what. How it hurt to disappoint, but she needed to get it over with. She returned to the living room and to a handsome, smiling Frank Breck.

"Would you mind taking a stroll out to Harrington Park?" she asked. "It's such a beautiful night."

The moment Frank seized her hand, she turned to mush. They strolled along side-by-side. Like Big Ole, he smelled of a hint of after-shave and his hand felt warm and strong. When they reached the bench, he sidled up close, slipping an arm around her. Suddenly, out in the great outdoors she felt closed in.

"Frank?" she said, startled by the tone of her own voice.

In the dark, she could faintly see his forehead cinch and sensed his raw concern. "What is it, Jo? You sound worried."

She angled a turn toward him to gain distance. "I'm having a hard time knowing what to say or how to say it."

"Whatever it is, why do I get the uneasy feeling it's not going to be good?"

"It's not good or bad. It's neutral." She let out a breathy sigh and forced the words out. "It's us."

He pulled back defensively. "What do you mean? What about us?"

"I've been doing a lot of rationalizing and that's not fair."

"Rationalizing about what?"

Her eyebrows hiked involuntarily. "Us. I've been rationalizing about us. Every time you've called me for a date, I've said yes, when that wasn't necessarily the right thing to say."

"You're talking crazy, Jo."

She looked up at him, her heart a plea. "Am I? Every time I've said yes I've felt guilty about it."

"That's ridiculous," he said sharply. "What's there to feel guilty about?"

Jo drew back at the harshness of his tone and waited a lingering moment for him to calm. If Frank were Tryg, they wouldn't need to have this conversation. "It never dawned on me to simply tell you the truth."

"Which is?"

"I love spending time with you. I really do. Not passing time, but actually spending valuable time, and I want more than anything to continue enjoying our time together. But we have to face the fact that we're not sipping from the same wine glass. That could invite some serious problems farther down the road. I think we need to face that now before we go on."

"We what?" he said, sounding incredulous.

"I want to be your friend."

"Oh, that's a great line," he scoffed.

"No. Listen. Please. I want to feel free to call you the way I'd call a brother—"

He hopped up and hovered over her. "A brother?"

"That's right, but not in the way you're thinking."

"A brother is a brother."

"No. I mean something totally different. I've been freezing with fear that you would drop me if I was honest about my doubts about any kind of future I might have with you."

"Why would you have doubts?" Empathy appeared to replace his defensiveness as he sat again on the park bench. "You aren't making any sense."

Jo reached for his hands and looked up into his troubled eyes. "Remember on our first date how you told me you had fallen for a married woman?"

"Yes. That was a long time ago, but it's over. What about it?"

"My boundaries are set tighter than yours, Frank, and the problem on my end is that I don't want to widen mine. Do you remember how you responded when I asked if you were concerned about her husband? You didn't say anything. Why?"

Frank bent over and clasping his hands, he rested his forearms on his thighs and looked off into the night, his voice sounding far away. "He's a grown man. Why would I be?"

Jo's supper backed up into her throat. "There's no question he had his faults. We all do. But from where I'm standing, you didn't value his needs or the needs of his children. In doing that, you've also opened the door further down the road to not valuing me. That's a foundation builder, and I want and need a solid foundation."

"And you think I can't give that to you?" he said softly. "You don't trust me."

Jo thought for a long moment. "You're right. If I'm honest, I don't."

"What?" he asked in utter disbelief.

"Look, Frank. Trust isn't something we deserve. It's something we need to earn—each and every one of us. And speaking of trust, there has to be a story behind the figurine Brue picked up when she and I were at your home on the Fourth of July. The one she didn't drop or break. I saw you flinch."

Jo stared into the telling silence that followed. "Oh, dear," she said finally. "I guess the better question would be who is the story behind the figurine?" She squeezed her eyes closed, as if that could squeeze out a distressing reality it hurt desperately to face. "Then there was that lipstick on Brue's milk glass, and your trip out of town. It's early in our relationship, I know that. You have every right to your privacy. Unfortunately, you're choosing to exercise that right over building trust with me."

Sooner than she had hoped, Frank trudged down Jo's front porch steps with his head hung low, yet moving swiftly enough that the soles of his shoes barely touched the stairs. Watching him drive away, Jo touched the window lightly, her heart aching. Had what she feared come upon her? Was Frank's affection so fragile that an ounce of reality would crush it by its weight? Or was his affection not fragile at all? Was it merely unavailable? She then recalled Ardena's words the day Jo received his roses. "It's like buying something new and valuable," she had said, "and fearing you're going to lose it, or scratch it, or break it, before it has a chance to become nothing more than another possession."

Jo gazed up the road and watched the Hudson's headlights fade as it crossed over the top of the hill. With only an inkling of who the man really was, she'd lost, scratched, and broken a new relationship.

And the disappointment hurt something awful.

CHAPTER SEVENTY-FOUR

T ryg's heart thumping in his throat, bile from his stomach, and air from his lungs all competed for space. What was he supposed to say to Jo? At one o'clock this afternoon he would stand at her front door feeling like an absolute idiot. No Sarah. No Charlie. What was worse, it was too late to back out.

He dove into the morning paper, but only saw words, words floating on the surface of the page. Like little toy boats on the surface of a lake, they refused to sink in. He tossed *The Amber Leaf Tribune* on an end table then stepped out onto the sun porch to lounge with a steaming cup of coffee. It was watery, but he drank it anyway. He could pray for rain, but peering out the windows, that would take a miracle. Not a cloud in the robin-egg-blue sky. Dry breeze. Not too warm, not too cool. No place to dart off to. No place to take cover. Not that his pride would let him.

But first he had to face seeing her at Village Church. He wouldn't have to worry about running into her in the alcove or his eyes meeting hers as he walked up the aisle—alone—if he settled in a pew before she got there. That's what he would do. Get there early. Get lost reading the bulletin. Why make this any harder than it needed to be?

He arrived at a quarter to nine. And squirmed. He was being ridiculous. When Jo arrived, he glanced her way, but she was too busy fussing with Brue to notice. All that worry for nothing.

At nine o'clock straight up, Big Ole led the singing of the *Doxology* then gave Tryg an unusually bright grin as he made his way back down the aisle. Had he found out about what happened with Sarah last night? Didn't he care? And where was she this morning, anyway? Tryg then read the scriptures the way he had every Sunday morning. After he returned to his pew, Calvin stepped up to the lectern and paused, his eyes resting briefly—deliberately?—on Tryg before delivering the sermon. That was unusual.

"This morning I thought we would explore what heaven is like," he said. "Let's begin by taking a look at what we experience here on earth with our God-given senses. It's almost like a preview, isn't it? Think about it. The sun poking through the windows in the morning, bringing with it the promise of a beautiful day. The heartwarming sound of the words I love you from someone who means them. Babies cooing. Birds warbling in the trees. Supper on the stove. The sweet fragrance of bread baking in the oven. Fire crackling on the hearth on a cold winter's night.

"Or how about the heaven on earth we experience only through our obedience?" Calvin scanned the congregation, and then appeared to fix an admiring gaze on Big Ole. "Regaining our honor when we've been dishonored in the worst way. That amazing feeling of freedom when we've exercised forgiveness. Looking for and finding God in the midst of our catastrophes. Isn't that what we're called to do? To set our wants and needs aside and choose obedience to Him over our hunger for revenge? How gratifying the taste of victory.

"But now back to what heaven is like. The concept seems too great to grasp, doesn't it? We've all heard stories about the bright light at the end of the tunnel. Kind of makes you wonder if that brightness might be nothing more than a receding light in an operating room when a patient is slipping away. Are the accounts merely illusions? Like a mirage on a sun-baked desert? There are many who have experienced it that would challenge that notion.

"In reading the scriptures, there are some undeniable truths we can explore. Time on earth is linear, but in heaven, we read in Revelation, chapter ten, verse six, 'And sware by him that liveth for ever and ever, who created heaven, and the things that therein are, and the earth, and the things that therein are, and the sea, and the things which are therein, that there should be time no longer.' Let me repeat that. '...that there should be time no longer.' Time in heaven is not linear then, is it? The beginning, the middle, and the ending are omnipresent. That stated, if God is love and heaven is His home, how could hatred abide there?"

Calvin looked at Tryg and continued on as if Calvin's message was aimed at him.

"No anger. No jealousy. No grieving. No resentment. No worrying. Think about it. Think about how freeing it must be to reside there, a place where everything is perfect and no negative emotions can possibly exist."

Calvin then shifted his gaze toward the congregation in general.

"No greed, no deceit, lust, arrogance, feelings of inferiority or superiority, depression, pain, sickness, poverty. No competing to be the best—or the worst. The list goes on and on, doesn't it?"

He seized the lectern and slowly scanned the congregation as if trying to drive home a point. Then Calvin's gaze appeared to rest briefly on Jo. That was interesting.

"Let's say that you're in a relationship with someone here on earth," Calvin continued, "and that relationship is cut short by his or her premature passing."

He's talking about Case. How could he do that to her?

"Now help me with this," Calvin said then paused again, as if for effect. "If there are no negative thoughts in heaven, how can we possibly believe that the saints are pacing up there, worrying about us, and about what's happening with our puny lives down here on earth below?" Calvin smiled confidently. "Think about it. Really think about it. Somehow I don't believe that's possible, do you?"

Tryg fixed his stare on the wooden pew in front of him. He had only thought of Case in terms of strolling along the golden streets of heaven, protective of Jo and Brue, but that could not be. Not if he's in heaven where no negative thoughts exist, where no worrying and pacing exist. For the first time since the accident, Tryg felt a weight release. He felt as if he could breathe and live again, not merely endure. He gave Jo an indirect glance, which she appeared to catch equally as quickly.

Could she possibly be feeling unshackled, too?

CHAPTER SEVENTY-FIVE

Nine minutes to go. The wait was driving Jo nuts. She switched on the radio. Perry Como's new hit, *Till the End of Time,* had started playing. Suddenly she became aware of her shallow breath and beating heart ... thump, thump ... thump, thump. She snapped the radio off and leafed through a magazine.

One minute before the hour of one, Jo's stomach lurched when she heard a car engine and the grating sound of an emergency brake. She glanced at the door, fearful of the knock she was about to hear. But she didn't hear a knock. Instead she heard that whistle, that familiar chirpy whistle that gave her gooseflesh.

"Where's Brue?" Tryg said brightly as he stepped into Jo's living room.

"Some of her friends were having a last-minute party she didn't want to miss."

He nodded approvingly. Jo tried hard to suppress a heavenly tingling as he offered her his arm and escorted her toward the car, but her efforts were in vain.

It felt strange sitting in the front seat, but she would move to the back the instant they picked up Sarah and Charlie. What an interesting afternoon this was going to be.

But Tryg did not swing by the O.M. Harrington, and Jo wasn't about to ask questions. Instead he drove on, turning on Newton and again on Main. In a few minutes' time the car headed up a two-lane road toward Clarks Grove.

"What a relief Japan has finally surrendered," Tryg said breaking the silence.

Jo nodded. "Maybe things can get back to normal now."

"They will."

Jo sat quietly. Listening to the whir of the tires. Wondering what Tryg was up to. Somehow she got the feeling he wasn't thinking about Japan or Europe or any other aspect of the war. When he made a purposeful right-hand turn in Clarks Grove and headed down the road toward the east, she turned toward him. "Where are we going?" she said uneasily. "I assume we're meeting Sarah and Charlie somewhere, right?"

He looked straight ahead. "No. We're not meeting them at all, Jo. We're going to Hollandale."

Her stomach tightened. *"Hollandale?"*

"That's right. We're going to do something we should have done a long time ago."

"Which is?"

He glanced at her, his expression serious. "Face our past ... and our future."

Please, no.

For the first time since the onset of gas rationing, Jo felt appreciation for the 35 mile-per-hour speed limit—anything to buy time. When they reached the cemetery, her breathing slowed. Crawling with apprehension, she shivered despite the warm and perfect weather.

Tryg stepped around the car, opened her door, and held out a hand. In a twinkling, she switched from shivering to melting at the light touch of his fingertips. But then he secured her hand, holding it firmly, and guided her forward until they reached Case's final resting place.

Holding Case's best friend's hand felt strangely natural out here in the cemetery, here where ... she looked up, her cheeks feeling kissed by a gentle, exonerating breeze.

Tryg released Jo's hand and, although he grimaced briefly at the physical pain he must have been feeling in his bad leg, he slowly knelt on one knee. He stayed there, quiet for a long while, but then began talking to Case as if he were alive and could hear Tryg's every word. "After all this time, I still can't do anything behind your back, buddy. Our friendship's always been too strong for that. You deserve better. So I brought your wife, your greatest treasure here on earth, with me today, and I want to ask your permission to marry her."

Jo gasped. Tears stung her eyes and her heart hammered, but Tryg did not look up.

"I'm embarrassed to admit this," he said, "but I've found myself becoming increasingly jealous of anyone who gives her a second look, and because of my deep feelings for her, I've hurt one too many women. They never stood a chance. Not only was I not fair to them, I wasn't fair to myself either. I've paid a hefty price for my actions." Tryg looked up toward the heavens as if he could see Case looking down between a cloud break. "What do you say, Case? I promise I'll take excellent care of her."

Tryg listened for a long moment and then, gazing deeply into Jo's eyes, he grinned. "Did you hear that? Did you hear that, Jo?" He looked up again and searched the sky. "A whisper on the wind. That was Case. He said yes. He gave us his blessings."

Feeling lightheaded, Jo fell into Tryg's welcoming arms. In the midst of a crushing embrace, tears trickled down her cheeks as his words continued to flow. "Some time ago," he whispered tenderly, "I asked God for three things. I asked for a woman I could love with all my heart, a woman I could trust with all my soul, and a woman I could respect with all my being, but I never was able to find her. It never dawned on me to search in the most obvious place of all. I never expected that woman to be you."

Jo reached up and lightly touched his cheek. "I hope you aren't disappointed."

"Not disappointed, Jo. Wonderfully, wonderfully relieved."

Jo couldn't stop smiling. It wasn't possible for God to throw open the windows of heaven any wider.

Tryg pulled off the main road immediately east of Amber Leaf and headed down a remote country road.

"Where are we going now?" she asked.

"There's something I'd like to show you."

No more than a quarter of a mile up the gravel path, he turned right again, drove another mile or so, and stopped the car. "Do you see that beautiful piece of land?" he said, pointing at a small, rolling knoll with a lone oak reaching its strong arms toward the sky.

"It's lovely. Looks like a picture," Jo said, wondering why Tryg would be so enthralled by a small hill and a single oak tree.

"Would you like to live there?"

"But there's no house," she said unthinkingly.

"You're right, at least not yet. I've been thinking about buying that piece of land and building a home there, a fine home, a home that looks like a smaller version of the O.M. Harrington House with French windows and a wrap-around porch. Think of it Jo—a library bursting with books, a huge cherrywood desk, and a crackling fireplace. A great room with staircases running up either side, leading to an upstairs with spacious bedrooms and walkout balconies. A large kitchen with a breakfast nook and a bay window, so we can read the morning paper under full sunlight. A master bedroom with double doors and a huge four-poster bed." Tryg reached for Jo's hand. "Do you think you might have any interest in helping me build our dream home?"

Jo felt dizzy with joy.

"Come," he said. "Let's take a look around."

When they reached the top of the knoll, Tryg plucked up a twig and drew a sketch of his floor plans in the grass, showing Jo the tentative size, location, and view of every room in his imagined home. When he reached the great room, he grinned coyly and said, "I believe I hear the violins playing." He held out a hand. "May I have this dance?"

"I'd be honored." Jo eased into his arms and yielded to the silent music playing only in their hearts. "To what tune are we dancing? I need to know so I can keep better time."

"It's the I-Have-the-Most-Wonderful-Fianceé-in-the-World Waltz."

"Instrumental?"

"Yes, ma'am," he said, a smile still evident in his soothing voice. "Woodwinds and strings."

"Who wrote it?"

"I did."

"Very nice." Jo's feet danced on air, then slowing, she looked up and said, "Beautiful, really!"

To hear a whisper on the wind,
To know the meaning therein;
And to see pure love in another's eyes
Is to be at peace again.

The End

QUESTIONS FOR DISCUSSION

1. Who was your favorite character and why?

2. Did you find yourself transported back in time as you read A Whisper on the Wind and at the same time see how the problems they faced back then were nothing more than a different version of the problems we face today?

3. Could you identify with the challenges Jo, Tryg, and Big Ole faced? If so, which challenges did you find the most compelling?

4. What do you consider Jo's greatest weakness and her greatest strength? Tryg's? Big Ole's?

5. Can you identify with Big Ole's resolve to forgive Wil's egregious offense and reshape the young boy's life? Did you find it believable?

6. How did you feel about Jo's relationship with Farmer Frank? Were you pulling for her or were you hoping she would turn and walk away?

7. How did you feel about Sarah's relationship with Tryg? Were you pulling for her to live happily ever after with him or with Charlie?

8. Were you able to see what Big Ole saw in Wil and did you find yourself wanting Wil to overcome his shattered life?

9. Did you find Calvin Doherty's sermon about heaven compelling? Could you see how it had the power to set Tryg and Jo free?

10. What did you feel were the book's greatest weaknesses and strengths?